The Collector's Wodehouse

P. G. WODEHOUSE

The Heart of a Goof

THE OVERLOOK PRESS
NEW YORK

This edition first published in the United States in 2006 by
The Overlook Press, Peter Mayer Publishers, Inc.

141 Wooster Street
New York, NY 10012
www.overlookpress.com

For bulk and special sales, please contact sales@overlookny.com
or write to us at the address above.

First published in the UK by Herbert Jenkins, 1926
Copyright by the Trustees of the Wodehouse Estate
Originally published in the USA in 1926 under the title *Divots*

Cataloging-in-Publication Data is available from the Library of Congress

Manufactured in Germany

ISBN 978-1-58567-837-2

5 7 9 8 6 4

The Heart of a Goof

CONTENTS

TO
MY DAUGHTER

LEONORA

WITHOUT WHOSE NEVER-FAILING
SYMPATHY AND ENCOURAGEMENT
THIS BOOK
WOULD HAVE BEEN FINISHED
IN
HALF THE TIME

Before leading the reader out on to this little nine-hole course, I should like to say a few words on the club-house steps with regard to the criticisms of my earlier book of Golf stories, *The Clicking of Cuthbert*. In the first place, I noticed with regret a disposition on the part of certain writers to speak of Golf as a trivial theme, unworthy of the pen of a thinker. In connection with this, I can only say that right through the ages the mightiest brains have occupied themselves with this noble sport, and that I err, therefore, if I do err, in excellent company.

Apart from the works of such men as James Braid, John Henry Taylor and Horace Hutchinson, we find Publius Syrius not disdaining to give advice on the back-swing ('He gets through too late who goes too fast'); Diogenes describing the emotions of a cheery player at the water-hole ('Be of good cheer. I see land'); and Doctor Watts, who, watching one of his drives from the tee, jotted down the following couplet on the back of his score-card:

> Fly, like a youthful hart or roe,
> Over the hills where spices grow.

And, when we consider that Chaucer, the father of English poetry, inserted in his Squiere's Tale the line

Therefore behoveth him a ful long spoone

(though, of course, with the modern rubber-cored ball an iron would have got the same distance) and that Shakespeare himself, speaking querulously in the character of a weak player who held up an impatient foursome, said:

Four rogues in buckram let drive at me

we may, I think, consider these objections answered.

A far more serious grievance which I have against my critics is that many of them confessed to the possession of but the slightest knowledge of the game, and one actually stated in cold print that he did not know what a niblick was. A writer on golf is certainly entitled to be judged by his peers – which, in my own case, means men who do one good drive in six, four reasonable approaches in an eighteen-hole round, and average three putts per green: and I think I am justified in asking of editors that they instruct critics of this book to append their handicaps in brackets at the end of their remarks. By this means the public will be enabled to form a fair estimate of the worth of the volume, and the sting in such critiques as 'We laughed heartily while reading these stories – once – at a misprint' will be sensibly diminished by the figures (36) at the bottom of the paragraph. While my elation will be all the greater should the words 'A genuine masterpiece' be followed by a simple (scr.).

One final word. The thoughtful reader, comparing this book with *The Clicking of Cuthbert*, will, no doubt, be struck by the poignant depth of feeling which pervades the present volume like the scent of muddy shoes in a locker-room: and it may be that he will conclude that, like so many English writers, I have fallen under the spell of the great Russians.

This is not the case. While it is, of course, true that my style owes much to Dostoievsky, the heart-wringing qualities of such stories as 'The Awakening of Rollo Podmarsh' and 'Keeping in with Vosper' is due entirely to the fact that I have spent much time recently playing on the National Links at Southampton, Long Island, U.S.A. These links were constructed by an exiled Scot who conceived the dreadful idea of assembling on one course all the really foul holes in Great Britain. It cannot but leave its mark on a man when, after struggling through the Sahara at Sandwich and the Alps at Prestwick, he finds himself faced by the Station-Master's Garden hole at St. Andrew's and knows that the Redan and the Eden are just round the corner. When you turn in a medal score of a hundred and eight on two successive days, you get to know something about Life.

And yet it may be that there are a few gleams of sunshine in the book. If so, it is attributable to the fact that some of it was written before I went to Southampton and immediately after I had won my first and only trophy – an umbrella in a hotel tournament at Aiken, South Carolina, where, playing to a handi-cap of sixteen, I went through a field consisting of some of the fattest retired business-men in America like a devouring flame. If we lose the Walker Cup this year, let England remember that.

P. G. WODEHOUSE

The Sixth Bunker
  Addington

It was a morning when all nature shouted 'Fore!' The breeze, as it blew gently up from the valley, seemed to bring a message of hope and cheer, whispering of chip-shots holed and brassies landing squarely on the meat. The fairway, as yet unscarred by the irons of a hundred dubs, smiled greenly up at the azure sky; and the sun, peeping above the trees, looked like a giant golf-ball perfectly lofted by the mashie of some unseen god and about to drop dead by the pin of the eighteenth. It was the day of the opening of the course after the long winter, and a crowd of considerable dimensions had collected at the first tee. Plus fours gleamed in the sunshine, and the air was charged with happy anticipation.

In all that gay throng there was but one sad face. It belonged to the man who was waggling his driver over the new ball perched on its little hill of sand. This man seemed careworn, hopeless. He gazed down the fairway, shifted his feet, waggled, gazed down the fairway again, shifted the dogs once more, and waggled afresh. He waggled as Hamlet might have waggled, moodily, irresolutely. Then, at last, he swung, and, taking from his caddie the niblick which the intelligent lad had been holding in readiness from the moment when he had walked on to the tee, trudged wearily off to play his second.

The Oldest Member, who had been observing the scene with a benevolent eye from his favourite chair on the terrace, sighed.

'Poor Jenkinson,' he said, 'does not improve.'

'No,' agreed his companion, a young man with open features and a handicap of six. 'And yet I happen to know that he has been taking lessons all the winter at one of those indoor places.'

'Futile, quite futile,' said the Sage with a shake of his snowy head. 'There is no wizard living who could make that man go round in an average of sevens. I keep advising him to give up the game.'

'You!' cried the young man, raising a shocked and startled face from the driver with which he was toying. '*You* told him to give up golf! Why I thought—'

'I understand and approve of your horror,' said the Oldest Member, gently. 'But you must bear in mind that Jenkinson's is not an ordinary case. You know and I know scores of men who have never broken a hundred and twenty in their lives, and yet contrive to be happy, useful members of society. However badly they may play, they are able to forget. But with Jenkinson it is different. He is not one of those who can take it or leave it alone. His only chance of happiness lies in complete abstinence. Jenkinson is a goof.'

'A what?'

'A goof,' repeated the Sage. 'One of those unfortunate beings who have allowed this noblest of sports to get too great a grip upon them, who have permitted it to eat into their souls, like some malignant growth. The goof, you must understand, is not like you and me. He broods. He becomes morbid. His goofery unfits him for the battles of life. Jenkinson, for example, was once a man with a glowing future in the hay, corn, and feed business, but a constant stream of hooks, tops, and slices gradually made him so diffident and mistrustful of himself, that he let opportunity after opportunity slip, with the result that other, sterner, hay, corn, and feed merchants passed him in the race. Every time he had the chance to carry through some big deal in hay, or to execute some flashing *coup* in corn and feed, the fatal diffidence generated by a hundred rotten rounds would undo him. I understand his bankruptcy may be expected at any moment.'

'My golly!' said the young man, deeply impressed. 'I hope I never become a goof. Do you mean to say there is really no cure except giving up the game?'

The Oldest Member was silent for a while.

'It is curious that you should have asked that question,' he said at last, 'for only this morning I was thinking of the one case in my experience where a goof was enabled to overcome his deplorable malady. It was owing to a girl, of course. The longer I live, the more I come to see that most things are. But you will, no doubt, wish to hear the story from the beginning.'

The young man rose with the startled haste of some wild creature, which, wandering through the undergrowth, perceives the trap in his path.

'I should love to,' he mumbled, 'only I shall be losing my place at the tee.'

'The goof in question,' said the Sage, attaching himself with quiet firmness to the youth's coat-button, 'was a man of about your age, by name Ferdinand Dibble. I knew him well. In fact, it was to me—'

'Some other time, eh?'

'It was to me,' proceeded the Sage, placidly, 'that he came for sympathy in the great crisis of his life, and I am not ashamed to say that when he had finished laying bare his soul to me there were tears in my eyes. My heart bled for the boy.'

'I bet it did. But—'

The Oldest Member pushed him gently back into his seat.

'Golf,' he said, 'is the Great Mystery. Like some capricious goddess—'

The young man, who had been exhibiting symptoms of feverishness, appeared to become resigned. He sighed softly.

'Did you ever read "The Ancient Mariner"?' he said.

'Many years ago,' said the Oldest Member. 'Why do you ask?'

'Oh, I don't know,' said the young man. 'It just occurred to me.'

Golf (resumed the Oldest Member) is the Great Mystery. Like some capricious goddess, it bestows its favours with what would appear an almost fat-headed lack of method and discrimination. On every side we see big two-fisted he-men floundering round in three figures, stopping every few minutes to let through little shrimps with knock knees and hollow cheeks, who are tearing off snappy seventy-fours. Giants of finance have to accept a stroke per from their junior clerks. Men capable of governing empires fail to control a small, white ball, which presents no difficulties whatever to others with one ounce more brain than a cuckoo-clock. Mysterious, but there it is. There was no apparent reason why Ferdinand Dibble should not have been a competent golfer. He had strong wrists and a good eye. Nevertheless, the fact remains that he was a dub. And on a certain evening in June I realised that he was also a goof. I found it out quite suddenly as the result of a conversation which we had on this very terrace.

I was sitting here that evening thinking of this and that, when by the corner of the club-house I observed young Dibble in conversation with a girl in white. I could not see who she was, for her back was turned. Presently they parted and Ferdinand came slowly across to where I sat. His air was dejected. He had had the boots licked off him earlier in the afternoon by Jimmy Fothergill, and it was to this that I attributed his gloom. I was to find out in a few moments that I was partly but not entirely correct in this surmise. He took the next chair to mine, and for several minutes sat staring moodily down into the valley.

'I've just been talking to Barbara Medway,' he said, suddenly breaking the silence.

'Indeed?' I said. 'A delightful girl.'

'She's going away for the summer to Marvis Bay.'

'She will take the sunshine with her.'

'You bet she will!' said Ferdinand Dibble, with extraordinary warmth, and there was another long silence.

Presently Ferdinand uttered a hollow groan.

'I love her, dammit!' he muttered brokenly. 'Oh, golly, how I love her!'

I was not surprised at his making me the recipient of his confidences like this. Most of the young folk in the place brought their troubles to me sooner or later.

'And does she return your love?'

'I don't know. I haven't asked her.'

'Why not? I should have thought the point not without its interest for you.'

Ferdinand gnawed the handle of his putter distractedly.

'I haven't the nerve,' he burst out at length. 'I simply can't summon up the cold gall to ask a girl, least of all an angel like her, to marry me. You see, it's like this. Every time I work myself up to the point of having a dash at it, I go out and get trimmed by someone giving me a stroke a hole. Every time I feel I've mustered up enough pep to propose, I take ten on a bogey three. Every time I think I'm in good mid-season form for putting my fate to the test, to win or lose it all, something goes all blooey with my swing, and I slice into the rough at every tee. And then my self-confidence leaves me. I become nervous, tongue-tied, diffident. I wish to goodness I knew the man who invented this infernal game. I'd strangle him. But I suppose he's been dead for ages. Still, I could go and jump on his grave.'

It was at this point that I understood all, and the heart within me sank like lead. The truth was out. Ferdinand Dibble was a goof.

'Come, come, my boy,' I said, though feeling the uselessness of any words. 'Master this weakness.'

'I can't.'

'Try!'

'I have tried.'

He gnawed his putter again.

'She was asking me just now if I couldn't manage to come to Marvis Bay, too,' he said.

'That surely is encouraging? It suggests that she is not entirely indifferent to your society.'

'Yes, but what's the use? Do you know,' a gleam coming into his eyes for a moment, 'I have a feeling that if I could ever beat some really fairly good player – just once – I could bring the thing off.' The gleam faded. 'But what chance is there of that?'

It was a question which I did not care to answer. I merely patted his shoulder sympathetically, and after a little while he left me and walked away. I was still sitting there, thinking over his hard case, when Barbara Medway came out of the club-house.

She, too, seemed grave and pre-occupied, as if there was

something on her mind. She took the chair which Ferdinand had vacated, and sighed wearily.

'Have you ever felt,' she asked, 'that you would like to bang a man on the head with something hard and heavy? With knobs on?'

I said I had sometimes experienced such a desire, and asked if she had any particular man in mind. She seemed to hesitate for a moment before replying, then, apparently, made up her mind to confide in me. My advanced years carry with them certain pleasant compensations, one of which is that nice girls often confide in me. I frequently find myself enrolled as a father-confessor on the most intimate matters by beautiful creatures from whom many a younger man would give his eye-teeth to get a friendly word. Besides, I had known Barbara since she was a child. Frequently – though not recently – I had given her her evening bath. These things form a bond.

'Why are men such chumps?' she exclaimed.

'You still have not told me who it is that has caused these harsh words. Do I know him?'

'Of course you do. You've just been talking to him.'

'Ferdinand Dibble? But why should you wish to bang Ferdinand Dibble on the head with something hard and heavy with knobs on?'

'Because he's such a goop.'

'You mean a goof?' I queried, wondering how she could have penetrated the unhappy man's secret.

'No, a goop. A goop is a man who's in love with a girl and won't tell her so. I am as certain as I am of anything that Ferdinand is fond of me.'

'Your instinct is unerring. He has just been confiding in me on that very point.'

'Well, why doesn't he confide in *me*, the poor fish?' cried the high-spirited girl, petulantly flicking a pebble at a passing grasshopper. 'I can't be expected to fling myself into his arms unless he gives some sort of a hint that he's ready to catch me.'

'Would it help if I were to repeat to him the substance of this conversation of ours?'

'If you breathe a word of it, I'll never speak to you again,' she cried. 'I'd rather die an awful death than have any man think I wanted him so badly that I had to send relays of messengers begging him to marry me.'

I saw her point.

'Then I fear,' I said, gravely, 'that there is nothing to be done. One can only wait and hope. It may be that in the years to come Ferdinand Dibble will acquire a nice lissom, wristy swing, with the head kept rigid and the right leg firmly braced and—'

'What are you talking about?'

'I was toying with the hope that some sunny day Ferdinand Dibble would cease to be a goof.'

'You mean a goop?'

'No, a goof. A goof is a man who—' And I went on to explain the peculiar psychological difficulties which lay in the way of any declaration of affection on Ferdinand's part.

'But I never heard of anything so ridiculous in my life,' she ejaculated. 'Do you mean to say that he is waiting till he is good at golf before he asks me to marry him?'

'It is not quite so simple as that,' I said sadly. 'Many bad golfers marry, feeling that a wife's loving solicitude may improve their game. But they are rugged, thick-skinned men, not sensitive and introspective, like Ferdinand. Ferdinand has allowed himself to become morbid. It is one of the chief merits of golf that non-success at the game induces a certain amount of decent humility, which keeps a man from pluming himself too much on any petty triumphs he may achieve in other walks of life; but in all things there is a happy mean, and with Ferdinand this humility has gone too far. It has taken all the spirit out of him. He feels crushed and worthless. He is grateful to caddies when they accept a tip instead of drawing themselves up to their full height and flinging the money in his face.'

'Then do you mean that things have got to go on like this for ever?'

I thought for a moment.

'It is a pity,' I said, 'that you could not have induced Ferdinand to go to Marvis Bay for a month or two.'

'Why?'

'Because it seems to me, thinking the thing over, that it is just possible that Marvis Bay might cure him. At the hotel there he would find collected a mob of golfers – I used the term in its broadest sense, to embrace the paralytics and the men who play left-handed – whom even he would be able to beat. When I was last at Marvis Bay, the hotel links were a sort of Sargasso Sea into which had drifted all the pitiful flotsam and jetsam of golf. I have seen things done on that course at which I shuddered and averted my eyes – and I am not a weak man. If Ferdinand can polish up his game so as to go round in a fairly steady hundred and five, I fancy there is hope. But I understand he is not going to Marvis Bay.'

'Oh yes, he is,' said the girl.

'Indeed! He did not tell me that when we were talking just now.'

'He didn't know it then. He will when I have had a few words with him.'

And she walked with firm steps back into the club-house.

* * *

It has been well said that there are many kinds of golf, beginning at the top with the golf of professionals and the best amateurs and working down through the golf of ossified men to that of Scotch University professors. Until recently this last was looked upon as the lowest possible depth; but nowadays, with the growing popularity of summer hotels, we are able to add a brand still lower, the golf you find at places like Marvis Bay.

To Ferdinand Dibble, coming from a club where the standard of play was rather unusually high, Marvis Bay was a revelation, and for some days after his arrival there he went about dazed, like a man who cannot believe it is really true. To go out on the links at this summer resort was like entering a new world. The hotel was full of stout, middle-aged men, who, after a mis-spent youth devoted to making money, had taken to a game at which real proficiency can only be acquired by those who start playing in their cradles and keep their weight down. Out on the course each morning you could see representatives of every nightmare style that was ever invented. There was the man who seemed to be attempting to deceive his ball and lull it into a false security by looking away from it and then making a lightning slash in the apparent hope of catching it off its guard. There was the man who wielded his mid-iron like one killing snakes. There was the man who addressed his ball as if he were stroking a cat, the man who drove as if he were cracking a whip, the man who brooded over each shot like one whose heart is bowed down by bad news from home, and the man who scooped with his mashie as if he were ladling soup. By the end of the first week Ferdinand Dibble was the acknowledged champion of the place. He had gone through the entire menagerie like a bullet through a cream puff.

First, scarcely daring to consider the possibility of success, he had taken on the man who tried to catch his ball off its guard and had beaten him five up and four to play. Then, with gradually growing confidence, he tackled in turn the Cat-Stroker, the Whip-Cracker, the Heart Bowed Down, and the Soup-Scooper, and walked all over their faces with spiked shoes. And as these were the leading local amateurs, whose prowess the octogenarians and the men who went round in bath-chairs vainly strove to emulate, Ferdinand Dibble was faced on the eighth morning of his visit by the startling fact that he had no more worlds to conquer. He was monarch of all he surveyed, and, what is more, had won his first trophy, the prize in the great medal-play handicap tournament, in which he had nosed in ahead of the field by two strokes, edging out his nearest rival, a venerable old gentleman, by means of a brilliant and unexpected four on the last hole. The prize was a handsome pewter mug, about the size of the old oaken bucket, and Ferdinand used to go to his room immediately after dinner to croon over it like a mother over her child.

You are wondering, no doubt, why, in these circumstances, he did not take advantage of the new spirit of exhilarated pride which had replaced his old humility and instantly propose to Barbara Medway. I will tell you. He did not propose to Barbara because Barbara was not there. At the last moment she had been detained at home to nurse a sick parent and had been compelled to postpone her visit for a couple of weeks. He could, no doubt, have proposed in one of the daily letters which he wrote to her, but somehow, once he started writing, he found that he used up so much space describing his best shots on the links that day that it was difficult to squeeze in a declaration of undying passion. After all, you can hardly cram that sort of thing into a postscript.

He decided, therefore, to wait till she arrived, and meanwhile pursued his conquering course. The longer he waited the better, in one way, for every morning and afternoon that passed was adding new layers to his self-esteem. Day by day in every way he grew chestier and chestier.

Meanwhile, however, dark clouds were gathering. Sullen mutterings were to be heard in corners of the hotel lounge, and the spirit of revolt was abroad. For Ferdinand's chestiness had not escaped the notice of his defeated rivals. There is nobody so chesty as a normally unchesty man who suddenly becomes chesty, and I am sorry to say that the chestiness which had come to Ferdinand was the aggressive type of chestiness which breeds enemies. He had developed a habit of holding the game up in order to give his opponent advice. The Whip-Cracker had not forgiven, and never would forgive, his well-meant but galling criticism of his backswing. The Scooper, who had always scooped since the day when, at the age of sixty-four, he subscribed to the Correspondence Course which was to teach him golf in twelve lessons by mail, resented being told by a snip of a boy that the mashie-stroke should be a smooth, unhurried swing. The Snake-Killer— But I need not weary you with a detailed recital of these men's grievances; it is enough to say that they all had it in for Ferdinand, and one night, after dinner, they met in the lounge to decide what was to be done about it.

A nasty spirit was displayed by all.

'A mere lad telling me how to use my mashie!' growled the Scooper. 'Smooth and unhurried my left eyeball! I get it up, don't I? Well, what more do you want?'

'I keep telling him that mine is the old, full St. Andrews

swing,' muttered the Whip-Cracker, between set teeth, 'but he won't listen to me.'

'He ought to be taken down a peg or two,' hissed the Snake-Killer. It is not easy to hiss a sentence without a single 's' in it, and the fact that he succeeded in doing so shows to what a pitch of emotion the man had been goaded by Ferdinand's maddening air of superiority.

'Yes, but what can we do?' queried an octogenarian, when this last remark had been passed on to him down his ear-trumpet.

'That's the trouble,' sighed the Scooper. 'What can we do?' And there was a sorrowful shaking of heads.

'I know!' exclaimed the Cat-Stroker, who had not hitherto spoken. He was a lawyer, and a man of subtle and sinister mind. 'I have it! There's a boy in my office – young Parsloe – who could beat this man Dibble hollow. I'll wire him to come down here and we'll spring him on this fellow and knock some of the conceit out of him.'

There was a chorus of approval.

'But are you sure he can beat him?' asked the Snake-Killer, anxiously. 'It would never do to make a mistake.'

'Of course I'm sure,' said the Cat-Stroker. 'George Parsloe once went round in ninety-four.'

'Many changes there have been since ninety-four,' said the octogenarian, nodding sagely. 'Ah, many, many changes. None of these motor-cars then, tearing about and killing—'

Kindly hands led him off to have an egg-and-milk, and the remaining conspirators returned to the point at issue with bent brows.

'Ninety-four?' said the Scooper, incredulously. 'Do you mean counting every stroke?'

'Counting every stroke.'

'Not conceding himself any putts?'

'Not one.'

'Wire him to come at once,' said the meeting with one voice.

That night the Cat-Stroker approached Ferdinand, smooth, subtle, lawyer-like.

'Oh, Dibble,' he said, 'just the man I wanted to see. Dibble, there's a young friend of mine coming down here who goes in for golf a little. George Parsloe is his name. I was wondering if you could spare time to give him a game. He is just a novice, you know.'

'I shall be delighted to play a round with him,' said Ferdinand, kindly.

'He might pick up a pointer or two from watching you,' said the Cat-Stroker.

'True, true,' said Ferdinand.

'Then I'll introduce you when he shows up.'

'Delighted,' said Ferdinand.

He was in excellent humour that night, for he had had a letter from Barbara saying that she was arriving on the next day but one.

It was Ferdinand's healthy custom of a morning to get up in good time and take a dip in the sea before breakfast. On the morning of the day of Barbara's arrival, he arose, as usual, donned his flannels, took a good look at the cup, and started out. It was a fine, fresh morning, and he glowed both externally and internally. As he crossed the links, for the nearest route to the water was through the fairway of the seventh, he was whistling happily and rehearsing in his mind the opening sentences of his proposal. For it was his firm resolve that night after dinner to ask Barbara to marry him. He was proceeding over the smooth turf without a care in the world, when there was a sudden cry of 'Fore!' and the next moment a golf ball, missing him by inches, sailed up the fairway and came to a rest fifty yards from where he stood. He looked round and observed a figure coming towards him from the tee.

The distance from the tee was fully a hundred and thirty yards. Add fifty to that, and you have a hundred and eighty yards. No such drive had been made on the Marvis Bay links since their foundation, and such is the generous spirit of the true golfer that Ferdinand's first emotion, after the not inexcusable spasm of panic caused by the hum of the ball past his ear, was one of cordial admiration. By some kindly miracle, he supposed, one of his hotel acquaintances had been permitted for once in his life to time a drive right. It was only when the other man came up that there began to steal over him a sickening apprehension. The faces of all those who hewed divots on the hotel course were familiar to him, and the fact that this fellow was a stranger seemed to point with dreadful certainty to his being the man he had agreed to play.

'Sorry,' said the man. He was a tall, strikingly handsome youth, with brown eyes and a dark moustache.

'Oh, that's all right,' said Ferdinand. 'Er – do you always drive like that?'

'Well, I generally get a bit longer ball, but I'm off my drive this morning. It's lucky I came out and got this practice. I'm playing a match to-morrow with a fellow named Dibble, who's a local champion, or something.'

'Me,' said Ferdinand, humbly.

'Eh? Oh, you?' Mr Parsloe eyed him appraisingly. 'Well, may the best man win.'

As this was precisely what Ferdinand was afraid was going to happen, he nodded in a sickly manner and tottered off to his bathe. The magic had gone out of the morning. The sun still shone, but in a silly, feeble way; and a cold and depressing wind had sprung up. For Ferdinand's inferiority complex, which had seemed cured for ever, was back again, doing business at the old stand.

How sad it is in this life that the moment to which we have looked forward with the most glowing anticipation so often turns out on arrival, flat, cold, and disappointing. For ten days Barbara Medway had been living for that meeting with Ferdinand, when, getting out of the train, she would see him popping about on the horizon with the love-light sparkling in his eyes and words of devotion trembling on his lips. The poor girl never doubted for an instant that he would unleash his pent-up emotions inside the first five minutes, and her only worry was lest he should give an embarrassing publicity to the sacred scene by falling on his knees on the station platform.

'Well, here I am at last,' she cried gaily.

'Hullo!' said Ferdinand, with a twisted smile.

The girl looked at him, chilled. How could she know that his peculiar manner was due entirely to the severe attack of cold feet resultant upon his meeting with George Parsloe that morning? The interpretation which she placed upon it was that he was not glad to see her. If he had behaved like this before, she would, of course, have put it down to ingrowing goofery, but now she had his written statements to prove that for the last ten days his golf had been one long series of triumphs.

'I got your letters,' she said, persevering bravely.

'I thought you would,' said Ferdinand, absently.

'You seem to have been doing wonders.'

'Yes.'

There was a silence.

'Have a nice journey?' said Ferdinand.

'Very,' said Barbara.

She spoke coldly, for she was madder than a wet hen. She saw it all now. In the ten days since they had parted, his love, she realised, had waned. Some other girl, met in the romantic surroundings of this picturesque resort, had supplanted her in his affections. She knew how quickly Cupid gets off the mark at a summer hotel, and for an instant she blamed herself for ever having been so ivory-skulled as to let him come to this place alone. Then regret was swallowed up in wrath, and she became so glacial that Ferdinand, who had been on the point of telling her the secret of his gloom, retired into his shell and conversation during the drive to the hotel never soared above a certain level. Ferdinand said the sunshine was nice and Barbara said yes, it was nice, and Ferdinand said it looked pretty on the water, and Barbara said yes, it did look pretty on the water, and Ferdinand said he hoped it was not going to rain, and Barbara said yes, it would be a pity if it rained. And then there was another lengthy silence.

'How is my uncle?' asked Barbara at last.

I omitted to mention that the individual to whom I have referred as the Cat-Stroker was Barbara's mother's brother, and her host at Marvis Bay.

'Your uncle?'

'His name is Tuttle. Have you met him?'

'Oh yes. I've seen a good deal of him. He has got a friend staying with him,' said Ferdinand, his mind returning to the matter nearest his heart. 'A fellow named Parsloe.'

'Oh, is George Parsloe here? How jolly!'

'Do you know him?' barked Ferdinand, hollowly. He would not have supposed that anything could have added to his existing depression, but he was conscious now of having slipped a few rungs farther down the ladder of gloom. There had been a horribly joyful ring in her voice. Ah, well, he reflected morosely, how like life it all was! We never know what the morrow may bring forth. We strike a good patch and are beginning to think pretty well of ourselves, and along comes a George Parsloe.

'Of course I do,' said Barbara. 'Why, there he is.'

The cab had drawn up at the door of the hotel, and on the porch George Parsloe was airing his graceful person. To Ferdinand's fevered eye he looked like a Greek god, and his inferiority complex began to exhibit symptoms of elephantiasis. How could he compete at love or golf with a fellow who looked as if he had stepped out of the movies and considered himself off his drive when he did a hundred and eighty yards?

'Geor-gee!' cried Barbara, blithely. 'Hullo, George!'

'Why, hullo, Barbara!'

They fell into pleasant conversation, while Ferdinand hung miserably about in the offing. And presently, feeling that his society was not essential to their happiness, he slunk away.

George Parsloe dined at the Cat-Stroker's table that night, and it was with George Parsloe that Barbara roamed in the moonlight after dinner. Ferdinand, after a profitless hour at the billiard-table, went early to his room. But not even the rays of the moon, glinting on his cup, could soothe the fever in his soul. He practised putting sombrely into his tooth-glass for a while; then, going to bed, fell at last into a troubled sleep.

Barbara slept late the next morning and breakfasted in her room. Coming down towards noon, she found a strange emptiness in the hotel. It was her experience of summer hotels that a really fine day like this one was the cue for half the inhabitants to collect in the lounge, shut all the windows, and talk about conditions in the jute industry. To her surprise, though the sun was streaming down from a cloudless sky, the only occupant of the lounge was the octogenarian with the ear-trumpet. She observed that he was chuckling to himself in a senile manner.

'Good morning,' she said, politely, for she had made his acquaintance on the previous evening.

'Hey?' said the octogenarian, suspending his chuckling and getting his trumpet into position.

'I said "Good morning!"' roared Barbara into the receiver.

'Hey?'

'Good morning!'

'Ah! Yes, it's a very fine morning, a very fine morning. If it wasn't for missing my bun and glass of milk at twelve sharp,' said the octogenarian, 'I'd be down on the links. That's where I'd be, down on the links. If it wasn't for missing my bun and glass of milk.'

This refreshment arriving at this moment, he dismantled the radio outfit and began to restore his tissues.

'Watching the match,' he explained, pausing for a moment in his bun-mangling.

'What match?'

The octogenarian sipped his milk.

'What match?' repeated Barbara.

'Hey?'

'What match?'

The octogenarian began to chuckle again and nearly swallowed a crumb the wrong way.

'Take some of the conceit out of him,' he gurgled.

'Out of who?' asked Barbara, knowing perfectly well that she should have said 'whom.'

'Yes,' said the octogenarian.

'Who is conceited?'

'Ah! This young fellow, Dibble. Very conceited. I saw it in his eye from the first, but nobody would listen to me. Mark my words, I said, that boy needs taking down a peg or two. Well, he's going to be this morning. Your uncle wired to young Parsloe to come down, and he's arranged a match between them. Dibble—' Here the octogenarian choked again and had to rinse himself out with milk, 'Dibble doesn't know that Parsloe once went round in ninety-four!'

'What?'

Everything seemed to go black to Barbara. Through a murky mist she appeared to be looking at a negro octogenarian, sipping ink. Then her eyes cleared, and she found herself clutching for support at the back of a chair. She understood now. She realised why Ferdinand had been so distrait, and her whole heart went out to him in a spasm of maternal pity. How she had wronged him!

'Take some of the conceit out of him,' the octogenarian was mumbling, and Barbara felt a sudden sharp loathing for the old man. For two pins she could have dropped a beetle in his milk. Then the need for action roused her. What action? She did not know. All she knew was that she must act.

'Oh!' she cried.

'Hey?' said the octogenarian, bringing his trumpet to the ready.

But Barbara had gone.

It was not far to the links, and Barbara covered the distance on flying feet. She reached the club-house, but the course was empty except for the Scooper, who was preparing to drive off the first tee. In spite of the fact that something seemed to tell her subconsciously that this was one of the sights she ought not to miss, the girl did not wait to watch. Assuming that the match had started soon after breakfast, it must by now have reached one of the holes on the second nine. She ran down the hill, looking to left and right, and was presently aware of a group of spectators clustered about a green in the distance. As she hurried towards them they moved away, and now she could see Ferdinand advancing to the next tee. With a thrill that shook her whole body she realised that he had the honour. So he must have won one hole, at any rate. Then she saw her uncle.

'How are they?' she gasped.

Mr Tuttle seemed moody. It was apparent that things were not going altogether to his liking.

'All square at the fifteenth,' he replied, gloomily.

'All square!'

'Yes. Young Parsloe,' said Mr Tuttle with a sour look in the direction of that lissom athlete, 'doesn't seem to be able to do a thing right on the greens. He has been putting like a sheep with the botts.'

From the foregoing remark of Mr Tuttle you will, no doubt, have gleaned at least a clue to the mystery of how Ferdinand Dibble had managed to hold his long-driving adversary up to the fifteenth green, but for all that you will probably consider that some further explanation of this amazing state of affairs is required. Mere bad putting on the part of George Parsloe is not, you feel, sufficient to cover the matter entirely. You are right. There was another very important factor in the situation – to wit, that by some extraordinary chance Ferdinand Dibble had started right off from the first tee, playing the game of a lifetime. Never had he made such drives, never chipped his chips so shrewdly.

About Ferdinand's driving there was as a general thing a fatal stiffness and over-caution which prevented success. And with his chip-shots he rarely achieved accuracy owing to his habit of rearing his head like the lion of the jungle just before the club struck the ball. But to-day he had been swinging with a careless freedom, and his chips had been true and clean. The thing had puzzled him all the way round. It had not elated him, for, owing to Barbara's aloofness and the way in which she had gambolled about George Parsloe, like a young lamb in the springtime, he was in too deep a state of dejection to be elated by anything. And now, suddenly, in a flash of clear vision, he perceived the reason why he had been playing so well to-day. It was just because he was not elated. It was simply because he was so profoundly miserable.

That was what Ferdinand told himself as he stepped off the sixteenth, after hitting a screamer down the centre of the fairway, and I am convinced that he was right. Like so many indifferent golfers, Ferdinand Dibble had always made the game hard for himself by thinking too much. He was a deep student of the works of the masters, and whenever he prepared to play a stroke he had a complete mental list of all the mistakes which it was possible to make. He would remember how Taylor had warned against dipping the right shoulder, how Vardon had inveighed against any movement of the head; he would recall how Ray had mentioned the tendency to snatch back the club, how Braid had spoken sadly of those who sin against their better selves by stiffening the muscles and heaving.

The consequence was that when, after waggling in a frozen manner till mere shame urged him to take some definite course of action, he eventually swung, he invariably proceeded to dip his right shoulder, stiffen his muscles, heave, and snatch back the club, at the same time raising his head sharply as in the illustrated plate ('Some Frequent Faults of Beginners – No. 3 – Lifting the Bean') facing page thirty-four of James Braid's *Golf Without Tears*. To-day he had been so preoccupied with his broken heart that he had made his shots absently, almost carelessly, with the result that at least one in every three had been a lallapaloosa.

Meanwhile, George Parsloe had driven off and the match was progressing. George was feeling a little flustered by now. He had been given to understand that this bird Dibble was a hundred-at-his-best man, and all the way round the fellow had been reeling off fives in great profusion, and had once actually got a four. True, there had been an occasional six, and even a seven, but that did not alter the main fact that the man was making the dickens of a game of it. With the haughty spirit of one who had once done a ninety-four, George Parsloe had anticipated being at least three up at the turn. Instead of which he had been two down, and had had to fight strenuously to draw level.

Nevertheless, he drove steadily and well, and would certainly have won the hole had it not been for his weak and sinful putting. The same defect caused him to halve the seventeenth, after being on in two, with Ferdinand wandering in the desert and only reaching the green with his fourth. Then, however, Ferdinand holed out from a distance of seven yards, getting a five; which George's three putts just enabled him to equal.

Barbara had watched the proceedings with a beating heart. At first she had looked on from afar; but now, drawn as by a magnet, she approached the tee. Ferdinand was driving off. She held her breath. Ferdinand held his breath. And all around one could see their respective breaths being held by George Parsloe, Mr Tuttle, and the enthralled crowd of spectators. It was a moment of the acutest tension, and it was broken by the crack of Ferdinand's driver as it met the ball and sent it hopping along the ground for a mere thirty yards. At this supreme crisis in the match Ferdinand Dibble had topped.

George Parsloe teed up his ball. There was a smile of quiet satisfaction on his face. He snuggled the driver in his hands, and gave it a preliminary swish. This, felt George Parsloe, was where the happy ending came. He could drive as he had never driven before. He would so drive that it would take his opponent at least three shots to catch up with him. He drew back his club with infinite caution, poised it at the top of the swing—

'I always wonder—' said a clear, girlish voice, ripping the silence like the explosion of a bomb.

George Parsloe started. His club wobbled. It descended. The ball trickled into the long grass in front of the tee. There was a grim pause.

'You were saying, Miss Medway—' said George Parsloe, in a small, flat voice.

'Oh, I'm so sorry,' said Barbara. 'I'm afraid I put you off.'

'A little, perhaps. Possibly the merest trifle. But you were saying you wondered about something. Can I be of any assistance?'

'I was only saying,' said Barbara, 'that I always wonder why tees are called tees.'

George Parsloe swallowed once or twice. He also blinked a little feverishly. His eyes had a dazed, staring expression.

'I am afraid I cannot tell you off-hand,' he said, 'but I will make a point of consulting some good encyclopædia at the earliest opportunity.'

'Thank you so much.'

'Not at all. It will be a pleasure. In case you were thinking of inquiring at the moment when I am putting why greens are called greens, may I venture the suggestion now that it is because they are green?'

And, so saying, George Parsloe stalked to his ball and found it nestling in the heart of some shrub of which, not being a botanist, I cannot give you the name. It was a close-knit, adhesive shrub, and it twined its tentacles so lovingly around George Parsloe's niblick that he missed his first shot altogether. His second made the ball rock, and his third dislodged it. Playing a full swing with his brassie and being by now a mere cauldron of seething emotions he missed his fourth. His fifth came to within a few inches of Ferdinand's drive, and he picked it up and hurled it from him into the rough as if it had been something venomous.

'Your hole and match,' said George Parsloe, thinly.

Ferdinand Dibble sat beside the glittering ocean. He had hurried off the course with swift strides the moment George Parsloe had spoken those bitter words. He wanted to be alone with his thoughts.

They were mixed thoughts. For a moment joy at the reflection that he had won a tough match came irresistibly to the surface, only to sink again as he remembered that life, whatever its triumphs, could hold nothing for him now that Barbara Medway loved another.

'Mr Dibble!'

He looked up. She was standing at his side. He gulped and rose to his feet.

'Yes?'

There was a silence.

'Doesn't the sun look pretty on the water?' said Barbara.

Ferdinand groaned. This was too much.

'Leave me,' he said, hollowly. 'Go back to your Parsloe, the man with whom you walked in the moonlight beside this same water.'

'Well, why shouldn't I walk with Mr Parsloe in the moonlight beside this same water?' demanded Barbara, with spirit.

'I never said,' replied Ferdinand, for he was a fair man at heart, 'that you shouldn't walk with Mr Parsloe beside this same water. I simply said you did walk with Mr Parsloe beside this same water.'

'I've a perfect right to walk with Mr Parsloe beside this same water,' persisted Barbara. 'He and I are old friends.'

Ferdinand groaned again.

'Exactly! There you are! As I suspected. Old friends. Played together as children, and what not, I shouldn't wonder.'

'No, we didn't. I've only known him five years. But he is engaged to be married to my greatest chum, so that draws us together.'

Ferdinand uttered a strangled cry.

'Parsloe engaged to be married!'

'Yes. The wedding takes place next month.'

'But look here.' Ferdinand's forehead was wrinkled. He was thinking tensely. 'Look here,' said Ferdinand, a close reasoner. 'If Parsloe's engaged to your greatest chum, he can't be in love with *you*.'

'No.'

'And you aren't in love with him?'

'No.'

'Then, by gad,' said Ferdinand, 'how about it?'

'What do you mean?'

'Will you marry me?' bellowed Ferdinand.

'Yes.'

'You will?'

'Of course I will.'

'Darling!' cried Ferdinand.

'There is only one thing that bothers me a bit,' said Ferdinand, thoughtfully, as they strolled together over the scented meadows, while in the trees above them a thousand birds trilled Mendelssohn's Wedding March.

'What is that?'

'Well, I'll tell you,' said Ferdinand. 'The fact is, I've just discovered the great secret of golf. You can't play a really hot game unless you're so miserable that you don't worry over your shots. Take the case of a chip-shot, for instance. If you're really wretched, you don't care where the ball is going and so you don't raise your head to see. Grief automatically prevents pressing and over-swinging. Look at the top-notchers. Have you ever seen a happy pro?'

'No. I don't think I have.'

'Well, then!'

'But pros are all Scotchmen,' argued Barbara.

'It doesn't matter. I'm sure I'm right. And the darned thing is that I'm going to be so infernally happy all the rest of my life that I suppose my handicap will go up to thirty or something.'

Barbara squeezed his hand lovingly. 'Don't worry, precious,' she said, soothingly. 'It will be all right. I am a woman, and, once we are married, I shall be able to think of at least a hundred ways of snootering you to such an extent that you'll be fit to win the Amateur Championship.'

'You will?' said Ferdinand, anxiously. 'You're sure?'

'Quite, quite sure, dearest,' said Barbara.

'My angel!' said Ferdinand.

He folded her in his arms, using the interlocking grip.

The summer day was drawing to a close. Over the terrace outside the club-house the chestnut trees threw long shadows, and such bees as still lingered in the flower-beds had the air of tired business-men who are about ready to shut up the office and go off to dinner and a musical comedy. The Oldest Member, stirring in his favourite chair, glanced at his watch and yawned.

As he did so, from the neighbourhood of the eighteenth green, hidden from his view by the slope of the ground, there came suddenly a medley of shrill animal cries, and he deduced that some belated match must just have reached a finish. His surmise was correct. The babble of voices drew nearer, and over the brow of the hill came a little group of men. Two, who appeared to be the ringleaders in the affair, were short and stout. One was cheerful and the other dejected. The rest of the company consisted of friends and adherents; and one of these, a young man who seemed to be amused, strolled to where the Oldest Member sat.

'What,' inquired the Sage, 'was all the shouting for?'

The young man sank into a chair and lighted a cigarette.

'Perkins and Broster,' he said, 'were all square at the seventeenth, and they raised the stakes to fifty pounds. They were both on the green in seven, and Perkins had a two-foot putt to halve the match. He missed it by six inches. They play pretty high, those two.'

'It is a curious thing,' said the Oldest Member, 'that men whose golf is of a kind that makes hardened caddies wince always do. The more competent a player, the smaller the stake that contents him. It is only when you get down into the submerged tenth of the golfing world that you find the big gambling. However, I would not call fifty pounds anything sensational in the case of two men like Perkins and Broster. They are both well provided with the world's goods. If you would care to hear the story—'

The young man's jaw fell a couple of notches.

'I had no idea it was so late,' he bleated. 'I ought to be—'

'—of a man who played for really high stakes—'

'I promised to—'

'—I will tell it to you,' said the Sage.

'Look here,' said the young man, sullenly, 'it isn't one of those stories about two men who fall in love with the same girl and play a match to decide which is to marry her, is it? Because if so—'

'The stake to which I allude,' said the Oldest Member, 'was something far higher and bigger than a woman's love. Shall I proceed?'

'All right,' said the young man, resignedly. 'Snap into it.'

It has been well said – I think by the man who wrote the subtitles for 'Cage-Birds of Society' (began the Oldest Member) – that wealth does not always bring happiness. It was so with Bradbury Fisher, the hero of the story which I am about to relate. One of America's most prominent tainted millionaires, he had two sorrows in life – his handicap refused to stir from twenty-four and his wife disapproved of his collection of famous golf relics. Once, finding him crooning over the trousers in which Ouimet had won his historic replay against Vardon and Ray in the American Open, she had asked him why he did not collect something worth while, like Old Masters or first editions.

Worth while! Bradbury had forgiven, for he loved the woman, but he could not forget.

For Bradbury Fisher, like so many men who have taken to the game in middle age, after a youth mis-spent in the pursuits of commerce, was no half-hearted enthusiast. Although he still occasionally descended on Wall Street in order to pry the small investor loose from another couple of million, what he really lived for now was golf and his collection. He had begun the collection in his first year as a golfer, and he prized it dearly. And when he reflected that his wife had stopped him purchasing J. H. Taylor's shirt-stud, which he could have had for a few hundred pounds, the iron seemed to enter into his soul.

The distressing episode had occurred in London, and he was now on his way back to New York, having left his wife to continue her holiday in England. All through the voyage he remained moody and distrait; and at the ship's concert, at which he was forced to take the chair, he was heard to observe to the purser that if the alleged soprano who had just sung 'My Little Grey Home in the West' had the immortal gall to take a second encore he hoped that she would trip over a high note and dislocate her neck.

Such was Bradbury Fisher's mood throughout the ocean journey, and it remained constant until he arrived at his palatial home at Goldenville, Long Island, where, as he sat smoking a moody after-dinner cigar in the Versailles drawing-room, Blizzard, his English butler, informed him that Mr Gladstone Bott desired to speak to him on the telephone.

'Tell him to go and boil himself,' said Bradbury.

'Very good, sir.'

'No, I'll tell him myself,' said Bradbury. He strode to the telephone. 'Hullo!' he said, curtly.

He was not fond of this Bott. There are certain men who seem fated to go through life as rivals. It was so with Bradbury Fisher and J. Gladstone Bott. Born in the same town within a few days of one another, they had come to New York in the same week; and from that moment their careers had run side by side. Fisher had made his first million two days before Bott, but Bott's first divorce had got half a column and two sticks more publicity than Fisher's.

At Sing-Sing, where each had spent several happy years of early manhood, they had run neck and neck for the prizes which that institution has to offer. Fisher secured the position of catcher on the baseball nine in preference to Bott, but Bott just nosed Fisher out when it came to the choice of a tenor for the glee club. Bott was selected for the debating contest against Auburn, but Fisher got the last place on the crossword puzzle team, with Bott merely first reserve.

They had taken up golf simultaneously, and their handicaps had remained level ever since. Between such men it is not surprising that there was little love lost.

'Hullo!' said Gladstone Bott. 'So you're back? Say, listen, Fisher. I think I've got something that'll interest you. Something you'll be glad to have in your golf collection.'

Bradbury Fisher's mood softened. He disliked Bott, but that was no reason for not doing business with him. And though he had little faith in the man's judgment it might be that he had stumbled upon some valuable antique. There crossed his mind the comforting thought that his wife was three thousand miles away and that he was no longer under her penetrating eye – that eye which, so to speak, was always 'about his bath and about his bed and spying out all his ways.'

'I've just returned from a trip down South,' proceeded Bott, 'and I have secured the authentic baffy used by Bobby Jones in his first important contest – the Infants' All-In Championship of Atlanta, Georgia, open to those of both sexes not yet having finished teething.'

Bradbury gasped. He had heard rumours that this treasure was in existence, but he had never credited them.

'You're sure?' he cried. 'You're positive it's genuine?'

'I have a written guarantee from Mr Jones, Mrs Jones, and the nurse.'

'How much, Bott, old man?' stammered Bradbury. 'How much do you want for it, Gladstone, old top? I'll give you a hundred thousand dollars.'

'Ha!'

'Five hundred thousand.'

'Ha, ha!'

'A million.'

'Ha, ha, ha!'

'Two million.'

'Ha, ha, ha, ha!'

Bradbury Fisher's strong face twisted like that of a tortured fiend. He registered in quick succession rage, despair, hate, fury, anguish, pique, and resentment. But when he spoke again his voice was soft and gentle.

'Gladdy, old socks,' he said, 'we have been friends for years.'

'No, we haven't,' said Gladstone Bott.

'Yes, we have.'

'No, we haven't.'

'Well, anyway, what about two million five hundred?'

'Nothing doing. Say, listen. Do you really want that baffy?'

'I do, Botty, old egg, I do indeed.'

'Then listen. I'll exchange it for Blizzard.'

'For Blizzard?' quavered Fisher.

'For Blizzard.'

It occurs to me that, when describing the closeness of the rivalry between these two men I may have conveyed the impression that in no department of life could either claim a definite advantage over the other. If that is so, I erred. It is true that in a general way, whatever one had, the other had something equally good to counterbalance it; but in just one matter Bradbury Fisher had triumphed completely over Gladstone Bott. Bradbury Fisher had the finest English butler on Long Island.

Blizzard stood alone. There is a regrettable tendency on the part of English butlers to-day to deviate more and more from the type which made their species famous. The modern butler has a nasty knack of being a lissom young man in perfect condition who looks like the son of the house. But Blizzard was of the fine old school. Before coming to the Fisher home he had been for fifteen years in the service of an earl, and his appearance suggested that throughout those fifteen years he had not let a day pass without its pint of port. He radiated port and pop-eyed dignity. He had splay feet and three chins, and when he walked his curving waistcoat preceded him like the advance guard of some royal procession.

From the first, Bradbury had been perfectly aware that Bott

coveted Blizzard, and the knowledge had sweetened his life. But this was the first time he had come out into the open and admitted it.

'Blizzard?' whispered Fisher.

'Blizzard,' said Bott firmly. 'It's my wife's birthday next week, and I've been wondering what to give her.'

Bradbury Fisher shuddered from head to foot, and his legs wobbled like asparagus stalks. Beads of perspiration stood out on his forehead. The serpent was tempting him – tempting him grievously.

'You're sure you won't take three million – or four – or something like that?'

'No; I want Blizzard.'

Bradbury Fisher passed his handkerchief over his streaming brow.

'So be it,' he said in a low voice.

The Jones baffy arrived that night, and for some hours Bradbury Fisher gloated over it with the unmixed joy of a collector who has secured the prize of a lifetime. Then, stealing gradually over him, came the realisation of what he had done.

He was thinking of his wife and what she would say when she heard of this. Blizzard was Mrs Fisher's pride and joy. She had never, like the poet, nursed a dear gazelle, but, had she done so, her attitude towards it would have been identical with her attitude towards Blizzard. Although so far away, it was plain that her thoughts still lingered with the pleasure she had left at home, for on his arrival Bradbury had found three cables awaiting him.

The first ran:

'How is Blizzard? Reply.'

The second:

'How is Blizzard's sciatica? Reply.'

The third:

'Blizzard's hiccups. How are they? Suggest Doctor Murphy's Tonic Swamp-Juice. Highly spoken of. Three times a day after meals. Try for week and cable result.'

It did not require a clairvoyant to tell Bradbury that, if on her return she found that he had disposed of Blizzard in exchange for a child's cut-down baffy, she would certainly sue him for divorce. And there was not a jury in America that would not give their verdict in her favour without a dissentient voice. His first wife, he recalled, had divorced him on far flimsier grounds. So had his second, third, and fourth. And Bradbury loved his wife. There had been a time in his life when, if he lost a wife, he had felt philosophically that there would be another along in a minute; but, as a man grows older, he tends to become set in his habits, and he could not contemplate existence without the company of the present incumbent.

What, therefore, to do? What, when you came right down to it, to do?

There seemed no way out of the dilemma. If he kept the Jones baffy, no other price would satisfy Bott's jealous greed. And to part with the baffy, now that it was actually in his possession, was unthinkable.

And then, in the small hours of the morning, as he tossed sleeplessly on his Louis Quinze bed, his giant brain conceived a plan.

On the following afternoon he made his way to the clubhouse, and was informed that Bott was out playing a round with another millionaire of his acquaintance. Bradbury waited, and presently his rival appeared.

'Hey!' said Gladstone Bott, in his abrupt uncouth way. 'When are you going to deliver that butler?'

'I will make the shipment at the earliest date,' said Bradbury.

'I was expecting him last night.'

'You shall have him shortly.'

'What do you feed him on?' asked Gladstone Bott.

'Oh, anything you have yourselves. Put sulphur in his port in the hot weather. Tell me, how did your match go?'

'He beat me. I had rotten luck.'

Bradbury Fisher's eyes gleamed. His moment had come.

'Luck?' he said. 'What do you mean, luck? Luck has nothing to do with it. You're always beefing about your luck. The trouble with you is that you play rottenly.'

'What!'

'It is no use trying to play golf unless you learn the first principles and do it properly. Look at the way you drive.'

'What's wrong with my driving?'

'Nothing, except that you don't do anything right. In driving, as the club comes back in the swing, the weight should be shifted by degrees, quietly and gradually, until, when the club has reached its top-most point, the whole weight of the body is supported by the right leg, the left foot being turned at the time and the left knee bent in towards the right leg. But, regardless of how much you perfect your style, you cannot develop any method which will not require you to keep your head still so that you can see your ball clearly.'

'Hey!'

'It is obvious that it is impossible to introduce a jerk or a sudden violent effort into any part of the swing without disturbing the balance or moving the head. I want to drive home the fact that it is absolutely essential to—'

'Hey!' cried Gladstone Bott.

The man was shaken to the core. From the local pro, and from scratch men of his acquaintance, he would gladly have listened to this sort of thing by the hour, but to hear these words from Bradbury Fisher, whose handicap was the same as his own, and out of whom it was his unperishable conviction that he could hammer the tar any time he got him out on the links, was too much.

'Where do you get off,' he demanded, heatedly, 'trying to teach me golf?'

Bradbury Fisher chuckled to himself. Everything was working out as his subtle mind had foreseen.

'My dear fellow,' he said, 'I was only speaking for your good.'

'I like your nerve! I can lick you any time we start.'

'It's easy enough to talk.'

'I trimmed you twice the week before you sailed to England.'

'Naturally,' said Bradbury Fisher, 'in a friendly round, with only a few thousand dollars on the match, a man does not extend himself. You wouldn't dare to play me for anything that really mattered.'

'I'll play you when you like for anything you like.'

'Very well. I'll play you for Blizzard.'

'Against what?'

'Oh, anything you please. How about a couple of railroads?'

'Make it three.'

'Very well.'

'Next Friday suit you?'

'Sure,' said Bradbury Fisher.

It seemed to him that his troubles were over. Like all twenty-four handicap men, he had the most perfect confidence in his ability to beat all other twenty-four handicap men. As for Gladstone Bott, he knew that he could disembowel him any time he was able to lure him out of the club-house.

Nevertheless, as he breakfasted on the morning of the fateful match, Bradbury Fisher was conscious of an unwonted nervousness. He was no weakling. In Wall Street his phlegm in moments of stress was a by-word. On the famous occasion when the B. and G. crowd had attacked C. and D., and in order to keep control of L. and M. he had been compelled to buy so largely of S. and T., he had not turned a hair. And yet this morning, in endeavouring to prong up segments of bacon, he twice missed the plate altogether and on a third occasion speared himself in the cheek with his fork. The spectacle of Blizzard, so calm, so competent, so supremely the perfect butler, unnerved him.

'I am jumpy to-day, Blizzard,' he said, forcing a laugh.

'Yes, sir. You do, indeed, appear to have the willies.'

'Yes. I am playing a very important golf-match this morning.'

'Indeed, sir?'

'I must pull myself together, Blizzard.'

'Yes, sir. And, if I may respectfully make the suggestion, you should endeavour, when in action, to keep the head down and the eye rigidly upon the ball.'

'I will, Blizzard, I will,' said Bradbury Fisher, his keen eyes clouding under a sudden mist of tears. 'Thank you, Blizzard, for the advice.'

'Not at all, sir.'

'How is your sciatica, Blizzard?'

'A trifle improved, I thank you, sir.'

'And your hiccups?'

'I am conscious of a slight though possibly only a temporary relief, sir.'

'Good,' said Bradbury Fisher.

He left the room with a firm step; and proceeding to his library, read for a while portions of that grand chapter in James Braid's *Advanced Golf* which deals with driving into the wind. It was a fair and cloudless morning, but it was as well to be prepared for emergencies. Then, feeling that he had done all that could be done, he ordered the car and was taken to the links.

Gladstone Bott was awaiting him on the first tee, in company with two caddies. A curt greeting, a spin of the coin, and Gladstone Bott, securing the honour, stepped out to begin the contest.

Although there are, of course, endless sub-species in their ranks, not all of which have yet been classified by science, twenty-four handicap golfers may be stated broadly to fall in to two classes, the dashing and the cautious – those, that is to say, who endeavour to do every hole in a brilliant one and those who are content to win with a steady nine. Gladstone Bott was one of the cautious brigade. He fussed about for a few moments like a hen scratching gravel, then with a stiff quarter-swing sent his ball straight down the fairway for a matter of seventy yards, and it was Bradbury Fisher's turn to drive.

Now, normally, Bradbury Fisher was essentially a dasher. It was his habit, as a rule, to raise his left foot some six inches from the ground, and having swayed forcefully back on to his right leg, to sway sharply forward again and lash out with sickening violence in the general direction of the ball. It was a method which at times produced excellent results, though it had the flaw that it was somewhat uncertain. Bradbury Fisher was the only member of the club, with the exception of the club champion, who had ever carried the second green with his drive; but, on the other hand, he was also the only member who had ever laid his drive on the eleventh dead to the pin of the sixteenth.

But to-day the magnitude of the issues at stake had wrought a change in him. Planted firmly on both feet, he fiddled at the ball in the manner of one playing spillikens. When he swung, it was with a swing resembling that of Gladstone Bott; and, like Bott, he achieved a nice, steady, rainbow-shaped drive of some seventy yards straight down the middle. Bott replied with an eighty-yard brassy shot. Bradbury held him with another. And so, working their way cautiously across the prairie, they came to the green, where Bradbury, laying his third putt dead, halved the hole.

The second was a repetition of the first, the third and fourth repetitions of the second. But on the fifth green the fortunes of the match began to change. Here Gladstone Bott, faced with a fifteen-foot putt to win, smote his ball firmly off the line, as had been his practice at each of the preceding holes, and the ball, hitting a worm-cast and bounding off to the left, ran on a couple of yards, hit another worm-cast, bounded to the right, and finally, bumping into a twig, leaped to the left again and clattered into the tin.

'One up,' said Gladstone Bott. 'Tricky, some of these greens are. You have to gauge the angles to a nicety.'

At the sixth a donkey in an adjoining field uttered a raucous bray just as Bott was addressing his ball with a mashie-niblick on the edge of the green. He started violently and, jerking his club with a spasmodic reflex action of the forearm, holed out.

'Nice work,' said Gladstone Bott.

The seventh was a short hole, guarded by two large bunkers between which ran a narrow footpath of turf. Gladstone Bott's mashie-shot, falling short, ran over the rough, peered for a moment into the depths to the left, then, winding up the path, trickled on to the green, struck a fortunate slope, acquired momentum, ran on, and dropped into the hole.

'Nearly missed it,' said Gladstone Bott, drawing a deep breath.

Bradbury Fisher looked out upon a world that swam and danced before his eyes. He had not been prepared for this sort of thing. The way things were shaping, he felt that it would hardly surprise him now if the cups were to start jumping up and snapping at Bott's ball like starving dogs.

'Three up,' said Gladstone Bott.

With a strong effort Bradbury Fisher mastered his feelings. His mouth set grimly. Matters, he perceived, had reached a crisis. He saw now that he had made a mistake in allowing himself to be intimidated by the importance of the occasion into being scientific. Nature had never intended him for a scientific golfer, and up till now he had been behaving like an animated illustration out of a book by Vardon. He had taken his club back along and near the turf, allowing it to trend around the legs as far as was permitted by the movement of the arms. He had kept his right elbow close to the side, this action coming into operation before the club was allowed to describe a section of a circle in an upward direction, whence it was carried by means of a slow, steady, swinging movement. He had pivoted, he had pronated the wrists, and he had been careful about the lateral hip-shift.

And it had been all wrong. That sort of stuff might suit some people, but not him. He was a biffer, a swatter, and a slosher;

and it flashed upon him now that only by biffing, swatting, and sloshing as he had never biffed, swatted, and sloshed before could he hope to recover the ground he had lost.

Gladstone Bott was not one of those players who grow careless with success. His drive at the eighth was just as steady and short as ever. But this time Bradbury Fisher made no attempt to imitate him. For seven holes he had been checking his natural instincts, and now he drove with all the banked-up fury that comes with release from long suppression.

For an instant he remained poised on one leg like a stork; then there was a whistle and a crack, and the ball, smitten squarely in the midriff, flew down the course and, soaring over the bunkers, hit the turf and gambolled to within twenty yards of the green.

He straightened out the kinks in his spine with a grim smile. Allowing himself the regulation three putts, he would be down in five, and only a miracle could give Gladstone Bott anything better than a seven.

'Two down,' he said some minutes later, and Gladstone Bott nodded sullenly.

It was not often that Bradbury Fisher kept on the fairway with two consecutive drives, but strange things were happening to-day. Not only was his drive at the ninth a full two hundred and forty yards, but it was also perfectly straight.

'One down,' said Bradbury Fisher, and Bott nodded even more sullenly than before.

There are few things more demoralising than to be consistently outdriven; and when he is outdriven by a hundred and seventy yards at two consecutive holes the bravest man is apt to be shaken. Gladstone Bott was only human. It was with a sinking heart that he watched his opponent heave and sway on the tenth tee; and when the ball once more flew straight and far down the course a strange weakness seemed to come over him. For the first time he lost his morale and topped. The ball trickled into the long grass, and after three fruitless stabs at it with a niblick he picked up, and the match was squared.

At the eleventh Bradbury Fisher also topped, and his tee-shot, though nice and straight, travelled only a couple of feet. He had to scramble to halve in eight.

The twelfth was another short hole; and Bradbury, unable to curb the fine, careless rapture which had crept into his game, had the misfortune to overshoot the green by some sixty yards, thus enabling his opponent to take the lead once more.

The thirteenth and fourteenth were halved, but Bradbury, driving another long ball, won the fifteenth, squaring the match.

It seemed to Bradbury Fisher, as he took his stand on the sixteenth tee, that he now had the situation well in hand. At the thirteenth and fourteenth his drive had flickered, but on the fifteenth it had come back in all its glorious vigour and there appeared to be no reason to suppose that it had not come to stay. He recollected exactly how he had done that last colossal slosh, and he now prepared to reproduce the movements precisely as before. The great thing to remember was to hold the breath on the back-swing and not to release it before the moment of impact. Also, the eyes should not be closed until late in the down-swing. All great golfers have their little secrets, and that was Bradbury's.

With these aids to success firmly fixed in his mind, Bradbury Fisher prepared to give the ball the nastiest bang that a golf-ball had ever had since Edward Blackwell was in his prime. He drew in his breath and, with lungs expanded to their fullest capacity, heaved back on to his large, flat right foot. Then, clenching his teeth, he lashed out.

When he opened his eyes, they fell upon a horrid spectacle. Either he had closed those eyes too soon or else he had breathed too precipitately – whatever the cause, the ball, which should have gone due south, was travelling with great speed sou'-sou'-east. And, even as he gazed, it curved to earth and fell into as uninviting a bit of rough as he had ever penetrated. And he was a man who had spent much time in many roughs.

Leaving Gladstone Bott to continue his imitation of a spavined octogenarian rolling peanuts with a toothpick, Bradbury Fisher, followed by his caddie, set out on the long trail into the jungle.

Hope did not altogether desert him as he walked. In spite of its erratic direction, the ball had been so shrewdly smitten that it was not far from the green. Provided luck was with him and the lie not too desperate, a mashie would put him on the carpet. It was only when he reached the rough and saw what had happened that his heart sank. There the ball lay, half hidden in the grass, while above it waved the straggling tentacle of some tough-looking shrub. Behind it was a stone, and behind the stone, at just the elevation required to catch the back-swing of the club, was a tree. And, by an ironical stroke of fate which drew from Bradbury a hollow, bitter laugh, only a few feet to the right was a beautiful smooth piece of turf from which it would have been a pleasure to play one's second.

Dully, Bradbury looked round to see how Bott was getting on. And then suddenly, as he found that Bott was completely invisible behind the belt of bushes through which he had just passed, a voice seemed to whisper to him, 'Why not?'

Bradbury Fisher, remember, had spent thirty years in Wall Street.

It was at this moment that he realised that he was not alone. His caddie was standing at his side.

Bradbury Fisher gazed upon the caddie, whom until now he had not had any occasion to observe with any closeness.

The caddie was not a boy. He was a man, apparently in the middle forties, with bushy eyebrows and a walrus moustache; and there was something about his appearance which suggested to Bradbury that here was a kindred spirit. He reminded Bradbury a little of Spike Huggins, the safe-blower, who had been a fresher with him at Sing-Sing. It seemed to him that this caddie could be trusted in a delicate matter involving secrecy and silence. Had he been some babbling urchin, the risk might have been too great.

'Caddie,' said Bradbury.

'Sir?' said the caddie.

'Yours is an ill-paid job,' said Bradbury.

'It is, indeed, sir,' said the caddie.

'Would you like to earn fifty dollars?'

'I would prefer to earn a hundred.'

'I meant a hundred,' said Bradbury.

He produced a roll of bills from his pocket, and peeled off one of that value. Then, stooping, he picked up his ball and placed it on the little oasis of turf. The caddie bowed intelligently.

'You mean to say,' cried Gladstone Bott, a few moments later, 'that you were out with your second? With your second!'

'I had a stroke of luck.'

'You're sure it wasn't about six strokes of luck?'

'My ball was right out in the open in an excellent lie.'

'Oh!' said Gladstone Bott, shortly.

'I have four for it, I think.'

'One down,' said Gladstone Bott.

'And two to play,' trilled Bradbury.

It was with a light heart that Bradbury Fisher teed up on the seventeenth. The match, he felt, was as good as over. The whole essence of golf is to discover a way of getting out of rough without losing strokes; and with this sensible, broad-minded man of the world caddying for him he seemed to have discovered the ideal way. It cost him scarcely a pang when he saw his drive slice away into a tangle of long grass, but for the sake of appearances he affected a little chagrin.

'Tut, tut!' he said.

'I shouldn't worry,' said Gladstone Bott. 'You will probably find it sitting upon an india-rubber tee which someone has dropped there.'

He spoke sardonically, and Bradbury did not like his manner. But then he never had liked Gladstone Bott's manner, so what of that? He made his way to where the ball had fallen. It was lying under a bush.

'Caddie,' said Bradbury.

'Sir?' said the caddie.

'A hundred?'

'And fifty.'

'And fifty,' said Bradbury Fisher.

Gladstone Bott was still toiling along the fairway when Bradbury reached the green.

'How many?' he asked, eventually winning to the goal.

'On in two,' said Bradbury. 'And you?'

'Playing seven.'

'Then let me see. If you take two putts, which is most unlikely, I shall have six for the hole and match.'

A minute later Bradbury had picked up his ball out of the cup. He stood there, basking in the sunshine, his heart glowing with quiet happiness. It seemed to him that he had never seen the countryside looking so beautiful. The birds appeared to be singing as they had never sung before. The trees and the rolling turf had taken on a charm beyond anything he had ever encountered. Even Gladstone Bott looked almost bearable.

'A very pleasant match,' he said, cordially, 'conducted throughout in the most sporting spirit. At one time I thought you were going to pull it off, old man, but there – class will tell.'

'I will now make my report,' said the caddie with the walrus moustache.

'Do so,' said Gladstone Bott, briefly.

Bradbury Fisher stared at the man with blanched cheeks. The sun had ceased to shine, the birds had stopped singing. The trees and the rolling turf looked pretty rotten, and Gladstone Bott perfectly foul. His heart was leaden with a hideous dread.

'Your report? Your – your report? What do you mean?'

'You don't suppose,' said Gladstone Bott, 'that I would play you an important match unless I had detectives watching you, do you? This gentleman is from the Quick Results Agency. What have you to report?' he said, turning to the caddie.

The caddie removed his bushy eyebrows, and with a quick gesture swept off his moustache.

'On the twelfth inst.,' he began in a monotonous, sing-song voice, 'acting upon instructions received, I made my way to the Goldenville Golf Links in order to observe the movements of the man Fisher. I had adopted for the occasion the Number Three disguise and—'

'All right, all right,' said Gladstone Bott, impatiently. 'You can skip all that. Come down to what happened at the sixteenth.'

The caddie looked wounded, but he bowed deferentially.

'At the sixteenth hole the man Fisher moved his ball into what – from his actions and furtive manner – I deduced to be a more favourable position.'

'Ah!' said Gladstone Bott.

'On the seventeenth the man Fisher picked up his ball and threw it with a movement of the wrist on to the green.'

'It's a lie. A foul and contemptible lie,' shouted Bradbury Fisher.

'Realising that the man Fisher might adopt this attitude, sir,' said the caddie, 'I took the precaution of snapshotting him in the act with my miniature wrist-watch camera, the detective's best friend.'

Bradbury Fisher covered his face with his hands and uttered a hollow groan.

'My match,' said Gladstone Bott, with vindictive triumph. 'I'll trouble you to deliver that butler to me f.o.b. at my residence not later than noon to-morrow. Oh yes, and I was forgetting. You owe me three railroads.'

Blizzard, dignified but kindly, met Bradbury in the Byzantine hall on his return home.

'I trust your golf-match terminated satisfactorily, sir?' said the butler.

A pang, almost too poignant to be borne, shot through Bradbury.

'No, Blizzard,' he said. 'No. Thank you for your kind inquiry, but I was not in luck.'

'Too bad, sir,' said Blizzard, sympathetically. 'I trust the prize at stake was not excessive?'

'Well – er – well, it was rather big. I should like to speak to you about that a little later, Blizzard.'

'At any time that is suitable to you, sir. If you will ring for one of the assistant-under-footmen when you desire to see me, sir, he will find me in my pantry. Meanwhile, sir, this cable arrived for you a short while back.'

Bradbury took the envelope listlessly. He had been expecting a communication from his London agents announcing that they had bought Kent and Sussex, for which he had instructed them to make a firm offer just before he left England. No doubt this was their cable.

He opened the envelope, and started as if it had contained a scorpion. It was from his wife.

'Returning immediately "Aquitania,"' (it ran). 'Docking Friday night. Meet without fail.'

Bradbury stared at the words, frozen to the marrow. Although he had been in a sort of trance ever since that dreadful moment on the seventeenth green, his great brain had not altogether ceased to function; and, while driving home in the car, he had sketched out roughly a plan of action which, he felt, might meet the crisis. Assuming that Mrs Fisher was to remain abroad for another month he had practically decided to buy a daily paper, insert in it a front-page story announcing the death of Blizzard, forward the clipping to his wife, and then sell his house and move to another neighbourhood. In this way it might be that she would never learn of what had occurred.

But if she was due back next Friday, the scheme fell through and exposure was inevitable.

He wondered dully what had caused her change of plans, and

came to the conclusion that some feminine sixth sense must have warned her of peril threatening Blizzard. With a good deal of peevishness he wished that Providence had never endowed women with this sixth sense. A woman with merely five took quite enough handling.

'Sweet suffering soup-spoons!' groaned Bradbury.

'Sir?' said Blizzard.

'Nothing,' said Bradbury.

'Very good, sir,' said Blizzard.

For a man with anything on his mind, any little trouble calculated to affect the *joie de vivre*, there are few spots less cheering than the Customs sheds of New York. Draughts whistle dismally there – now to, now fro. Strange noises are heard. Customs officials chew gum and lurk grimly in the shadows, like tigers awaiting the luncheon-gong. It is not surprising that Bradbury's spirits, low when he reached the place, should have sunk to zero long before the gangplank was lowered and the passengers began to stream down it.

His wife was among the first to land. How beautiful she looked, thought Bradbury, as he watched her. And, alas, how intimidating. His tastes had always lain in the direction of spirited women. His first wife had been spirited. So had his second, third, and fourth. And the one at the moment holding office was perhaps the most spirited of the whole platoon. For one long instant, as he went to meet her, Bradbury Fisher was conscious of a regret that he had not married one of those meek, mild girls who suffer uncomplainingly at their husband's hands in the more hectic type of feminine novel. What he felt he could have done with at the moment was the sort of wife who thinks herself dashed lucky if the other half of the sketch does not drag her round the billiard-room by her hair, kicking her the while with spiked shoes.

Three conversational openings presented themselves to him as he approached her.

'Darling, there is something I want to tell you—'

'Dearest, I have a small confession to make—'

'Sweetheart, I don't know if by any chance you remember Blizzard, our butler. Well, it's like this—'

But, in the event, it was she who spoke first.

'Oh, Bradbury,' she cried, rushing into his arms, 'I've done the most awful thing, and you must try to forgive me!'

Bradbury blinked. He had never seen her in this strange mood before. As she clung to him, she seemed timid, fluttering, and – although a woman who weighed a full hundred and fifty-seven pounds – almost fragile.

'What is it?' he inquired, tenderly. 'Has somebody stolen your jewels?'

'No, no.'

'Have you been losing money at bridge?'

'No, no. Worse than that.'

Bradbury started.

'You didn't sing "My Little Grey Home in the West" at the ship's concert?' he demanded, eyeing her closely.

'No, no! Ah, how can I tell you? Bradbury, look! You see that man over there?'

Bradbury followed her pointing finger. Standing in an attitude of negligent dignity beside a pile of trunks under the letter V was a tall, stout, ambassadorial man, at the very sight of whom, even at this distance, Bradbury Fisher felt an odd sense of inferiority. His pendulous cheeks, his curving waistcoat, his protruding eyes, and the sequence of rolling chins combined to produce in

Bradbury that instinctive feeling of being in the presence of a superior which we experience when meeting scratch golfers, head-waiters of fashionable restaurants, and traffic-policemen. A sudden pang of suspicion pierced him.

'Well?' he said, hoarsely. 'What of him?'

'Bradbury, you must not judge me too harshly. We were thrown together and I was tempted—'

'Woman,' thundered Bradbury Fisher, 'who is this man?'

'His name is Vosper.'

'And what is there between you and him, and when did it start, and why and how and where?'

Mrs Fisher dabbed at her eyes with her handkerchief.

'It was at the Duke of Bootle's, Bradbury. I was invited there for the weekend.'

'And this man was there?'

'Yes.'

'Ha! Proceed!'

'The moment I set eyes on him, something seemed to go all over me.'

'Indeed!'

'At first it was his mere appearance. I felt that I had dreamed of such a man all my life, and that for all these wasted years I had been putting up with the second-best.'

'Oh, you did, eh? Really? Is that so? You did, did you?' snorted Bradbury Fisher.

'I couldn't help it, Bradbury. I know I have always seemed so devoted to Blizzard, and so I was. But, honestly, there is no comparison between them – really there isn't. You should see the way Vosper stood behind the Duke's chair. Like a high priest presiding over some mystic religious ceremony. And his voice when he asks you if you will have sherry or hock! Like the music of some wonderful organ. I couldn't resist him. I approached him delicately, and found that he was willing to come to America. He had been eighteen years with the Duke, and he told me he couldn't stand the sight of the back of his head any longer. So—'

Bradbury Fisher reeled.

'This man – this Vosper. Who is he?'

'Why, I'm telling you, honey. He was the Duke's butler, and now he's ours. Oh, you know how impulsive I am. Honestly, it wasn't till we were half-way across the Atlantic that I suddenly said to myself, "What about Blizzard?" What am I to do, Bradbury? I simply haven't the nerve to fire Blizzard. And yet what will happen when he walks into his pantry and finds Vosper there? Oh, think, Bradbury, think!'

Bradbury Fisher was thinking – and for the first time in a week without agony.

'Evangeline,' he said, gravely, 'this is awkward.'

'I know.'

'Extremely awkward.'

'I know, I know. But surely you can think of some way out of the muddle!'

'I may. I cannot promise, but I may.' He pondered deeply. 'Ha! I have it! It is just possible that I may be able to induce Gladstone Bott to take on Blizzard.'

'Do you really think he would?'

'He may – if I play my cards carefully. At any rate, I will try to persuade him. For the moment you and Vosper had better remain in New York, while I go home and put the negotiations in train. If I am successful, I will let you know.'

'Do try your very hardest.'

'I think I shall be able to manage it. Gladstone and I are old friends, and he would stretch a point to oblige me. But let this be a lesson to you, Evangeline.'

'Oh, I will.'

'By the way,' said Bradbury Fisher, 'I am cabling my London agents to-day to instruct them to buy J. H. Taylor's shirt-stud for my collection.'

'Quite right, Bradbury darling. And anything else you want in that way you will get, won't you?'

'I will,' said Bradbury Fisher.

The young man in the heather-mixture plus fours, who for some time had been pacing the terrace above the ninth green like an imprisoned jaguar, flung himself into a chair and uttered a snort of anguish.

'Women,' said the young man, 'are the limit.'

The Oldest Member, ever ready to sympathise with youth in affliction, turned a courteous ear.

'What,' he inquired, 'has the sex been pulling on you now?'

'My wife is the best little woman in the world.'

'I can readily believe it.'

'But,' continued the young man, 'I would like to bean her with a brick, and bean her good. I told her, when she wanted to play a round with me this afternoon, that we must start early, as the days are drawing in. What did she do? Having got into her things, she decided that she didn't like the look of them and made a complete change. She then powdered her nose for ten minutes. And when finally I got her on to the first tee, an hour late, she went back into the club-house to 'phone to her dressmaker. It will be dark before we've played six holes. If I had my way, golf-clubs would make a rigid rule that no wife be allowed to play with her husband.'

The Oldest Member nodded gravely.

THE HEART OF A GOOF

'Until this is done,' he agreed, 'the millennium cannot but be set back indefinitely. Although we are told nothing about it, there can be little doubt that one of Job's chief trials was that his wife insisted on playing golf with him. And, as we are on this topic, it may interest you to hear a story.'

'I have no time to listen to stories now.'

'If your wife is telephoning to her dress-maker, you have ample time,' replied the Sage. 'The story which I am about to relate deals with a man named Bradbury Fisher—'

'You told me that one.'

'I think not.'

'Yes, you did. Bradbury Fisher was a Wall Street millionaire who had an English butler named Blizzard, who had been fifteen years with an earl. Another millionaire coveted Blizzard, and they played a match for him, and Fisher lost. But, just as he was wondering how he could square himself with his wife, who valued Blizzard very highly, Mrs Fisher turned up from England with a still finer butler named Vosper, who had been eighteen years with a duke. So all ended happily.'

'Yes,' said the Sage. 'You appear to have the facts correctly. The tale which I am about to relate is a sequel to that story, and runs as follows:

You say (began the Oldest Member) that all ended happily. That was Bradbury Fisher's opinion, too. It seemed to Bradbury in the days that followed Vosper's taking of office as though Providence, recognising his sterling merits, had gone out of its way to smooth the path of life for him. The weather was fine; his handicap, after remaining stationary for many years, had begun to decrease; and his old friend Rupert Worple had just come out of Sing-Sing, where he had been taking a post-graduate course, and was paying him a pleasant visit at his house in Goldenville, Long Island.

The only thing, in fact, that militated against Bradbury's complete tranquillity was the information he had just received from his wife that her mother, Mrs Lora Smith Maplebury, was about to infest the home for an indeterminate stay.

Bradbury had never liked his wives' mothers. His first wife, he recalled, had had a particularly objectionable mother. So had his second, third, and fourth. And the present holder of the title appeared to him to be scratch. She had a habit of sniffing in a significant way whenever she looked at him, and this can never make for a spirit of easy comradeship between man and woman. Given a free hand, he would have tied a brick to her neck and dropped her in the water-hazard at the second; but, realising that this was but a Utopian dream, he sensibly decided to make the best of things and to content himself with jumping out of window whenever she came into a room in which he happened to be sitting.

His mood, therefore, as he sat in his Louis Quinze library on the evening on which this story opens, was perfectly contented. And when there was a knock at the door and Vosper entered, no foreboding came to warn him that the quiet peace of his life was about to be shattered.

'Might I have a word, sir?' said the butler.

'Certainly, Vosper. What is it?'

Bradbury Fisher beamed upon the man. For the hundredth time, as he eyed him, he reflected how immeasurably superior he was to the departed Blizzard. Blizzard had been fifteen years with an earl, and no one disputes that earls are all very well in their way. But they are not dukes. About a butler who has served in a ducal household there is something which cannot be duplicated by one who has passed the formative years of his butlerhood in humbler surroundings.

'It has to do with Mr Worple, sir.'

'What about him?'

'Mr Worple,' said the butler, gravely, 'must go. I do not like his laugh, sir.'

'Eh?'

'It is too hearty, sir. It would not have done for the Duke.'

Bradbury Fisher was an easy-going man, but he belonged to a free race. For freedom his fathers had fought and, if he had heard the story correctly, bled. His eyes flashed.

'Oh!' he cried. 'Oh, indeed!'

'Yes, sir.'

'Is zat so?'

'Yes, sir.'

'Well, let me tell you something, Bill—'

'My name is Hildebrand, sir.'

'Well, let me tell you, whatever your scarlet name is, that no butler is going to boss me in my own home. You can darned well go yourself.'

'Very good, sir.'

Vosper withdrew like an ambassador who has received his papers; and presently there was a noise without like hens going through a hedge, and Mrs Fisher plunged in.

'Bradbury,' she cried, 'are you mad? Of course Mr Worple must go if Vosper says so. Don't you realise that Vosper will leave us if we don't humour him?'

'I should worry about him leaving!'

A strange, set look came into Mrs Fisher's face.

'Bradbury,' she said, 'if Vosper leaves us, I shall die. And, what is more, just before dying I shall get a divorce. Yes, I will.'

'But, darling,' gasped Bradbury, 'Rupert Worple! Old Rupie Worple! We've been friends all our lives.'

'I don't care.'

'We were freshers at Sing-Sing together.'

'I don't care.'

'We were initiated into the same Frat, the dear old Cracka-Bitta-Rock, on the same day.'

'I don't care. Heaven has sent me the perfect butler, and I'm not going to lose him.'

There was a tense silence.

'Ah, well!' said Bradbury Fisher with a deep sigh.

That night he broke the news to Rupert Worple.

'I never thought,' said Rupert Worple sadly, 'when we sang together on the glee-club at the old Alma Mater, that it would ever come to this.'

'Nor I,' said Bradbury Fisher. 'But so it must be. You wouldn't have done for the Duke, Rupie, you wouldn't have done for the Duke.'

'Good-bye, Number 8,097,564,' said Rupert Worple in a low voice.

'Good-bye, Number 8,097,565,' whispered Bradbury Fisher.

And with a silent hand-clasp the two friends parted.

With the going of Rupert Worple a grey cloud seemed to settle upon the glowing radiance of Bradbury Fisher's life. Mrs Lora Smith Maplebury duly arrived; and, having given a series of penetrating sniffs as he greeted her in the entrance-hall, dug herself in and settled down to what looked like the visit of a lifetime. And then, just as Bradbury's cup seemed to be full to over-flowing, Mrs Fisher drew him aside one evening.

'Bradbury,' said Mrs Fisher. 'I have some good news for you.'

'Is your mother leaving?' asked Bradbury eagerly.

'Of course not. I said good news. I am taking up golf again.'

Bradbury Fisher clutched at the arms of his chair, and an ashen pallor spread itself over his clean-cut face.

'What did you say?' he muttered.

'I'm taking up golf again. Won't it be nice? We'll be able to play together every day.'

Bradbury Fisher shuddered strongly. It was many years since he had played with his wife, but, like an old wound, the memory of it still troubled him occasionally.

'It was Vosper's idea.'

'Vosper!'

A sudden seething fury gripped Bradbury. This pestilent butler was an absolute home-wrecker. He toyed with the idea of poisoning Vosper's port. Surely, if he were to do so, a capable lawyer could smooth things over and get him off with, at the worst, a nominal fine.

'Vosper says I need exercise. He says he does not like my wheezing.'

'Your what?'

'My wheezing. I do wheeze, you know.'

'Well, so does he.'

'Yes, but a good butler is expected to wheeze. A wheezing woman is quite a different thing. My wheezing would never have done for the Duke, Vosper says.'

Bradbury Fisher breathed tensely.

'Ha!' he said.

'I think it's so nice of him, Bradbury. It shows he has our interests at heart, just like a faithful old retainer. He says wheezing is an indication of heightened blood-pressure and can be remedied by gentle exercise. So we'll have our first round to-morrow morning, shall we?'

'Just as you say,' said Bradbury dully. 'I had a sort of date to make one of a foursome with three men at the club, but—'

'Oh, you don't want to play with those silly men any more. It will be much nicer, just you and I playing together.'

It has always seemed to me a strange and unaccountable thing that nowadays, when gloom is at such a premium in the world's literature and all around us stern young pessimists are bringing home the bacon with their studies in the greyly grim, no writer has thought of turning his pen to a realistic portrayal of the golfing wife. No subject could be more poignant, and yet it has been completely neglected. One can only suppose that even modern novelists feel that the line should be drawn somewhere.

Bradbury Fisher's emotions, as he stood by the first tee watching his wife prepare to drive off, were far beyond my poor power to describe. Compared with him at that moment, the hero of a novel of the Middle West would have seemed almost offensively chirpy. This was the woman he loved, and she was behaving in a manner that made the iron sink deep into his soul.

Most women golfers are elaborate wagglers, but none that Bradbury had ever seen had made quite such a set of Swedish exercises out of the simple act of laying the clubhead behind the ball and raising it over the right shoulder. For fully a minute, it seemed to him, Mrs Fisher fiddled and pawed at the ball; while Bradbury, realising that there are eighteen tees on a course and that this Russian Ballet stuff was consequently going to happen at least seventeen times more, quivered in agony and clenched his hands till the knuckles stood out white under the strain.

Then she drove, and the ball trickled down the hill into a patch of rough some five yards distant.

'Tee-hee!' said Mrs Fisher.

Bradbury uttered a sharp cry. He was married to a golfing giggler.

'What did I do then?'

'God help you, woman,' said Bradbury, 'you jerked your head up till I wonder it didn't come off at the neck.'

It was at the fourth hole that further evidence was afforded the wretched man of how utterly a good, pure woman may change her nature when once she gets out on the links. Mrs Fisher had played her eleventh, and, having walked the intervening three yards, was about to play her twelfth when behind them, grouped upon the tee, Bradbury perceived two of his fellow-members of the club. Remorse and shame pierced him.

'One minute, honey,' he said, as his life's partner took a stranglehold on her mashie and was about to begin the movements. 'We'd better let these men through.'

'What men?'

'We're holding up a couple of fellows. I'll wave to them.'

'You will do nothing of the sort,' cried Mrs Fisher. 'The idea!'

'But, darling—'

'Why should they go through us? We started before them.'

'But, pettie—'

'They shall not pass!' said Mrs Fisher. And, raising her mashie, she dug a grim divot out of the shrinking turf. With bowed head, Bradbury followed her on the long, long trail.

The sun was sinking as they came at last to journey's end.

'How right Vosper is!' said Mrs Fisher, nestling into the cushions of the automobile. 'I feel ever so much better already.'

'Do you?' said Bradbury wanly. 'Do you?'

'We'll play again to-morrow afternoon,' said his wife.

Bradbury Fisher was a man of steel. He endured for a week. But on the last day of the week Mrs Fisher insisted on taking as a companion on the round Alfred, her pet Airedale. In vain Bradbury spoke of the Green Committee and their prejudice against dogs on the links. Mrs Fisher – and Bradbury, as he heard the ghastly words, glanced involuntarily up at the summer sky, as if preparing to dodge the lightning-bolt which could scarcely fail to punish such blasphemy – said that the Green Committee were a lot of silly, fussy old men, and she had no patience with them.

So Alfred came along – barking at Bradbury as he endeavoured to concentrate on the smooth pronation of the wrists, pounding ahead to frolic round distant players who were shaping for delicate chip-shots, and getting a deep toe-hold on the turf of each successive green. Hell, felt Bradbury, must be something like this; and he wished that he had led a better life.

But that retribution which waits on all, both small and great, who defy Green Committees had marked Alfred down. Taking up a position just behind Mrs Fisher as she began her down swing on the seventh, he received so shrewd a blow on his right foreleg that with a sharp yelp he broke into a gallop, raced through a foursome on the sixth green, and, charging across country, dived headlong into the water-hazard on the second; where he remained until Bradbury, who had been sent in pursuit, waded in and fished him out.

Mrs Fisher came panting up, full of concern. 'What shall we do? The poor little fellow is quite lame. I know, you can carry him, Bradbury.'

Bradbury Fisher uttered a low, bleating sound. The water had had the worst effect on the animal. Even when dry, Alfred was always a dog of powerful scent. Wet, he had become definitely one of the six best smellers. His aroma had what the advertisement-writers call 'strong memory value.'

'Carry him? To the car, do you mean?'

'Of course not. Round the links. I don't want to miss a day's golf. You can put him down when you play your shots.'

For a long instant Bradbury hesitated. The words 'Is zat so?' trembled on his lips.

'Very well,' he said, swallowing twice.

That night, in his du Barri bedroom, Bradbury Fisher lay sleepless far into the dawn. A crisis, he realised, had come in his domestic affairs. Things, he saw clearly, could not go on like this. It was not merely the awful spiritual agony of playing these daily rounds of golf with his wife that was so hard to endure. The real trouble was that the spectacle of her on the links was destroying his ideals, sapping away that love and respect which should have been as imperishable as steel.

To a good man his wife should be a goddess, a being far above him to whom he can offer worship and reverence, a beacon-star guiding him over the tossing seas of life. She should be ever on a pedestal and in a shrine. And when she waggles for a minute and a half and then jerks her head and tops the ball, she ceases to be so. And Mrs Fisher was not merely a head-lifter and a super-waggler; she was a scoffer at Golf's most sacred things. She held up scratch-men. She omitted to replace divots. She spoke lightly of Green Committees.

The sun was gilding Goldenville in its morning glory when Bradbury made up his mind. He would play with her no more.

To do so would be fair neither to himself nor to her. At any moment, he felt, she might come out on the links in high heels or stop to powder her nose on the green while frenzied foursomes waited to play their approach-shots. And then love would turn to hate, and he and she would go through life estranged. Better to end it now, while he still retained some broken remains of the old esteem.

He had got everything neatly arranged. He would plead business in the City and sneak off each day to play on another course five miles away.

'Darling,' he said at breakfast, 'I'm afraid we shan't be able to have our game for a week or so. I shall have to be at the office early and late.'

'Oh, what a shame!' said Mrs Fisher.

'You will, no doubt, be able to get a game with the pro or somebody. You know how bitterly this disappoints me. I had come to look on our daily round as the bright spot of the day. But business is business.'

'I thought you had retired from business,' said Mrs Lora Smith Maplebury, with a sniff that cracked a coffee-cup.

Bradbury Fisher looked at her coldly. She was a lean, pale-eyed woman with high cheek-bones, and for the hundredth time since she had come into his life he felt how intensely she needed a punch on the nose.

'Not altogether,' he said. 'I still retain large interests in this and that, and I am at the moment occupied with affairs which I cannot mention without revealing secrets which might – which would – which are—Well, anyway, I've got to go to the office.'

'Oh, quite,' said Mrs Maplebury.

'What do you mean, quite?' demanded Bradbury.

'I mean just what I say. Quite!'

'Why quite?'

'Why not quite? I suppose I can say "Quite!" can't I?'

'Oh, quite,' said Bradbury.

He kissed his wife and left the room. He felt a little uneasy. There had been something in the woman's manner which had caused him a vague foreboding.

Had he been able to hear the conversation that followed his departure, he would have been still more uneasy.

'Suspicious!' said Mrs Maplebury.

'What is?' asked Mrs Fisher.

'That man's behaviour.'

'What do you mean?'

'Did you observe him closely while he was speaking?'

'No.'

'The tip of his nose wiggled. Always distrust a man who wiggles the tip of his nose.'

'I am sure Bradbury would not deceive you.'

'So am I. But he might try to.'

'I don't understand, mother. Do you mean you think Bradbury is not going to the office?'

'I am sure he is not.'

'You think—?'

'I do.'

'You are suggesting—?'

'I am.'

'You would imply—?'

'I would.'

A moan escaped Mrs Fisher.

'Oh, mother, mother!' she cried. 'If I thought Bradbury was untrue to me, what I wouldn't do to that poor clam!'

KEEPING IN WITH VOSPER

'I certainly think that the least you can do, as a good womanly woman, is to have a capable lawyer watching your interests.'

'But we can easily find out if he is at the office. We can ring them up on the 'phone and ask.'

'And be told that he is in conference. He will not have neglected to arrange for that.'

'Then what shall I do?'

'Wait,' said Mrs Maplebury. 'Wait and be watchful.'

The shades of night were falling when Bradbury returned to his home. He was fatigued but jubilant. He had played forty-five holes in the society of his own sex. He had kept his head down and his eye on the ball. He had sung negro spirituals in the locker-room.

'I trust, Bradbury,' said Mrs Maplebury, 'that you are not tired after your long day?'

'A little,' said Bradbury. 'Nothing to signify.' He turned radiantly to his wife.

'Honey,' he said, 'you remember the trouble I was having with my iron? Well, to-day—'

He stopped aghast. Like every good husband it had always been his practice hitherto to bring his golfing troubles to his wife, and in many a cosy after-dinner chat he had confided to her the difficulty he was having in keeping his iron-shots straight. And he had only just stopped himself now from telling her that to-day he had been hitting 'em sweetly on the meat right down the middle.

'Your iron?'

'Er – ah – yes. I have large interests in Iron – as also in Steel, Jute, Woollen Fabrics, and Consolidated Peanuts. A gang has been trying to hammer down my stock. To-day I fixed them.'

'You did, did you?' said Mrs Maplebury.

THE HEART OF A GOOF

'I said I did,' retorted Bradbury, defiantly.

'So did I. I said you did, did you?'

'What do you mean, did you?'

'Well, you did, didn't you?'

'Yes, I did.'

'Exactly what I said. You did. Didn't you?'

'Yes, I did.'

'Yes, you did!' said Mrs Maplebury.

Once again Bradbury felt vaguely uneasy. There was nothing in the actual dialogue which had just taken place to cause him alarm – indeed, considered purely as dialogue, it was bright and snappy and well calculated to make things gay about the home. But once more there had been a subtle something in his mother-in-law's manner which had jarred upon him. He mumbled and went off to dress for dinner.

'Ha!' said Mrs Maplebury, as the door closed.

Such, then, was the position of affairs in the Fisher home. And now that I have arrived thus far in my story and have shown you this man systematically deceiving the woman he had vowed – at one of the most exclusive altars in New York – to love and cherish, you – if you are the sort of husband I hope you are – must be saying to yourself: 'But what of Bradbury Fisher's conscience?' Remorse, you feel, must long since have begun to gnaw at his vitals; and the thought suggests itself to you that surely by this time the pangs of self-reproach must have interfered seriously with his short game, even if not as yet sufficiently severe to affect his driving off the tee.

You are overlooking the fact that Bradbury Fisher's was the trained and educated conscience of a man who had passed a large portion of his life in Wall Street; and years of practice had enabled him to reduce the control of it to a science. Many a time in the past, when an active operator on the Street, he had done things to the Small Investor which would have caused raised eyebrows in the fo'c'sle of a pirate sloop – and done them without a blush. He was not the man, therefore, to suffer torment merely because he was slipping one over on the Little Woman.

Occasionally he would wince a trifle at the thought of what would happen if she ever found out; but apart from that, I am doing no more than state the plain truth when I say that Bradbury Fisher did not care a whoop.

Besides, at this point his golf suddenly underwent a remarkable improvement. He had always been a long driver, and quite abruptly he found that he was judging them nicely with the putter. Two weeks after he had started on his campaign of deception he amazed himself and all who witnessed the performance by cracking a hundred for the first time in his career. And every golfer knows that in the soul of the man who does that there is no room for remorse. Conscience may sting the player who is going round in a hundred and ten, but when it tries to make itself unpleasant to the man who is doing ninety-sevens and ninety-eights, it is simply wasting its time.

I will do Bradbury Fisher justice. He did regret that he was not in a position to tell his wife all about that first ninety-nine of his. He would have liked to take her into a corner and show her with the aid of a poker and a lump of coal just how he had chipped up to the pin on the last hole and left himself a simple two-foot putt. And the forlorn feeling of being unable to confide his triumphs to a sympathetic ear deepened a week later when, miraculously achieving ninety-six in the medal round, he qualified for the sixth sixteen in the annual invitation tournament of the club to which he had attached himself.

'Shall I?' he mused, eyeing her wistfully across the Queen Anne table in the Crystal Boudoir, to which they had retired to drink their after-dinner coffee. 'Better not, better not,' whispered Prudence in his ear.

'Bradbury,' said Mrs Fisher.

'Yes, darling?'

'Have you been hard at work to-day?'

'Yes, precious. Very, very hard at work.'

'Ho!' said Mrs Maplebury.

'What did you say?' said Bradbury.

'I said ho!'

'What do you mean, ho?'

'Just ho. There is no harm, I imagine, in my saying ho, if I wish to.'

'Oh no,' said Bradbury. 'By no means. Not at all. Pray do so.'

'Thank you,' said Mrs Maplebury. 'Ho!'

'You do have to slave at the office, don't you?' said Mrs Fisher.

'I do, indeed.'

'It must be a great strain.'

'A terrible strain. Yes, yes, a terrible strain.'

'Then you won't object to giving it up, will you?'

Bradbury started.

'Giving it up?'

'Giving up going to the office. The fact is, dear,' said Mrs Fisher, 'Vosper has complained.'

'What about?'

'About you going to the office. He says he has never been in the employment of anyone engaged in commerce, and he doesn't like it. The Duke looked down on commerce very much. So I'm afraid, darling, you will have to give it up.'

Bradbury Fisher stared before him, a strange singing in his ears. The blow had been so sudden that he was stunned.

His fingers picked feverishly at the arm of his chair. He had paled to the very lips. If the office was barred to him, on what pretext could he sneak away from home? And sneak he must, for to-morrow and the day after the various qualifying sixteens were to play the match-rounds for the cups; and it was monstrous and impossible that he should not be there. He must be there. He had done a ninety-six, and the next best medal score in his sixteen was a hundred and one. For the first time in his life he had before him the prospect of winning a cup; and, highly though the poets have spoken of love, that emotion is not to be compared with the frenzy which grips a twenty-four handicap man who sees himself within reach of a cup.

Blindly he tottered from the room and sought his study. He wanted to be alone. He had to think, think.

The evening paper was lying on the table. Automatically he picked it up and ran his eye over the front page. And, as he did so, he uttered a sharp exclamation.

He leaped from his chair and returned to the boudoir, carrying the paper.

'Well, what do you know about this?' said Bradbury Fisher, in a hearty voice.

'We know a great deal about a good many things,' said Mrs Maplebury.

'What is it, Bradbury?' said Mrs Fisher.

'I'm afraid I shall have to leave you for a couple of days. Great nuisance, but there it is. But, of course, I must be there.'

'Where?'

'Ah, where?' said Mrs Maplebury.

'At Sing-Sing. I see in the paper that to-morrow and the day after they are inaugurating the new Osborne Stadium. All the men of my class will be attending, and I must go, too.'

'Must you really?'

'I certainly must. Not to do so would be to show a lack of college spirit. The boys are playing Yale, and there is to be a big dinner afterwards. I shouldn't wonder if I had to make a speech. But don't worry, honey,' he said, kissing his wife affectionately. 'I shall be back before you know I've gone.' He turned sharply to Mrs Maplebury. 'I beg your pardon?' he said, stiffly.

'I did not speak.'

'I thought you did.'

'I merely inhaled. I simply drew in air through my nostrils. If I am not at liberty to draw in air through my nostrils in your house, pray inform me.'

'I would prefer that you didn't,' said Bradbury, between set teeth.

'Then I would suffocate.'

'Yes,' said Bradbury Fisher.

Of all the tainted millionaires who, after years of plundering the widow and the orphan, have devoted the evening of their life to the game of golf, few can ever have been so boisterously exhilarated as was Bradbury Fisher when, two nights later, he returned to his home. His dreams had all come true. He had won his way to the foot of the rainbow. In other words, he was the possessor of a small pewter cup, value three dollars, which he had won by beating a feeble old gentleman with one eye in the final match of the competition for the sixth sixteen at the Squashy Hollow Golf Club Invitation Tournament.

He entered the house, radiant.

'Tra-la!' sang Bradbury Fisher. 'Tra-la!'

'I beg your pardon, sir?' said Vosper, who had encountered him in the hall.

'Eh? Oh, nothing. Just tra-la.'

'Very good, sir.'

Bradbury Fisher looked at Vosper. For the first time it seemed to sweep over him like a wave that Vosper was an uncommonly good fellow. The past was forgotten, and he beamed upon Vosper like the rising sun.

'Vosper,' he said, 'what wages are you getting?'

'I regret to say, sir,' replied the butler, 'that, at the moment, the precise amount of the salary of which I am in receipt has slipped my mind. I could refresh my memory by consulting my books, if you so desire it, sir.'

'Never mind. Whatever it is, it's doubled.'

'I am obliged, sir. You will, no doubt, send me a written memo, to that effect?'

'Twenty, if you like.'

'One will be ample, sir.'

Bradbury curveted past him through the baronial hall and into the Crystal Boudoir. His wife was there alone.

'Mother has gone to bed,' she said. 'She has a bad headache.'

'You don't say!' said Bradbury. It was as if everything was conspiring to make this a day of days. 'Well, it's great to be back in the old home.'

'Did you have a good time?'

'Capital.'

'You saw all your old friends?'

'Every one of them.'

'Did you make a speech at the dinner?'

'Did I! They rolled out of their seats and the waiters swept them up with dusters.'

'A very big dinner, I suppose?'

'Enormous.'

'How was the football game?'

'Best I've ever seen. We won. Number 432,986 made a hundred-and-ten-yard run for a touchdown in the last five minutes.'

'Really?'

'And that takes a bit of doing, with a ball and chain round your ankle, believe me!'

'Bradbury,' said Mrs Fisher, 'where have you been these last two days?'

Bradbury's heart missed a beat. His wife was looking exactly like her mother. It was the first time he had ever been able to believe that she could be Mrs Maplebury's daughter.

'Been? Why, I'm telling you.'

'Bradbury,' said Mrs Fisher, 'just one word. Have you seen the paper this morning?'

'Why, no. What with all the excitement of meeting the boys and this and that—'

'Then you have not seen that the inauguration of the new Stadium at Sing-Sing was postponed on account of an outbreak of mumps in the prison?'

Bradbury gulped.

'There was no dinner, no football game, no gathering of Old Grads – nothing! So – where have you been, Bradbury?'

Bradbury gulped again.

'You're sure you haven't got this wrong?' he said at length.

'Quite.'

'I mean, sure it wasn't some other place?'

'Quite.'

'Sing-Sing? You got the name correctly?'

'Quite. Where, Bradbury, have you been these last two days?'

'Well – er—'

Mrs Fisher coughed dryly.

'I merely ask out of curiosity. The facts will, of course, come out in court.'

'In court!'

'Naturally I propose to place this affair in the hands of my lawyer immediately.'

Bradbury started convulsively.

'You mustn't!'

'I certainly shall.'

A shudder shook Bradbury from head to foot. He felt worse than he had done when his opponent in the final had laid him a stymie on the last green, thereby squaring the match and taking it to the nineteenth hole.

'I will tell you all,' he muttered.

'Well?'

'Well – it was like this.'

'Yes?'

'Er – like this. In fact, this way.'

'Proceed.'

Bradbury clenched his hands; and, as far as that could be managed, avoided her eye.

'I've been playing golf,' he said in a low, toneless voice.

'Playing golf?'

'Yes.' Bradbury hesitated. 'I don't mean it in an offensive spirit, and no doubt most men would have enjoyed themselves thoroughly, but I – well, I am curiously constituted, angel, and the fact is I simply couldn't stand playing with you any longer. The fault, I am sure, was mine, but – well, there it is. If I had played another round with you, my darling, I think that I should have begun running about in circles, biting my best friends. So I thought it all over, and, not wanting to hurt your feelings by telling you the truth, I stooped to what I might call a ruse. I said I was going to the office; and, instead of going to the office, I went off to Squashy Hollow and played there.'

Mrs Fisher uttered a cry.

'You were there to-day and yesterday?'

In spite of his trying situation, the yeasty exhilaration which had been upon him when he entered the room returned to Bradbury.

'Was I!' he cried. 'You bet your Russian boots I was! Only winning a cup, that's all!'

'You won a cup?'

'You bet your diamond tiara I won a cup. Say, listen,' said Bradbury, diving for a priceless Boule table and wrenching a leg off it. 'Do you know what happened in the semi-final?' He clasped his fingers over the table-leg in the overlapping grip. 'I'm here, see, about fifteen feet off the green. The other fellow lying dead, and I'm playing the like. Best I could hope for was a half, you'll say, eh? Well, listen. I just walked up to that little white ball, and I gave it a little flick, and, believe me or believe me not, that little white ball never stopped running till it plunked into the hole.'

He stopped. He perceived that he had been introducing into the debate extraneous and irrelevant matter.

'Honey,' he said, fervently, 'you mustn't get mad about this. Maybe, if we try again, it will be all right. Give me another chance. Let me come out and play a round to-morrow. I think perhaps your style of play is a thing that wants getting used to. After all, I didn't like olives the first time I tried them. Or whisky. Or caviare, for that matter. Probably if—'

Mrs Fisher shook her head.

'I shall never play again.'

'Oh, but, listen—'

She looked at him fondly, her eyes dim with happy tears.

'I should have known you better, Bradbury. I suspected you. How foolish I was.'

'There, there,' said Bradbury.

'It was mother's fault. She put ideas into my head.'

There was much that Bradbury would have liked to say about her mother, but he felt that this was not the time.

'And you really forgive me for sneaking off and playing at Squashy Hollow?'

'Of course.'

'Then why not a little round to-morrow?'

'No, Bradbury, I shall never play again. Vosper says I mustn't.'

'What!'

'He saw me one morning on the links, and he came to me and told me – quite nicely and respectfully – that it must not occur again. He said with the utmost deference that I was making a spectacle of myself and that this nuisance must now cease. So I gave it up. But it's all right. Vosper thinks that gentle massage will cure my wheezing, so I'm having it every day, and really I do think there's an improvement already.'

'Where is Vosper?' said Bradbury, hoarsely.

'You aren't going to be rude to him, Bradbury? He is so sensitive.'

But Bradbury Fisher had left the room.

'You rang, sir?' said Vosper, entering the Byzantine smoking-room some few minutes later.

'Yes,' said Bradbury. 'Vosper, I am a plain, rugged man and

THE HEART OF A GOOF

I do not know all that there is to be known about these things. So do not be offended if I ask you a question.'

'Not at all, sir.'

'Tell me, Vosper, did the Duke ever shake hands with you?'

'Once only, sir – mistaking me in a dimly-lit hall for a visiting archbishop.'

'Would it be all right for me to shake hands with you now?'

'If you wish it, sir, certainly.'

'I want to thank you, Vosper. Mrs Fisher tells me that you have stopped her playing golf. I think that you have saved my reason, Vosper.'

'That is extremely gratifying, sir.'

'Your salary is trebled.'

'Thank you very much, sir. And, while we are talking, sir, if I might— There is one other little matter I wished to speak of, sir.'

'Shoot, Vosper.'

'It concerns Mrs Maplebury, sir.'

'What about her?'

'If I might say so, sir, she would scarcely have done for the Duke.'

A sudden wild thrill shot through Bradbury.

'You mean—?' he stammered.

'I mean, sir, that Mrs Maplebury must go. I make no criticism of Mrs Maplebury, you will understand, sir. I merely say that she would decidedly not have done for the Duke.'

Bradbury drew in his breath sharply.

'Vosper,' he said, 'the more I hear of that Duke of yours, the more I seem to like him. You really think he would have drawn the line at Mrs Maplebury?'

'Very firmly, sir.'

'Splendid fellow! Splendid fellow! She shall go to-morrow, Vosper.'

'Thank you very much, sir.'

'And, Vosper.'

'Sir?'

'Your salary. It is quadrupled.'

'I am greatly obliged, sir.'

'Tra-la, Vosper!'

'Tra-la, sir. Will that be all?'

'That will be all. Tra-la!'

'Tra-la, sir,' said the butler.

The afternoon was warm and heavy. Butterflies loafed languidly in the sunshine, birds panted in the shady recesses of the trees.

The Oldest Member, snug in his favourite chair, had long since succumbed to the drowsy influence of the weather. His eyes were closed, his chin sunk upon his breast. The pipe which he had been smoking lay beside him on the turf, and ever and anon there proceeded from him a muffled snore.

Suddenly the stillness was broken. There was a sharp, cracking sound as of splitting wood. The Oldest Member sat up, blinking. As soon as his eyes had become accustomed to the glare, he perceived that a foursome had holed out on the ninth and was disintegrating. Two of the players were moving with quick, purposeful steps in the direction of the side door which gave entrance to the bar; a third was making for the road that led to the village, bearing himself as one in profound dejection; the fourth came on to the terrace.

'Finished?' said the Oldest Member.

The other stopped, wiping a heated brow. He lowered himself into the adjoining chair and stretched his legs out.

'Yes. We started at the tenth. Golly, I'm tired. No joke playing in this weather.'

'How did you come out?'

'We won on the last green. Jimmy Fothergill and I were playing the vicar and Rupert Blake.'

'What was that sharp, cracking sound I heard?' asked the Oldest Member.

'That was the vicar smashing his putter. Poor old chap, he had rotten luck all the way round, and it didn't seem to make it any better for him that he wasn't able to relieve his feelings in the ordinary way.'

'I suspected some such thing,' said the Oldest Member, 'from the look of his back as he was leaving the green. His walk was the walk of an overwrought soul.'

His companion did not reply. He was breathing deeply and regularly.

'It is a moot question,' proceeded the Oldest Member, thoughtfully, 'whether the clergy, considering their peculiar position, should not be more liberally handicapped at golf than the laymen with whom they compete. I have made a close study of the game since the days of the feather ball, and I am firmly convinced that to refrain entirely from oaths during a round is almost equivalent to giving away three bisques. There are certain occasions when an oath seems to be so imperatively demanded that the strain of keeping it in must inevitably affect the ganglions or nerve-centres in such a manner as to diminish the steadiness of the swing.'

The man beside him slipped lower down in his chair. His mouth had opened slightly.

'I am reminded in this connection,' said the Oldest Member, 'of the story of young Chester Meredith, a friend of mine whom you have not, I think, met. He moved from this neighbourhood shortly before you came. There was a case where a man's whole happiness was very nearly wrecked purely because he tried to curb his instincts and thwart nature in this very respect. Perhaps you would care to hear the story?'

A snore proceeded from the next chair.

'Very well, then,' said the Oldest Member, 'I will relate it.'

Chester Meredith (said the Oldest Member) was one of the nicest young fellows of my acquaintance. We had been friends ever since he had come to live here as a small boy, and I had watched him with a fatherly eye through all the more important crises of a young man's life. It was I who taught him to drive, and when he had all that trouble in his twenty-first year with shanking his short approaches, it was to me that he came for sympathy and advice. It was an odd coincidence, therefore, that I should have been present when he fell in love.

I was smoking my evening cigar out here and watching the last couples finishing their rounds, when Chester came out of the club-house and sat by me. I could see that the boy was perturbed about something, and wondered why, for I knew that he had won his match.

'What,' I inquired, 'is on your mind?'

'Oh, nothing,' said Chester. 'I was only thinking that there are some human misfits who ought not to be allowed on any decent links.'

'You mean—?'

'The Wrecking Crew,' said Chester, bitterly. 'They held us up all the way round, confound them. Wouldn't let us through. What can you do with people who don't know enough of the etiquette of the game to understand that a single has right of way over a four-ball foursome? We had to loaf about for hours on end while they scratched at the turf like a lot of crimson hens. Eventually all four of them lost their balls simultaneously at the eleventh and we managed to get by. I hope they choke.'

I was not altogether surprised at his warmth. The Wrecking Crew consisted of four retired business-men who had taken up the noble game late in life because their doctors had ordered them air and exercise. Every club, I suppose, has a cross of this kind to bear, and it was not often that our members rebelled; but there was undoubtedly something particularly irritating in the methods of the Wrecking Crew. They tried so hard that it seemed almost inconceivable that they should be so slow.

'They are all respectable men,' I said, 'and were, I believe, highly thought of in their respective businesses. But on the links I admit that they are a trial.'

'They are the direct lineal descendants of the Gadarene swine,' said Chester firmly. 'Every time they come out I expect to see them rush down the hill from the first tee and hurl themselves into the lake at the second. Of all the—'

'Hush!' I said.

Out of the corner of my eye I had seen a girl approaching, and I was afraid lest Chester in his annoyance might use strong language. For he was one of those golfers who are apt to express themselves in moments of emotion with a good deal of generous warmth.

'Eh?' said Chester.

I jerked my head, and he looked round. And, as he did so, there came into his face an expression which I had seen there only once before, on the occasion when he won the President's Cup on the last green by holing a thirty-yard chip with his mashie. It was a look of ecstasy and awe. His mouth was open, his eyebrows raised, and he was breathing heavily through his nose.

'Golly!' I heard him mutter.

The girl passed by. I could not blame Chester for staring at her. She was a beautiful young thing, with a lissom figure and a perfect face. Her hair was a deep chestnut, her eyes blue, her nose small and laid back with about as much loft as a light iron. She disappeared, and Chester, after nearly dislocating his neck trying to see her round the corner of the club-house, emitted a deep, explosive sigh.

'Who is she?' he whispered.

I could tell him that. In one way and another I get to know most things around this locality.

'She is a Miss Blakeney. Felicia Blakeney. She has come to stay for a month with the Waterfields. I understand she was at school with Jane Waterfield. She is twenty-three, has a dog named Joseph, dances well, and dislikes parsnips. Her father is a distinguished writer on sociological subjects; her mother is Wilmot Royce, the well-known novelist, whose last work, *Sewers of the Soul*, was, you may recall, jerked before a tribunal by the Purity League. She has a brother, Crispin Blakeney, an eminent young reviewer and essayist, who is now in India studying local conditions with a view to a series of lectures. She only arrived here yesterday, so this is all I have been able to find out about her as yet.'

Chester's mouth was still open when I began speaking. By the time I had finished it was open still wider. The ecstatic look in his eyes had changed to one of dull despair.

'My God!' he muttered. 'If her family is like that, what chance is there for a rough-neck like me?'

'You admire her?'

'She is the alligator's Adam's apple,' said Chester, simply.

I patted his shoulder.

'Have courage, my boy,' I said. 'Always remember that the love of a good man, to whom the pro can give only a couple of strokes in eighteen holes, is not to be despised.'

'Yes, that's all very well. But this girl is probably one solid mass of brain. She will look on me as an uneducated wart-hog.'

'Well, I will introduce you, and we will see. She looked a nice girl.'

'You're a great describer, aren't you?' said Chester. 'A wonderful flow of language you've got, I don't think! Nice girl! Why, she's the only girl in the world. She's a pearl among women. She's the most marvellous, astounding, beautiful, heavenly thing that ever drew perfumed breath.' He paused, as if his train of thought had been interrupted by an idea. 'Did you say that her brother's name was Crispin?'

'I did. Why?'

Chester gave vent to a few manly oaths.

'Doesn't that just show you how things go in this rotten world?'

'What do you mean?'

'I was at school with him.'

'Surely that should form a solid basis for friendship?'

'Should it? Should it, by gad? Well, let me tell you that I probably kicked that blighted worm Crispin Blakeney a matter of seven hundred and forty-six times in the few years I knew him. He was the world's worst. He could have walked straight into the Wrecking Crew and no questions asked. Wouldn't it jar you? I have the luck to know her brother, and it turns out that we couldn't stand the sight of each other.'

'Well, there is no need to tell her that.'

'Do you mean—?' He gazed at me wildly. 'Do you mean I might pretend we were pals?'

'Why not? Seeing that he is in India, he can hardly contradict you.'

'My gosh!' He mused for a moment. I could see that the idea was beginning to sink in. It was always thus with Chester. You had to give him time. 'By Jove, it mightn't be a bad scheme at that. I mean, it would start me off with a rush, like being one up on bogey in the first two. And there's nothing like a good start. By gad, I'll do it.'

'I should.'

'Reminiscences of the dear old days when we were lads together, and all that sort of thing.'

'Precisely.'

'It isn't going to be easy, mind you,' said Chester, meditatively. 'I'll do it because I love her, but nothing else in this world would make me say a civil word about the blister. Well, then, that's settled. Get on with the introduction stuff, will you? I'm in a hurry.'

One of the privileges of age is that it enables a man to thrust his society on a beautiful girl without causing her to draw herself up and say 'Sir!' It was not difficult for me to make the acquaintance of Miss Blakeney, and, this done, my first act was to unleash Chester on her.

'Chester,' I said, summoning him as he loafed with an overdone carelessness on the horizon, one leg almost inextricably entwined about the other, 'I want you to meet Miss Blakeney. Miss Blakeney, this is my young friend Chester Meredith. He was at school with your brother Crispin. You were great friends, were you not?'

'Bosom,' said Chester, after a pause.

'Oh, really?' said the girl. There was a pause. 'He is in India now.'

'Yes,' said Chester.

There was another pause.

'Great chap,' said Chester, gruffly.

'Crispin is very popular,' said the girl, 'with some people.'

'Always been my best pal,' said Chester.

'Yes?'

I was not altogether satisfied with the way matters were developing. The girl seemed cold and unfriendly, and I was afraid that this was due to Chester's repellent manner. Shyness, especially when complicated by love at first sight, is apt to have strange effects on a man, and the way it had taken Chester was to make him abnormally stiff and dignified. One of the most charming things about him, as a rule, was his delightful boyish smile. Shyness had caused him to iron this out of his countenance till no trace of it remained. Not only did he not smile, he looked like a man who never had smiled and never would. His mouth was a thin, rigid line. His back was stiff with what appeared to be contemptuous aversion. He looked down his nose at Miss Blakeney as if she were less than the dust beneath his chariot-wheels.

I thought the best thing to do was to leave them alone together to get acquainted. Perhaps, I thought, it was my presence that was cramping Chester's style. I excused myself and receded.

It was some days before I saw Chester again. He came round to my cottage one night after dinner and sank into a chair, where he remained silent for several minutes.

'Well?' I said at last.

'Eh?' said Chester, starting violently.

'Have you been seeing anything of Miss Blakeney lately?'

'You bet I have.'

'And how do you feel about her on further acquaintance?'

'Eh?' said Chester, absently.

'Do you still love her?'

Chester came out of his trance.

'Love her?' he cried, his voice vibrating with emotion. 'Of course I love her. Who wouldn't love her? I'd be a silly chump not loving her. Do you know,' the boy went on, a look in his eyes like that of some young knight seeing the Holy Grail in a vision, 'do you know, she is the only woman I ever met who didn't overswing. Just a nice, crisp, snappy half-slosh, with a good full follow-through. And another thing. You'll hardly believe me, but she waggles almost as little as George Duncan. You know how women waggle as a rule, fiddling about for a minute and a half like kittens playing with a ball of wool. Well, she just makes one firm pass with the club and then *bing!* There is none like her, none.'

'Then you have been playing golf with her?'

'Nearly every day.'

'How is your game?'

'Rather spotty. I seem to be mistiming them.'

I was concerned.

'I do hope, my dear boy,' I said, earnestly, 'that you are taking care to control your feelings when out on the links with Miss Blakeney. You know what you are like. I trust you have not been using the sort of language you generally employ on occasions when you are not timing them right?'

'Me?' said Chester, horrified. 'Who, me? You don't imagine for a moment that I would dream of saying a thing that would bring a blush to her dear cheek, do you? Why, a bishop could have gone round with me and learned nothing new.'

I was relieved.

'How do you find you manage the dialogue these days?' I asked. 'When I introduced you, you behaved – you will forgive an old friend for criticising – you behaved a little like a stuffed frog with laryngitis. Have things got easier in that respect?'

'Oh yes. I'm quite the prattler now. I talk about her brother mostly. I put in the greater part of my time boosting the tick. It seems to be coming easier. Will-power, I suppose. And then, of course, I talk a good deal about her mother's novels.'

'Have you read them?'

'Every damned one of them – for her sake. And if there's a greater proof of love than that, show me! My gosh, what muck that woman writes! That reminds me, I've got to send to the bookshop for her latest – out yesterday. It's called *The Stench of Life*. A sequel, I understand, to *Grey Mildew*.'

'Brave lad,' I said, pressing his hand. 'Brave, devoted lad!'

'Oh, I'd do more than that for her.' He smoked for awhile in silence. 'By the way, I'm going to propose to her to-morrow.'

'Already?'

'Can't put it off a minute longer. It's been as much as I could manage, bottling it up till now. Where do you think would be the best place? I mean, it's not the sort of thing you can do while you're walking down the street or having a cup of tea. I thought of asking her to have a round with me and taking a stab at it on the links.'

'You could not do better. The links – Nature's cathedral.'

'Right-o, then! I'll let you know how I come out.'

'I wish you luck, my boy,' I said.

And what of Felicia, meanwhile? She was, alas, far from returning the devotion which scorched Chester's vital organs. He seemed to her precisely the sort of man she most disliked.

From childhood up Felicia Blakeney had lived in an atmosphere of highbrowism, and the type of husband she had always seen in her daydreams was the man who was simple and straightforward and earthy and did not know whether Artbashiekeff was a suburb of Moscow or a new kind of Russian drink. A man like Chester, who on his own statement would rather read one of her mother's novels than eat, revolted her. And his warm affection for her brother Crispin set the seal on her distaste.

Felicia was a dutiful child, and she loved her parents. It took a bit of doing, but she did it. But at her brother Crispin she drew the line. He wouldn't do, and his friends were worse than he was. They were high-voiced, supercilious, pince-nezed young men who talked patronisingly of Life and Art, and Chester's unblushing confession that he was one of them had put him ten down and nine to play right away.

You may wonder why the boy's undeniable skill on the links had no power to soften the girl. The unfortunate fact was that all the good effects of his prowess were neutralised by his behaviour while playing. All her life she had treated golf with a proper reverence and awe, and in Chester's attitude towards the game she seemed to detect a horrible shallowness. The fact is, Chester, in his efforts to keep himself from using strong language, had found a sort of relief in a girlish giggle, and it made her shudder every time she heard it.

His deportment, therefore, in the space of time leading up to the proposal could not have been more injurious to his cause. They started out quite happily, Chester doing a nice two-hundred-yarder off the first tee, which for a moment awoke the girl's respect. But at the fourth, after a lovely brassie-shot, he found his ball deeply embedded in the print of a woman's high heel. It was just one of those rubs of the green which normally would have caused him to ease his bosom with a flood of sturdy protest, but now he was on his guard.

'Tee-hee!' simpered Chester, reaching for his niblick. 'Too bad, too bad!' and the girl shuddered to the depths of her soul.

Having holed out, he proceeded to enliven the walk to the next tee with a few remarks on her mother's literary style, and it was while they were walking after their drives that he proposed.

His proposal, considering the circumstances, could hardly have been less happily worded. Little knowing that he was rushing upon his doom, Chester stressed the Crispin note. He gave Felicia the impression that he was suggesting this marriage more for Crispin's sake than anything else. He conveyed the idea that he thought how nice it would be for brother Crispin to have his old chum in the family. He drew a picture of their little home, with Crispin for ever popping in and out like a rabbit. It is not to be wondered at that, when at length he had finished and she had time to speak, the horrified girl turned him down with a thud.

It is at moments such as these that a man reaps the reward of a good upbringing.

In similar circumstances those who have not had the benefit of a sound training in golf are too apt to go wrong. Goaded by the sudden anguish, they take to drink, plunge into dissipation, and write *vers libre*. Chester was mercifully saved from this. I saw him the day after he had been handed the mitten, and was struck by the look of grim determination in his face. Deeply wounded though he was, I could see that he was the master of his fate and the captain of his soul.

'I am sorry, my boy,' I said, sympathetically, when he had told me the painful news.

'It can't be helped,' he replied, bravely.

'Her decision was final?'

'Quite.'

'You do not contemplate having another pop at her?'

'No good. I know when I'm licked.'

I patted him on the shoulder and said the only thing it seemed possible to say.

'After all, there is always golf.'

He nodded.

'Yes. My game needs a lot of tuning up. Now is the time to do it. From now on I go at this pastime seriously. I make it my life-work. Who knows?' he murmured, with a sudden gleam in his eyes. 'The Amateur Championship—'

'The Open!' I cried, falling gladly into his mood.

'The American Amateur,' said Chester, flushing.

'The American Open,' I chorused.

'No one has ever copped all four.'

'No one.'

'Watch me!' said Chester Meredith, simply.

It was about two weeks after this that I happened to look in on Chester at his house one morning. I found him about to start for the links. As he had foreshadowed in the conversation which I have just related, he now spent most of the daylight hours on the course. In these two weeks he had gone about his task of achieving perfection with a furious energy which made him the talk of the club. Always one of the best players in the place, he had developed an astounding brilliance. Men who had played him level were now obliged to receive two and even three strokes. The pro. himself, conceding one, had only succeeded in halving their match. The struggle for the President's Cup came round

once more, and Chester won it for the second time with ridiculous ease.

When I arrived, he was practising chip-shots in his sitting-
room. I noticed that he seemed to be labouring under some
strong emotion, and his first words gave me the clue.

'She's going away to-morrow,' he said, abruptly, lofting a ball
over the whatnot on to the Chesterfield.

I was not sure whether I was sorry or relieved. Her absence
would leave a terrible blank, of course, but it might be that it
would help him to get over his infatuation.

'Ah!' I said, non-committally.

Chester addressed his ball with a well-assumed phlegm, but
I could see by the way his ears wiggled that he was feeling deeply.
I was not surprised when he topped his shot into the coal-scuttle.

'She has promised to play a last round with me this morning,'
he said.

Again I was doubtful what view to take. It was a pretty, poetic
idea, not unlike Browning's 'Last Ride Together,' but I was not
sure if it was altogether wise. However, it was none of my
business, so I merely patted him on the shoulder and he gathered
up his clubs and went off.

Owing to motives of delicacy I had not offered to accompany
him on his round, and it was not till later that I learned the
actual details of what occurred. At the start, it seems, the spiritual
anguish which he was suffering had a depressing effect on his
game. He hooked his drive off the first tee and was only enabled
to get a five by means of a strong niblick shot out of the rough.
At the second, the lake hole, he lost a ball in the water and got
another five. It was only at the third that he began to pull himself
together.

The test of a great golfer is his ability to recover from a bad start. Chester had this quality to a pre-eminent degree. A lesser man, conscious of being three over bogey for the first two holes, might have looked on his round as ruined. To Chester it simply meant that he had to get a couple of 'birdies' right speedily, and he set about it at once. Always a long driver, he excelled himself at the third. It is, as you know, an uphill hole all the way, but his drive could not have come far short of two hundred and fifty yards. A brassie-shot of equal strength and unerring direction put him on the edge of the green, and he holed out with a long putt two under bogey. He had hoped for a 'birdie' and he had achieved an 'eagle.'

I think that this splendid feat must have softened Felicia's heart, had it not been for the fact that misery had by this time entirely robbed Chester of the ability to smile. Instead, therefore, of behaving in the wholesome, natural way of men who get threes at bogey five holes, he preserved a drawn, impassive countenance; and as she watched him tee up her ball, stiff, correct, polite, but to all outward appearance absolutely inhuman, the girl found herself stifling that thrill of what for a moment had been almost adoration. It was, she felt, exactly how her brother Crispin would have comported himself if he had done a hole in two under bogey.

And yet she could not altogether check a wistful sigh when, after a couple of fours at the next two holes, he picked up another stroke on the sixth and with an inspired spoon-shot brought his medal-score down to one better than bogey by getting a two at the hundred-and-seventy-yard seventh. But the brief spasm of tenderness passed, and when he finished the first nine with two more fours she refrained from anything warmer than a mere word of stereotyped congratulation.

'One under bogey for the first nine,' she said. 'Splendid!'

'One under bogey!' said Chester, woodenly.

'Out in thirty-four. What is the record for the course?'

Chester started. So great had been his pre-occupation that he had not given a thought to the course record. He suddenly realised now that the pro., who had done the lowest medal-score to date – the other course record was held by Peter Willard with a hundred and sixty-one, achieved in his first season – had gone out in only one better than his own figures that day.

'Sixty-eight,' he said.

'What a pity you lost those strokes at the beginning!'

'Yes,' said Chester.

He spoke absently – and, as it seemed to her, primly and without enthusiasm – for the flaming idea of having a go at the course record had only just occurred to him. Once before he had done the first nine in thirty-four, but on that occasion he had not felt that curious feeling of irresistible force which comes to a golfer at the very top of his form. Then he had been aware all the time that he had been putting chancily. They had gone in, yes, but he had uttered a prayer per putt. To-day he was superior to any weak doubtings. When he tapped the ball on the green, he knew it was going to sink. The course record? Why not? What a last offering to lay at her feet! She would go away, out of his life for ever; she would marry some other bird; but the memory of that supreme round would remain with her as long as she breathed. When he won the Open and Amateur for the second – the third – the fourth time, she would say to herself, 'I was with him when he dented the record for his home course!' And he had only to pick up a couple of strokes on the last nine, to do threes at holes where he was wont to be satisfied with fours. Yes, by Vardon, he would take a whirl at it.

* * *

You, who are acquainted with these links, will no doubt say that the task which Chester Meredith had sketched out for himself – cutting two strokes off thirty-five for the second nine – was one at which Humanity might well shudder. The pro. himself, who had finished sixth in the last Open Championship, had never done better than a thirty-five, playing perfect golf and being one under par. But such was Chester's mood that, as he teed up on the tenth, he did not even consider the possibility of failure. Every muscle in his body was working in perfect co-ordination with its fellows, his wrists felt as if they were made of tempered steel, and his eyes had just that hawk-like quality which enables a man to judge his short approaches to the inch. He swung forcefully, and the ball sailed so close to the direction-post that for a moment it seemed as if it had hit it.

'Oo!' cried Felicia.

Chester did not speak. He was following the flight of the ball. It sailed over the brow of the hill, and with his knowledge of the course he could tell almost the exact patch of turf on which it must have come to rest. An iron would do the business from there, and a single putt would give him the first of the 'birdies' he required. Two minutes later he had holed out a six-foot putt for a three.

'Oo!' said Felicia again.

Chester walked to the eleventh tee in silence. 'No, never mind,' she said, as he stooped to put her ball on the sand. 'I don't think I'll play any more. I'd much rather just watch you.'

'Oh, that you could watch me through life!' said Chester, but he said it to himself. His actual words were 'Very well!' and he spoke them with a stiff coldness which chilled the girl.

The eleventh is one of the trickiest holes on the course, as no doubt you have found out for yourself. It looks absurdly simple, but that little patch of wood on the right that seems so harmless is placed just in the deadliest position to catch even the most slightly sliced drive. Chester's lacked the austere precision of his last. A hundred yards from the tee it swerved almost imperceptibly, and, striking a branch, fell in the tangled undergrowth. It took him two strokes to hack it out and put it on the green, and then his long putt, after quivering on the edge of the hole, stayed there. For a swift instant red-hot words rose to his lips, but he caught them just as they were coming out and crushed them back. He looked at his ball and he looked at the hole.

'Tut!' said Chester.

Felicia uttered a deep sigh. The niblick-shot out of the rough had impressed her profoundly. If only, she felt, this superb golfer had been more human! If only she were able to be constantly in this man's society, to see exactly what it was that he did with his left wrist that gave that terrific snap to his drives, she might acquire the knack herself one of these days. For she was a clear-thinking, honest girl, and thoroughly realised that she did not get the distance she ought to with her wood. With a husband like Chester beside her to stimulate and advise, of what might she not be capable? If she got wrong in her stance, he could put her right with a word. If she had a bout of slicing, how quickly he would tell her what caused it. And she knew that she had only to speak the word to wipe out the effects of her refusal, to bring him to her side for ever.

But could a girl pay such a price? When he had got that 'eagle' on the third, he had looked bored. When he had missed this last putt, he had not seemed to care. 'Tut!' What a word to use at such a moment! No, she felt sadly, it could not be done. To marry Chester Meredith, she told herself, would be like marrying a composite of Soames Forsyte, Sir Willoughby Patterne, and all her brother Crispin's friends. She sighed and was silent.

Chester, standing on the twelfth tee, reviewed the situation swiftly, like a general before a battle. There were seven holes to play, and he had to do these in two better than bogey. The one that faced him now offered few opportunities. It was a long, slogging, dog-leg hole, and even Ray and Taylor, when they had played their exhibition game on the course, had taken fives. No opening there.

The thirteenth – up a steep hill with a long iron-shot for one's second and a blind green fringed with bunkers? Scarcely practicable to hope for better than a four. The fourteenth – into the valley with the ground sloping sharply down to the ravine? He had once done it in three, but it had been a fluke. No; on these three holes he must be content to play for a steady par and trust to picking up a stroke on the fifteenth.

The fifteenth, straightforward up to the plateau green with its circle of bunkers, presents few difficulties to the finished golfer who is on his game. A bunker meant nothing to Chester in his present conquering vein. His mashie-shot second soared almost contemptuously over the chasm and rolled to within a foot of the pin. He came to the sixteenth with the clear-cut problem before him of snipping two strokes off par on the last three holes.

To the unthinking man, not acquainted with the lay-out of our links, this would no doubt appear a tremendous feat. But the fact is, the Green Committee, with perhaps an unduly sentimental bias towards the happy ending, have arranged a comparatively easy finish to the course. The sixteenth is a perfectly plain hole with broad fairway and a down-hill run; the seventeenth, a one-shot affair with no difficulties for the man who keeps them straight; and the eighteenth, though its up-hill run makes it deceptive to the stranger and leads the unwary to take a mashie instead of a light iron for his second, has no real venom in it. Even Peter Willard has occasionally come home in a canter with a six, five, and seven, conceding himself only two eight-foot putts. It is, I think, this mild conclusion to a tough course that makes the refreshment-room of our club so noticeable for its sea of happy faces. The bar every day is crowded with rejoicing men who, forgetting the agonies of the first fifteen, are babbling of what they did on the last three. The seventeenth, with its possibilities of holing out a topped second, is particularly soothing.

Chester Meredith was not the man to top his second on any hole, so this supreme bliss did not come his way; but he laid a beautiful mashie-shot dead and got a three; and when with his iron he put his first well on the green at the seventeenth and holed out for a two, life, for all his broken heart, seemed pretty tolerable. He now had the situation well in hand. He had only to play his usual game to get a four on the last and lower the course record by one stroke.

It was at this supreme moment of his life that he ran into the Wrecking Crew.

You doubtless find it difficult to understand how it came about that if the Wrecking Crew were on the course at all he had not run into them long before. The explanation is that, with a regard for the etiquette of the game unusual in these miserable men, they had for once obeyed the law that enacts that foursomes shall start at the tenth. They had begun their dark work on the second nine, accordingly, at almost the exact moment when Chester Meredith was driving off at the first, and this had enabled them to keep ahead until now. When Chester came to the eighteenth tee, they were just leaving it, moving up the fairway with their caddies in mass formation and looking to his exasperated eye like one of those great race-migrations of the Middle Ages. Wherever Chester looked he seemed to see human, so to speak, figures. One was doddering about in the long grass fifty yards from the tee, others debouched to left and right. The course was crawling with them.

Chester sat down on the bench with a weary sigh. He knew these men. Self-centred, remorseless, deaf to all the promptings of their better nature, they never let anyone through. There was nothing to do but wait.

The Wrecking Crew scratched on. The man near the tee rolled his ball ten yards, then twenty, then thirty – he was improving. Ere long he would be out of range. Chester rose and swished his driver.

But the end was not yet. The individual operating in the rough on the left had been advancing in slow stages, and now, finding his ball teed up on a tuft of grass, he opened his shoulders and let himself go. There was a loud report, and the ball, hitting a tree squarely, bounded back almost to the tee, and all the weary work was to do again. By the time Chester was able to drive, he was reduced by impatience, and the necessity of refraining from commenting on the state of affairs as he would have wished to comment, to a frame of mind in which no man could have kept himself from pressing. He pressed, and topped. The ball skidded over the turf for a meagre hundred yards.

'D-d-d-dear me!' said Chester.

The next moment he uttered a bitter laugh. Too late a miracle had happened. One of the foul figures in front was waving its club. Other ghastly creatures were withdrawing to the side of the fairway. Now, when the harm had been done, these outcasts were signalling to him to go through. The hollow mockery of the thing swept over Chester like a wave. What was the use of going through now? He was a good three hundred yards from the green, and he needed bogey at this hole to break the record. Almost absently he drew his brassie from his bag; then, as the full sense of his wrongs bit into his soul, he swung viciously.

Golf is a strange game. Chester had pressed on the tee and foozled. He pressed now, and achieved the most perfect shot of his life. The ball shot from its place as if a charge of powerful explosive were behind it. Never deviating from a straight line, never more than six feet from the ground, it sailed up the hill, crossed the bunker, eluded the mounds beyond, struck the turf, rolled, and stopped fifty feet from the hole. It was a brassie-shot of a lifetime, and shrill senile yippings of excitement and congratulation floated down from the Wrecking Crew. For, degraded though they were, these men were not wholly devoid of human instincts.

Chester drew a deep breath. His ordeal was over. That third shot, which would lay the ball right up to the pin, was precisely the sort of thing he did best. Almost from boyhood he had been a wizard at the short approach. He could hole out in two now on his left ear. He strode up the hill to his ball. It could not have been lying better. Two inches away there was a nasty cup in the turf; but it had avoided this and was sitting nicely perched up, smiling an invitation to the mashie-niblick. Chester shuffled his feet and eyed the flag keenly. Then he stooped to play, and Felicia watched him breathlessly. Her whole being seemed to be concentrated on him. She had forgotten everything save that she was seeing a course record get broken. She could not have been more wrapped up in his success if she had had large sums of money on it.

The Wrecking Crew, meanwhile, had come to life again. They had stopped twittering about Chester's brassie-shot and were thinking of resuming their own game. Even in foursomes where fifty yards is reckoned a good shot somebody must be away, and the man whose turn it was to play was the one who had acquired from his brother-members of the club the nickname of the First Grave-Digger.

A word about this human wen. He was – if there can be said to be grades in such a sub-species – the star performer of the Wrecking Crew. The lunches of fifty-seven years had caused his chest to slip down into the mezzanine floor, but he was still a powerful man, and had in his youth been a hammer-thrower of some repute. He differed from his colleagues – the Man With the Hoe, Old Father Time, and Consul, the Almost Human – in that, while they were content to peck cautiously at the ball, he never spared himself in his efforts to do it a violent injury. Frequently he had cut a blue dot almost in half with his niblick. He was completely muscle-bound, so that he seldom achieved anything beyond a series of chasms in the turf, but he was always trying, and it was his secret belief that, given two or three miracles happening simultaneously, he would one of these days bring off a snifter. Years of disappointment had, however, reduced the flood of hope to a mere trickle, and when he took his brassie now and addressed the ball he had no immediate plans beyond a vague intention of rolling the thing a few yards farther up the hill.

The fact that he had no business to play at all till Chester had holed out did not occur to him; and even if it had occurred he would have dismissed the objection as finicking. Chester, bending over his ball, was nearly two hundred yards away – or the distance of three full brassie-shots. The First Grave-Digger did not hesitate. He whirled up his club as in distant days he had been wont to swing the hammer, and, with the grunt which this performance always wrung from him, brought it down.

Golfers – and I stretch this term to include the Wrecking Crew – are a highly imitative race. The spectacle of a flubber flubbing ahead of us on the fairway inclines to make us flub as well; and, conversely, it is immediately after we have seen a magnificent shot that we are apt to eclipse ourselves. Consciously, the Grave-Digger had no notion how Chester had made that superb brassie-biff of his, but all the while I suppose his subconscious self had been taking notes. At any rate, on this one occasion he, too, did the shot of a lifetime. As he opened his eyes, which he always shut tightly at the moment of impact, and started to unravel himself from the complicated tangle in which his follow-through had left him, he perceived the ball breasting the hill like some untamed jack-rabbit of the Californian prairie.

For a moment his only emotion was one of dreamlike amazement. He stood looking at the ball with a wholly impersonal wonder, like a man suddenly confronted with some terrific work of Nature. Then, as a sleep-walker awakens, he came to himself with a start. Directly in front of the flying ball was a man bending to make an approach-shot.

Chester, always a concentrated golfer when there was man's work to do, had scarcely heard the crack of the brassie behind him. Certainly he had paid no attention to it. His whole mind was fixed on his stroke. He measured with his eye the distance to the pin, noted the down-slope of the green, and shifted his stance a little to allow for it. Then, with a final swift waggle, he laid his club-head behind the ball and slowly raised it. It was just coming down when the world became full of shouts of 'Fore!' and something hard smote him violently on the seat of his plus-fours.

The supreme tragedies of life leave us momentarily stunned. For an instant which seemed an age Chester could not understand what had happened. True, he realised that there had been an earthquake, a cloud-burst, and a railway accident, and that a high building had fallen on him at the exact moment when somebody had shot him with a gun, but these happenings would account for only a small part of his sensations. He blinked several times, and rolled his eyes wildly. And it was while rolling them that he caught sight of the gesticulating Wrecking Crew on the lower slopes and found enlightenment. Simultaneously, he observed his ball only a yard and a half from where it had been when he addressed it.

Chester Meredith gave one look at his ball, one look at the flag, one look at the Wrecking Crew, one look at the sky. His lips writhed, his forehead turned vermilion. Beads of perspiration started out on his forehead. And then, with his whole soul seething like a cistern struck by a thunder-bolt, he spoke.

'!!!!!!!!!!!!!!' cried Chester.

Dimly he was aware of a wordless exclamation from the girl beside him, but he was too distraught to think of her now. It was as if all the oaths pent up within his bosom for so many weary days were struggling and jostling to see which could get out first. They cannoned into each other, they linked hands and formed parties, they got themselves all mixed up in weird vowel-sounds, the second syllable of some red-hot verb forming a temporary union with the first syllable of some blistering noun.

'—! —!! —!!! —!!!! —!!!!!' cried Chester.

Felicia stood staring at him. In her eyes was the look of one who sees visions.

'***!!! ***!!! ***!!! ***!!!' roared Chester, in part.

A great wave of emotion flooded over the girl. How she had misjudged this silver-tongued man! She shivered as she thought that, had this not happened, in another five minutes they would have parted for ever, sundered by seas of misunderstanding, she cold and scornful, he with all his music still within him.

'Oh, Mr Meredith!' she cried, faintly.

With a sickening abruptness Chester came to himself. It was as if somebody had poured a pint of ice-cold water down his back. He blushed vividly. He realised with horror and shame how grossly he had offended against all the canons of decency and good taste. He felt like the man in one of those 'What Is Wrong With This Picture?' things in the advertisements of the etiquette-books.

'I beg – I beg your pardon!' he mumbled, humbly. 'Please, please, forgive me. I should not have spoken like that.'

'You should! You should!' cried the girl, passionately. 'You should have said all that and a lot more. That awful man ruining your record round like that! Oh, why am I a poor weak woman with practically no vocabulary that's any use for anything!'

Quite suddenly, without knowing that she had moved, she found herself at his side, holding his hand.

'Oh, to think how I misjudged you!' she wailed. 'I thought you cold, stiff, formal, precise. I hated the way you sniggered when you foozled a shot. I see it all now! You were keeping it in for my sake. Can you ever forgive me?'

Chester, as I have said, was not a very quick-minded young man, but it would have taken a duller youth than he to fail to read the message in the girl's eyes, to miss the meaning of the pressure of her hand on his.

'My gosh!' he exclaimed wildly. 'Do you mean—? Do you

think—? Do you really—? Honestly, has this made a difference? Is there any chance for a fellow, I mean?'

Her eyes helped him on. He felt suddenly confident and masterful.

'Look here – no kidding – will you marry me?' he said.

'I will! I will!'

'Darling!' cried Chester.

He would have said more, but at this point he was interrupted by the arrival of the Wrecking Crew, who panted up full of apologies; and Chester, as he eyed them, thought that he had never seen a nicer, cheerier, pleasanter lot of fellows in his life. His heart warmed to them. He made a mental resolve to hunt them up some time and have a good long talk. He waved the Grave-Digger's remorse airily aside.

'Don't mention it,' he said. 'Not at all. Faults on both sides. By the way, my *fiancée*, Miss Blakeney.'

The Wrecking Crew puffed acknowledgment.

'But, my dear fellow,' said the Grave-Digger, 'it was – really it was – unforgivable. Spoiling your shot. Never dreamed I would send the ball that distance. Lucky you weren't playing an important match.'

'But he was,' moaned Felicia. 'He was trying for the course record, and now he can't break it.'

The Wrecking Crew paled behind their whiskers, aghast at this tragedy, but Chester, glowing with the yeasty intoxication of love, laughed lightly.

'What do you mean, can't break it?' he cried, cheerily. 'I've one more shot.'

And, carelessly addressing the ball, he holed out with a light flick of his mashie-niblick.

* * *

'Chester, darling!' said Felicia.

They were walking slowly through a secluded glade in the quiet evenfall.

'Yes, precious?'

Felicia hesitated. What she was going to say would hurt him, she knew, and her love was so great that to hurt him was agony.

'Do you think—' she began. 'I wonder whether— It's about Crispin.'

'Good old Crispin!'

Felicia sighed, but the matter was too vital to be shirked. Cost what it might, she must speak her mind.

'Chester, darling, when we are married, would you mind very, *very* much if we didn't have Crispin with us *all* the time?'

Chester started.

'Good Lord!' he exclaimed. 'Don't you like him?'

'Not very much,' confessed Felicia. 'I don't think I'm clever enough for him. I've rather disliked him ever since we were children. But I know what a friend he is of yours—'

Chester uttered a joyous laugh.

'Friend of mine! Why, I can't stand the blighter! I loathe the worm! I abominate the excrescence! I only pretended we were friends because I thought it would put me in solid with you. The man is a pest and should have been strangled at birth. At school I used to kick him every time I saw him. If your brother Crispin tries so much as to set foot across the threshold of our little home, I'll set the dog on him.'

'Darling!' whispered Felicia. 'We shall be very, very happy.' She drew her arm through his. 'Tell me, dearest,' she murmured, 'all about how you used to kick Crispin at school.'

And together they wandered off into the sunset.

'After all,' said the young man, 'golf is only a game.'

He spoke bitterly and with the air of one who has been following a train of thought. He had come into the smoking-room of the club-house in low spirits at the dusky close of a November evening, and for some minutes had been sitting, silent and moody, staring at the log fire.

'Merely a pastime,' said the young man.

The Oldest Member, nodding in his arm-chair, stiffened with horror, and glanced quickly over his shoulder to make sure that none of the waiters had heard these terrible words.

'Can this be George William Pennefather speaking!' he said, reproachfully. 'My boy, you are not yourself.'

The young man flushed a little beneath his tan: for he had had a good upbringing and was not bad at heart.

'Perhaps I ought not to have gone quite so far as that,' he admitted. 'I was only thinking that a fellow's got no right, just because he happens to have come on a bit in his form lately, to treat a fellow as if a fellow was a leper or something.'

The Oldest Member's face cleared, and he breathed a relieved sigh.

'Ah! I see,' he said. 'You spoke hastily and in a sudden fit of pique because something upset you out on the links to-day. Tell me all. Let me see, you were playing with Nathaniel Frisby this afternoon, were you not? I gather that he beat you.'

'Yes, he did. Giving me a third. But it isn't being beaten that I mind. What I object to is having the blighter behave as if he were a sort of champion condescending to a mere mortal. Dash it, it seemed to bore him playing with me! Every time I sliced off the tee he looked at me as if I were a painful ordeal. Twice when I was having a bit of trouble in the bushes I caught him yawning. And after we had finished he started talking about what a good game croquet was, and he wondered more people didn't take it up. And it's only a month or so ago that I could play the man level!'

The Oldest Member shook his snowy head sadly.

'There is nothing to be done about it,' he said. 'We can only hope that the poison will in time work its way out of the man's system. Sudden success at golf is like the sudden acquisition of wealth. It is apt to unsettle and deteriorate the character. And, as it comes almost miraculously, so only a miracle can effect a cure. The best advice I can give you is to refrain from playing with Nathaniel Frisby till you can keep your tee-shots straight.'

'Oh, but don't run away with the idea that I wasn't pretty good off the tee this afternoon!' said the young man. 'I should like to describe to you the shot I did on the—'

'Meanwhile,' proceeded the Oldest Member, 'I will relate to you a little story which bears on what I have been saying.'

'From the very moment I addressed the ball—'

'It is the story of two loving hearts temporarily estranged owing to the sudden and unforeseen proficiency of one of the couple—'

'I waggled quickly and strongly, like Duncan. Then, swinging smoothly back, rather in the Vardon manner—'

'But as I see,' said the Oldest Member, 'that you are all impatience for me to begin, I will do so without further preamble.'

To the philosophical student of golf like myself (said the Oldest Member) perhaps the most outstanding virtue of this noble pursuit is the fact that it is a medicine for the soul. Its great service to humanity is that it teaches human beings that, whatever petty triumphs they may have achieved in other walks of life, they are after all merely human. It acts as a corrective against sinful pride. I attribute the insane arrogance of the later Roman emperors almost entirely to the fact that, never having played golf, they never knew that strange chastening humility which is engendered by a topped chip-shot. If Cleopatra had been outed in the first round of the Ladies' Singles, we should have heard a lot less of her proud imperiousness. And, coming down to modern times, it was undoubtedly his rotten golf that kept Wallace Chesney the nice unspoiled fellow he was. For in every other respect he had everything in the world calculated to make a man conceited and arrogant. He was the best-looking man for miles around; his health was perfect; and, in addition to this, he was rich; danced, rode, played bridge and polo with equal skill; and was engaged to be married to Charlotte Dix. And when you saw Charlotte Dix you realised that being engaged to her would by itself have been quite enough luck for any one man.

But Wallace, as I say, despite all his advantages, was a thoroughly nice, modest young fellow. And I attribute this to the fact that, while one of the keenest golfers in the club, he was also one of the worst players. Indeed, Charlotte Dix used to say to me in his presence that she could not understand why people paid money to go to the circus when by merely walking over the

brow of a hill they could watch Wallace Chesney trying to get
out of the bunker by the eleventh green. And Wallace took
the gibe with perfect good humour, for there was a delightful
camaraderie between them which robbed it of any sting. Often
at lunch in the club-house I used to hear him and Charlotte
planning the handicapping details of a proposed match between
Wallace and a non-existent cripple whom Charlotte claimed to
have discovered in the village – it being agreed finally that he
should accept seven bisques from the cripple, but that, if the
latter ever recovered the use of his arms, Wallace should get a
stroke a hole.

In short, a thoroughly happy and united young couple. Two
hearts, if I may coin an expression, that beat as one.

I would not have you misjudge Wallace Chesney. I may have
given you the impression that his attitude towards golf was
light and frivolous, but such was not the case. As I have said,
he was one of the keenest members of the club. Love made
him receive the joshing of his *fiancée* in the kindly spirit in
which it was meant, but at heart he was as earnest as you could
wish, he practised early and late; he bought golf books; and
the mere sight of a patent club of any description acted on
him like catnip on a cat. I remember remonstrating with him
on the occasion of his purchasing a wooden-faced driving-
mashie which weighed about two pounds, and was, taking it
for all in all, as foul an instrument as ever came out of the
workshop of a clubmaker who had been dropped on the head
by his nurse when a baby.

'I know, I know,' he said, when I had finished indicating some
of the weapon's more obvious defects. 'But the point is, I believe
in it. It gives me confidence. I don't believe you could slice with
a thing like that if you tried.'

Confidence! That was what Wallace Chesney lacked, and that, as he saw it, was the prime grand secret of golf. Like an alchemist on the track of the Philosopher's Stone, he was for ever seeking for something which would really give him confidence. I recollect that he even tried repeating to himself fifty times every morning the words, 'Every day in every way I grow better and better.' This, however, proved such a black lie that he gave it up. The fact is, the man was a visionary, and it is to auto-hypnosis of some kind that I attribute the extraordinary change that came over him at the beginning of his third season.

You may have noticed in your perambulations about the City a shop bearing above its door and upon its windows the legend:

COHEN BROS.,
Second-hand Clothiers,

a statement which is borne out by endless vistas seen through the door of every variety of what is technically known as Gents' Wear. But the Brothers Cohen, though their main stock-in-trade is garments which have been rejected by their owners for one reason or another, do not confine their dealings to Gents' Wear. The place is a museum of derelict goods of every description. You can get a second-hand revolver there, or a second-hand sword, or a second-hand umbrella. You can do a cheap deal in field-glasses, trunks, dog collars, canes, photograph frames, attaché cases, and bowls for goldfish. And on the bright spring morning when Wallace Chesney happened to pass by there was exhibited in the window a putter of such pre-eminently lunatic design that he stopped dead as if he had run into an invisible wall, and then, panting like an overwrought fish, charged in through the door.

* * *

The shop was full of the Cohen family, sombre-eyed, smileless men with purposeful expressions; and two of these, instantly descending upon Wallace Chesney like leopards, began in swift silence to thrust him into a suit of yellow tweed. Having worked the coat over his shoulders with a shoe-horn, they stood back to watch the effect.

'A beautiful fit,' announced Isidore Cohen.

'A little snug under the arms,' said his brother Irving. 'But that'll give.'

'The warmth of the body will make it give,' said Isidore.

'Or maybe you'll lose weight in the summer,' said Irving.

Wallace, when he had struggled out of the coat and was able to breathe, said that he had come in to buy a putter. Isidore thereupon sold him the putter, a dog collar, and a set of studs, and Irving sold him a fire-man's helmet: and he was about to leave when their elder brother Lou, who had just finished fitting out another customer, who had come in to buy a cap, with two pairs of trousers and a miniature aquarium for keeping newts in, saw that business was in progress and strolled up. His fathomless eye rested on Wallace, who was toying feebly with the putter.

'You play golf?' asked Lou. 'Then looka here!'

He dived into an alleyway of dead clothing, dug for a moment, and emerged with something at the sight of which Wallace Chesney, hardened golfer that he was, blenched and threw up an arm defensively.

'No, no!' he cried.

The object which Lou Cohen was waving insinuatingly before his eyes was a pair of those golfing breeches which are technically known as Plus Fours. A player of two years' standing, Wallace Chesney was not unfamiliar with Plus Fours – all the club cracks wore them – but he had never seen Plus Fours like these. What might be termed the main *motif* of the fabric was a curious vivid pink, and with this to work on the architect had let his imagination run free, and had produced so much variety in the way of chessboard squares of white, yellow, violet, and green that the eye swam as it looked upon them.

'These were made to measure for Sandy McHoots, the Open Champion,' said Lou, stroking the left leg lovingly. 'But he sent 'em back for some reason or other.'

'Perhaps they frightened the children,' said Wallace, recollecting having heard that Mr McHoots was a married man.

'They'll fit you nice,' said Lou.

'Sure they'll fit him nice,' said Isidore, warmly.

'Why, just take a look at yourself in the glass,' said Irving, 'and see if they don't fit you nice.'

And, as one who wakes from a trance, Wallace discovered that his lower limbs were now encased in the prismatic garment. At what point in the proceedings the brethren had slipped them on him, he could not have said. But he was undeniably in.

Wallace looked in the glass. For a moment, as he eyed his reflection, sheer horror gripped him. Then suddenly, as he gazed, he became aware that his first feelings were changing. The initial shock over, he was becoming calmer. He waggled his right leg with a certain sang-froid.

There is a certain passage in the works of the poet Pope with which you may be familiar. It runs as follows:

> 'Vice is a monster of so frightful mien
> As to be hated needs but to be seen:
> Yet seen too oft, familiar with her face,
> We first endure, then pity, then embrace.'

Even so was it with Wallace Chesney and these Plus Fours. At first he had recoiled from them as any decent-minded man would have done. Then, after a while, almost abruptly he found himself in the grip of a new emotion. After an unsuccessful attempt to analyse this, he suddenly got it. Amazing as it may seem, it was pleasure that he felt. He caught his eye in the mirror, and it was smirking. Now that the things were actually on, by Hutchinson, they didn't look half bad. By Braid, they didn't. There was a sort of something about them. Take away that expanse of bare leg with its unsightly sock-suspender and substitute a woolly stocking, and you would have the lower section of a golfer. For the first time in his life, he thought, he looked like a man who could play golf.

There came to him an odd sensation of masterfulness. He was still holding the putter, and now he swung it up above his shoulder. A fine swing, all lissomness and supple grace, quite different from any swing he had ever done before.

Wallace Chesney gasped. He knew that at last he had discovered that prime grand secret of golf for which he had searched so long. It was the costume that did it. All you had to do was wear Plus Fours. He had always hitherto played in grey flannel trousers. Naturally he had not been able to do himself justice. Golf required an easy dash, and how could you be easily dashing in concertina-shaped trousers with a patch on the knee? He saw now – what he had never seen before – that it was not because they were crack players that crack players wore Plus Fours: it was because they wore Plus Fours that they were crack players. And these Plus Fours had been the property of an Open Champion. Wallace Chesney's bosom swelled, and he was filled, as by some strange gas, with joy – with excitement – with confidence. Yes, for the first time in his golfing life, he felt really confident.

True, the things might have been a shade less gaudy: they

might perhaps have hit the eye with a slightly less violent punch: but what of that? True, again, he could scarcely hope to avoid the censure of his club-mates when he appeared like this on the links: but what of *that*? His club-mates must set their teeth and learn to bear these Plus Fours like men. That was what Wallace Chesney thought about it. If they did not like his Plus Fours, let them go and play golf somewhere else.

'How much?' he muttered, thickly. And the Brothers Cohen clustered grimly round with notebooks and pencils.

In predicting a stormy reception for his new apparel, Wallace Chesney had not been unduly pessimistic. The moment he entered the club-house Disaffection reared its ugly head. Friends of years' standing called loudly for the committee, and there was a small and vehement party of the left wing, headed by Raymond Gandle, who was an artist by profession, and consequently had a sensitive eye, which advocated the tearing off and public burial of the obnoxious garment. But, prepared as he had been for some such demonstration on the part of the coarser-minded, Wallace had hoped for better things when he should meet Charlotte Dix, the girl who loved him. Charlotte, he had supposed, would understand and sympathise.

Instead of which, she uttered a piercing cry and staggered to a bench, whence a moment later she delivered her ultimatum.

'Quick!' she said. 'Before I have to look again.'

'What do you mean?'

'Pop straight back into the changing-room while I've got my eyes shut, and remove the fancy-dress.'

'What's wrong with them?'

'Darling,' said Charlotte, 'I think it's sweet and patriotic of you to be proud of your cycling club colours or whatever they are, but you mustn't wear them on the links. It will unsettle the caddies.'

'They *are* a trifle on the bright side,' admitted Wallace. 'But it helps my game, wearing them. I was trying a few practice-shots just now, and I couldn't go wrong. Slammed the ball on the meat every time. They inspire me, if you know what I mean. Come on, let's be starting.'

Charlotte opened her eyes incredulously. 'You can't seriously mean that you're really going to *play* in – those? It's against the rules. There must be a rule somewhere in the book against coming out looking like a sunset. Won't you go and burn them for my sake?'

'But I tell you they give me confidence. I sort of squint down at them when I'm addressing the ball, and I feel like a pro.'

'Then the only thing to do is for me to play you for them. Come on, Wally, be a sportsman. I'll give you a half and play you for the whole outfit – the breeches, the red jacket, the little cap, and the belt with the snake's-head buckle. I'm sure all those things must have gone with the breeches. Is it a bargain?'

Strolling on the club-house terrace some two hours later, Raymond Gandle encountered Charlotte and Wallace coming up from the eighteenth green.

'Just the girl I wanted to see,' said Raymond. 'Miss Dix, I represent a select committee of my fellow-members, and I have come to ask you on their behalf to use the influence of a good woman to induce Wally to destroy those Plus Fours of his, which we all consider nothing short of Bolshevik propaganda and a menace to the public weal. May I rely on you?'

'You may not,' retorted Charlotte. 'They are the poor boy's mascot. You've no idea how they have improved his game. He has just beaten me hollow. I am going to try to learn to bear them, so you must. Really, you've no notion how he has come on. My cripple won't be able to give him more than a couple of bisques if he keeps up this form.'

'It's something about the things,' said Wallace. 'They give me confidence.'

'They give *me* a pain in the neck,' said Raymond Gandle.

To the thinking man nothing is more remarkable in this life than the way in which Humanity adjusts itself to conditions which at their outset might well have appeared intolerable. Some great cataclysm occurs, some storm or earthquake, shaking the community to its foundations; and after the first pardonable consternation one finds the sufferers resuming their ordinary pursuits as if nothing had happened. There have been few more striking examples of this adaptability than the behaviour of the members of our golf-club under the impact of Wallace Chesney's Plus Fours. For the first few days it is not too much to say that they were stunned. Nervous players sent their caddies on in front of them at blind holes, so that they might be warned in time of Wallace's presence ahead and not have him happening to them all of a sudden. And even the pro. was not unaffected. Brought up in Scotland in an atmosphere of tartan kilts, he nevertheless winced, and a startled 'Hoots!' was forced from his lips when Wallace Chesney suddenly appeared in the valley as he was about to drive from the fifth tee.

But in about a week conditions were back to normalcy. Within ten days the Plus Fours became a familiar feature of the landscape, and were accepted as such without comment. They were pointed out to strangers together with the waterfall, the Lovers' Leap, and the view from the eighth green as things you ought not to miss when visiting the course; but apart from that one might almost say they were ignored. And meanwhile Wallace Chesney continued day by day to make the most extraordinary progress in his play.

As I said before, and I think you will agree with me when I have told you what happened subsequently, it was probably a case of auto-hypnosis. There is no other sphere in which a belief in oneself has such immediate effects as it has in golf. And Wallace, having acquired self-confidence, went on from strength to strength. In under a week he had ploughed his way through the Unfortunate Incidents – of which class Peter Willard was the best example – and was challenging the fellows who kept three shots in five somewhere on the fairway. A month later he was holding his own with ten-handicap men. And by the middle of the summer he was so far advanced that his name occasionally cropped up in speculative talks on the subject of the July medal. One might have been excused for supposing that, as far as Wallace Chesney was concerned, all was for the best in the best of all possible worlds.

And yet—

The first inkling I received that anything was wrong came through a chance meeting with Raymond Gandle, who happened to pass my gate on his way back from the links just as I drove up in my taxi; for I had been away from home for many weeks on a protracted business tour. I welcomed Gandle's advent and invited him in to smoke a pipe and put me abreast of local gossip. He came readily enough – and seemed, indeed, to have something on his mind and to be glad of the opportunity of revealing it to a sympathetic auditor.

'And how,' I asked him, when we were comfortably settled, 'did your game this afternoon come out?'

'Oh, he beat me,' said Gandle, and it seemed to me that there was a note of bitterness in his voice.

'Then He, whoever he was, must have been an extremely competent performer,' I replied, courteously, for Gandle was one of the finest players in the club. 'Unless, of course, you were giving him some impossible handicap?'

'No; we played level.'

'Indeed! Who was your opponent?'

'Chesney.'

'Wallace Chesney! And he beat you, playing level! This is the most amazing thing I have ever heard.'

'He's improved out of all knowledge.'

'He must have done. Do you think he would ever beat you again?'

'No. Because he won't have the chance.'

'You surely do not mean that you will not play him because you are afraid of being beaten?'

'It isn't being beaten I mind—'

And if I omit to report the remainder of his speech it is not merely because it contained expressions with which I am reluctant to sully my lips, but because, omitting these expletives, what he said was almost word for word what you were saying to me just now about Nathaniel Frisby. It was, it seemed, Wallace Chesney's manner, his arrogance, his attitude of belonging to some superior order of being that had so wounded Raymond Gandle. Wallace Chesney had, it appeared, criticised Gandle's mashie-play in no friendly spirit; had hung up the game on the fourteenth tee in order to show him how to place his feet; and on the way back to the club-house had said that the beauty of golf was that the best player could enjoy a round even with a dud, because, though there might be no interest in the match, he could always amuse himself by playing for his medal-score.

I was profoundly shaken.

'Wallace Chesney!' I exclaimed. 'Was it really Wallace Chesney who behaved in the manner you describe?'

'Unless he's got a twin brother of the same name, it was.'

'Wallace Chesney a victim to swelled head! I can hardly credit it.'

'Well, you needn't take my word for it unless you want to. Ask anybody. It isn't often he can get anyone to play with him now.'

'You horrify me!'

Raymond Gandle smoked awhile in brooding silence.

'You've heard about his engagement?' he said at length.

'I have heard nothing, nothing. What about his engagement?'

'Charlotte Dix has broken it off.'

'No!'

'Yes. Couldn't stand him any longer.'

I got rid of Gandle as soon as I could. I made my way as quickly as possible to the house where Charlotte lived with her aunt. I was determined to sift this matter to the bottom and to do all that lay in my power to heal the breach between two young people for whom I had a great affection.

'I have just heard the news,' I said, when the aunt had retired to some secret lair, as aunts do, and Charlotte and I were alone.

'What news?' said Charlotte, dully. I thought she looked pale and ill, and she had certainly grown thinner.

'This dreadful news about your engagement to Wallace Chesney. Tell me, why did you do this thing? Is there no hope of a reconciliation?'

'Not unless Wally becomes his old self again.'

'But I had always regarded you two as ideally suited to one another.'

'Wally has completely changed in the last few weeks. Haven't you heard?'

'Only sketchily, from Raymond Gandle.'

'I refuse,' said Charlotte, proudly, all the woman in her leaping to her eyes, 'to marry a man who treats me as if I were a kronen at the present rate of exchange, merely because I slice an occasional tee-shot. The afternoon I broke off the engagement' – her voice shook, and I could see that her indifference was but a mask – 'the afternoon I broke off the en-gug-gug-gagement, he t-told me I ought to use an iron off the tee instead of a dud-dud-driver.'

And the stricken girl burst into an uncontrollable fit of sobbing. And realising that, if matters had gone as far as that, there was little I could do, I pressed her hand silently and left her.

But though it seemed hopeless I decided to persevere. I turned my steps towards Wallace Chesney's bungalow, resolved to make one appeal to the man's better feelings. He was in his sitting-room when I arrived, polishing a putter; and it seemed significant to me, even in that tense moment, that the putter was quite an ordinary one, such as any capable player might use. In the brave old happy days of his dudhood, the only putters you ever found in the society of Wallace Chesney were patent self-adjusting things that looked like croquet mallets that had taken the wrong turning in childhood.

'Well, Wallace, my boy,' I said.

'Hallo!' said Wallace Chesney. 'So you're back?'

We fell into conversation, and I had not been in the room two minutes before I realised that what I had been told about the change in him was nothing more than the truth. The man's bearing and his every remark were insufferably bumptious. He spoke of his prospects in the July medal competition as if the issue were already settled. He scoffed at his rivals.

I had some little difficulty in bringing the talk round to the matter which I had come to discuss.

'My boy,' I said at length, 'I have just heard the sad news.'

'What sad news?'

'I have been talking to Charlotte—'

'Oh, that!' said Wallace Chesney.

'She was telling me—'

'Perhaps it's all for the best.'

'All for the best? What do you mean?'

'Well,' said Wallace, 'one doesn't wish, of course, to say anything ungallant, but, after all, poor Charlotte's handicap *is* fourteen and wouldn't appear to have much chance of getting any lower. I mean, there's such a thing as a fellow throwing himself away.'

Was I revolted at these callous words? For a moment, yes. Then it struck me that, though he had uttered them with a light laugh, that laugh had had in it more than a touch of bravado. I looked at him keenly. There was a bored, discontented expression in his eyes, a line of pain about his mouth.

'My boy,' I said, gravely, 'you are not happy.'

For an instant I think he would have denied the imputation. But my visit had coincided with one of those twilight moods in which a man requires, above all else, sympathy. He uttered a weary sigh.

'I'm fed up,' he admitted. 'It's a funny thing. When I was a dud, I used to think how perfect it must be to be scratch. I used to watch the cracks buzzing round the course and envy them.

It's all a fraud. The only time when you enjoy golf is when an occasional decent shot is enough to make you happy for the day. I'm plus two, and I'm bored to death. I'm too good. And what's the result? Everybody's jealous of me. Everybody's got it in for me. Nobody loves me.'

His voice rose in a note of anguish, and at the sound his terrier, which had been sleeping on the rug, crept forward and licked his hand.

'The dog loves you,' I said, gently, for I was touched.

'Yes, but I don't love the dog,' said Wallace Chesney.

'Now come, Wallace,' I said. 'Be reasonable, my boy. It is only your unfortunate manner on the links which has made you perhaps a little unpopular at the moment. Why not pull yourself up? Why ruin your whole life with this arrogance? All that you need is a little tact, a little forbearance. Charlotte, I am sure, is just as fond of you as ever, but you have wounded her pride. Why must you be unkind about her tee-shots?'

Wallace Chesney shook his head despondently.

'I can't help it,' he said. 'It exasperates me to see anyone foozling, and I have to say so.'

'Then there is nothing to be done,' I said, sadly.

All the medal competitions at our club are, as you know, important events; but, as you are also aware, none of them is looked forward to so keenly or contested so hotly as the one in July. At the beginning of the year of which I am speaking, Raymond Gandle had been considered the probable winner of the fixture; but as the season progressed and Wallace Chesney's skill developed to such a remarkable extent most of us were reluctantly inclined to put our money on the latter. Reluctantly, because Wallace's unpopularity was now so general that the thought of his winning was distasteful to all. It grieved me to see how cold his fellow-members were towards him. He drove off from the first tee without a solitary hand-clap; and, though the drive was of admirable quality and nearly carried the green, there was not a single cheer. I noticed Charlotte Dix among the spectators. The poor girl was looking sad and wan.

In the draw for partners Wallace had had Peter Willard allotted to him; and he muttered to me in a quite audible voice that it was as bad as handicapping him half-a-dozen strokes to make him play with such a hopeless performer. I do not think Peter heard, but it would not have made much difference to him if he had, for I doubt if anything could have had much effect for the worse on his game. Peter Willard always entered for the medal competition, because he said that competition-play was good for the nerves.

On this occasion he topped his ball badly, and Wallace lit his pipe with the exaggeratedly patient air of an irritated man. When Peter topped his second also, Wallace was moved to speech.

'For goodness' sake,' he snapped, 'what's the good of playing at all if you insist on lifting your head? Keep it down, man, keep it down. You don't need to watch to see where the ball is going. It isn't likely to go as far as all that. Make up your mind to count three before you look up.'

'Thanks,' said Peter, meekly. There was no pride in Peter to be wounded. He knew the sort of player he was.

The couples were now moving off with smooth rapidity, and the course was dotted with the figures of players and their accompanying spectators. A fair proportion of these latter had decided to follow the fortunes of Raymond Gandle, but by far the larger number were sticking to Wallace, who right from the start showed that Gandle or anyone else would have to return a very fine card to beat him. He was out in thirty-seven, two above bogey, and with the assistance of a superb second, which landed the ball within a foot of the pin, got a three on the tenth, where a four is considered good. I mention this to show that by the time he arrived at the short lake-hole Wallace Chesney was at the top of his form. Not even the fact that he had been obliged to let the next couple through owing to Peter Willard losing his ball had been enough to upset him.

The course has been rearranged since, but at that time the lake-hole, which is now the second, was the eleventh, and was generally looked on as the crucial hole in a medal round. Wallace no doubt realised this, but the knowledge did not seem to affect him. He lit his pipe with the utmost coolness: and, having replaced the match-box in his hip-pocket, stood smoking non-chalantly as he waited for the couple in front to get off the green.

They holed out eventually, and Wallace walked to the tee. As he did so, he was startled to receive a resounding smack.

'Sorry,' said Peter Willard, apologetically. 'Hope I didn't hurt you. A wasp.'

And he pointed to the corpse, which was lying in a used-up attitude on the ground.

'Afraid it would sting you,' said Peter.

'Oh, thanks,' said Wallace.

He spoke a little stiffly, for Peter Willard had a large, hard, flat hand, the impact of which had shaken him up considerably. Also, there had been laughter in the crowd. He was fuming as he bent to address his ball, and his annoyance became acute when, just as he reached the top of his swing, Peter Willard suddenly spoke.

'Just a second, old man,' said Peter. Wallace spun round, outraged.

'What *is* it? I do wish you would wait till I've made my shot.'

'Just as you like,' said Peter, humbly.

'There is no greater crime that a man can commit on the links than to speak to a fellow when he's making his stroke.'

'Of course, of course,' acquiesced Peter, crushed.

Wallace turned to his ball once more. He was vaguely conscious of a discomfort to which he could not at the moment give a name. At first he thought that he was having a spasm of lumbago, and this surprised him, for he had never in his life been subject to even a suspicion of that malady. A moment later he realised that this diagnosis had been wrong.

'Good heavens!' he cried, leaping nimbly some two feet into the air. 'I'm on fire!'

'Yes,' said Peter, delighted at his ready grasp of the situation. 'That's what I wanted to mention just now.'

Wallace slapped vigorously at the seat of his Plus Fours.

'It must have been when I killed that wasp,' said Peter, beginning to see clearly into the matter. 'You had a match-box in your pocket.'

Wallace was in no mood to stop and discuss first causes. He was springing up and down on his pyre, beating at the flames.

'Do you know what I should do if I were you?' said Peter Willard. 'I should jump into the lake.'

One of the cardinal rules of golf is that a player shall accept no advice from anyone but his own caddie; but the warmth about his lower limbs had now become so generous that Wallace was prepared to stretch a point. He took three rapid strides and entered the water with a splash.

The lake, though muddy, is not deep, and presently Wallace

was to be observed standing up to his waist some few feet from the shore.

'That ought to have put it out,' said Peter Willard. 'It was a bit of luck that it happened at this hole.' He stretched out a hand to the bather. 'Catch hold, old man, and I'll pull you out.'

'No!' said Wallace Chesney.

'Why not?'

'Never mind!' said Wallace, austerely. He bent as near to Peter as he was able.

'Send a caddie up to the club-house to fetch my grey flannel trousers from my locker,' he whispered, tensely.

'Oh, ah!' said Peter.

It was some little time before Wallace, encircled by a group of male spectators, was enabled to change his costume; and during the interval he continued to stand waist-deep in the water, to the chagrin of various couples who came to the tee in the course of their round and complained with not a little bitterness that his presence there added a mental hazard to an already difficult hole. Eventually, however, he found himself back ashore, his ball before him, his mashie in his hand.

'Carry on,' said Peter Willard, as the couple in front left the green. 'All clear now.'

Wallace Chesney addressed his ball. And, even as he did so, he was suddenly aware that an odd psychological change had taken place in himself. He was aware of a strange weakness. The charred remains of the Plus Fours were lying under an adjacent bush; and, clad in the old grey flannels of his early golfing days, Wallace felt diffident, feeble, uncertain of himself. It was as though virtue had gone out of him, as if some indispensable adjunct to good play had been removed. His corrugated trouser-leg caught his eye as he waggled, and all at once he became acutely alive to the fact that many eyes were watching him. The audience seemed to press on him like a blanket. He felt as he had been wont to feel in the old days when he had had to drive off the first tee in front of a terrace-full of scoffing critics.

The next moment his ball had bounded weakly over the intervening patch of turf and was in the water.

'Hard luck!' said Peter Willard, ever a generous foe. And the words seemed to touch some almost atrophied chord in Wallace's breast. A sudden love for his species flooded over him. Dashed decent of Peter, he thought, to sympathise. Peter was a good chap. So were the spectators good chaps. So was everybody, even his caddie.

Peter Willard, as if resolved to make his sympathy practical, also rolled his ball into the lake.

'Hard luck!' said Wallace Chesney, and started as he said it; for many weeks had passed since he had commiserated with an opponent. He felt a changed man. A better, sweeter, kindlier man. It was as if a curse had fallen from him.

He teed up another ball, and swung.

'Hard luck!' said Peter.

'Hard luck!' said Wallace, a moment later.

'Hard luck!' said Peter, a moment after that.

Wallace Chesney stood on the tee watching the spot in the water where his third ball had fallen. The crowd was now openly amused, and, as he listened to their happy laughter, it was borne in upon Wallace that he, too, was amused and happy. A weird, almost effervescent exhilaration filled him. He turned and beamed upon the spectators. He waved his mashie cheerily at them. This, he felt, was something like golf. This was golf as it should be – not the dull, mechanical thing which had bored him during all these past weeks of his perfection, but a gay, rollicking adventure. That was the soul of golf, the thing that made it the wonderful pursuit it was – that speculativeness, that not knowing where the dickens your ball was going when you hit it, that eternal hoping for the best, that never-failing chanciness. It is better to travel hopefully than to arrive, and at last this great truth had come home to Wallace Chesney. He realised now why pro's were all grave, silent men who seemed to struggle manfully against some secret sorrow. It was because they were too darned good. Golf had no surprises for them, no gallant spirit of adventure.

'I'm going to get a ball over if I stay here all night,' cried Wallace Chesney, gaily, and the crowd echoed his mirth. On the face of Charlotte Dix was the look of a mother whose prodigal son has rolled into the old home once more. She caught Wallace's eye and gesticulated to him blithely.

'The cripple says he'll give you a stroke a hole, Wally!' she shouted.

'I'm ready for him!' bellowed Wallace.

'Hard *luck!*' said Peter Willard.

Under their bush the Plus Fours, charred and dripping, lurked unnoticed. But Wallace Chesney saw them. They caught his eye as he sliced his eleventh into the marshes on the right. It seemed to him that they looked sullen. Disappointed. Baffled.

Wallace Chesney was himself again.

Down on the new bowling-green behind the club-house some sort of competition was in progress. The seats about the smooth strip of turf were crowded, and the weak-minded yapping of the patients made itself plainly audible to the Oldest Member as he sat in his favourite chair in the smoking-room. He shifted restlessly, and a frown marred the placidity of his venerable brow. To the Oldest Member a golf-club was a golf-club, and he resented the introduction of any alien element. He had opposed the institution of tennis-courts; and the suggestion of a bowling-green had stirred him to his depths.

A young man in spectacles came into the smoking-room. His high forehead was aglow, and he lapped up a ginger-ale with the air of one who considers that he has earned it.

'Capital exercise!' he said, beaming upon the Oldest Member.

The Oldest Member laid down his *Vardon On Casual Water*, and peered suspiciously at his companion.

'What did you go round in?' he asked.

'Oh, I wasn't playing golf,' said the young man. 'Bowls.'

'A nauseous pursuit!' said the Oldest Member, coldly, and resumed his reading.

The young man seemed nettled.

'I don't know why you should say that,' he retorted. 'It's a splendid game.'

'I rank it,' said the Oldest Member, 'with the juvenile pastime of marbles.'

The young man pondered for some moments.

'Well, anyway,' he said at length, 'it was good enough for Drake.'

'As I have not the pleasure of the acquaintance of your friend Drake, I am unable to estimate the value of his endorsement.'

'*The* Drake. The Spanish Armada Drake. He was playing bowls on Plymouth Hoe when they told him that the Armada was in sight. "There is time to finish the game," he replied. That's what Drake thought of bowls.'

'If he had been a golfer he would have ignored the Armada altogether.'

'It's easy enough to say that,' said the young man, with spirit, 'but can the history of golf show a parallel case?'

'A million, I should imagine.'

'But you've forgotten them, eh?' said the young man, satirically.

'On the contrary,' said the Oldest Member. 'As a typical instance, neither more nor less remarkable than a hundred others, I will select the story of Rollo Podmarsh.' He settled himself comfortably in his chair, and placed the tips of his fingers together. 'This Rollo Podmarsh—'

'No, I say!' protested the young man, looking at his watch.

'This Rollo Podmarsh—'

'Yes, but—'

This Rollo Podmarsh (said the Oldest Member) was the only son of his mother, and she was a widow; and like other young men in that position he had rather allowed a mother's tender care to take the edge off what you might call his rugged manliness. Not to put too fine a point on it, he had permitted his parent to coddle him ever since he had been in the nursery; and now, in his twenty-eighth year, he invariably wore flannel next his skin, changed his shoes the moment they got wet, and – from September to May, inclusive – never went to bed without partaking of a bowl of hot arrowroot. Not, you would say, the stuff of which heroes are made. But you would be wrong. Rollo Podmarsh was a golfer, and consequently pure gold at heart; and in his hour of crisis all the good in him came to the surface.

In giving you this character-sketch of Rollo, I have been at pains to make it crisp, for I observe that you are wriggling in a restless manner and you persist in pulling out that watch of yours and gazing at it. Let me tell you that, if a mere skeleton outline of the man has this effect upon you, I am glad for your sake that you never met his mother. Mrs Podmarsh could talk with enjoyment for hours on end about her son's character and habits. And, on the September evening on which I introduce her to you, though she had, as a fact, been speaking only for some ten minutes, it had seemed like hours to the girl, Mary Kent, who was the party of the second part to the conversation.

Mary Kent was the daughter of an old school-friend of Mrs Podmarsh, and she had come to spend the autumn and winter with her while her parents were abroad. The scheme had never looked particularly good to Mary, and after ten minutes of her hostess on the subject of Rollo she was beginning to weave dreams of knotted sheets and a swift getaway through the bedroom window in the dark of the night.

'He is a strict teetotaller,' said Mrs Podmarsh.

'Really?'

'And has never smoked in his life.'

'Fancy that!'

'But here is the dear boy now,' said Mrs Podmarsh, fondly.

Down the road towards them was coming a tall, well-knit figure in a Norfolk coat and grey flannel trousers. Over his broad shoulders was suspended a bag of golf-clubs.

'Is *that* Mr Podmarsh?' exclaimed Mary.

She was surprised. After all she had been listening to about the arrowroot and the flannel next the skin and the rest of it, she had pictured the son of the house as a far weedier specimen. She had been expecting to meet a small, slender young man with an eyebrow moustache, and pince-nez; and this person approaching might have stepped straight out of Jack Dempsey's training-camp.

'Does he play golf?' asked Mary, herself an enthusiast.

'Oh yes,' said Mrs Podmarsh. 'He makes a point of going out on the links once a day. He says the fresh air gives him such an appetite.'

Mary, who had taken a violent dislike to Rollo on the evidence of his mother's description of his habits, had softened towards him on discovering that he was a golfer. She now reverted to her previous opinion. A man who could play the noble game from such ignoble motives was beyond the pale.

'Rollo is exceedingly good at golf,' proceeded Mrs Podmarsh. 'He scores more than a hundred and twenty every time, while Mr Burns, who is supposed to be one of the best players in the club, seldom manages to reach eighty. But Rollo is very modest – modesty is one of his best qualities – and you would never guess he was so skilful unless you were told.'

'Well, Rollo darling, did you have a nice game? You didn't get your feet wet, I hope? This is Mary Kent, dear.'

THE AWAKENING OF ROLLO PODMARSH

Rollo Podmarsh shook hands with Mary. And at her touch the strange dizzy feeling which had come over him at the sight of her suddenly became increased a thousand-fold. As I see that you are consulting your watch once more, I will not describe his emotions as exhaustively as I might. I will merely say that he had never felt anything resembling this sensation of dazed ecstasy since the occasion when a twenty-foot putt of his, which had been going well off the line, as his putts generally did, had hit a worm-cast sou-sou-east of the hole and popped in, giving him a snappy six. Rollo Podmarsh, as you will have divined, was in love at first sight. Which makes it all the sadder to think Mary at the moment was regarding him as an outcast and a blister.

Mrs Podmarsh, having enfolded her son in a vehement embrace, drew back with a startled exclamation, sniffing.

'Rollo!' she cried. 'You smell of tobacco-smoke.'

Rollo looked embarrassed.

'Well, the fact is, mother—'

A hard protuberance in his coat-pocket attracted Mrs Podmarsh's notice. She swooped and drew out a big-bowled pipe.

'Rollo!' she exclaimed, aghast.

'Well, the fact is, mother—'

'Don't you know,' cried Mrs Podmarsh, 'that smoking is poisonous, and injurious to the health?'

'Yes. But the fact is mother—'

'It causes nervous dyspepsia, sleeplessness, gnawing of the stomach, headache, weak eyes, red spots on the skin, throat irritation, asthma, bronchitis, heart failure, lung trouble, catarrh, melancholy, neurasthenia, loss of memory, impaired will-power, rheumatism, lumbago, sciatica, neuritis, heartburn, torpid liver, loss of appetite, enervation, lassitude, lack of ambition, and falling out of hair.'

'Yes, I know, mother. But the fact is, Ted Ray smokes all the time he's playing, and I thought it might improve my game.'

And it was at these splendid words that Mary Kent felt for the first time that something might be made of Rollo Podmarsh. That she experienced one-millionth of the fervour which was gnawing at his vitals I will not say. A woman does not fall in love in a flash like a man. But at least she no longer regarded him with loathing. On the contrary, she found herself liking him. There was, she considered, the right stuff in Rollo. And if, as seemed probable from his mother's conversation, it would take a bit of digging to bring it up, well – she liked rescue-work and had plenty of time.

Mr Arnold Bennett, in a recent essay, advises young bachelors to proceed with a certain caution in matters of the heart. They should, he asserts, first decide whether or not they are ready for love; then, whether it is better to marry earlier or later; thirdly, whether their ambitions are such that a wife will prove a hindrance to their career. These romantic preliminaries concluded, they may grab a girl and go to it. Rollo Podmarsh would have made a tough audience for these precepts. Since the days of Antony and Cleopatra probably no one had ever got more swiftly off the mark. One may say that he was in love before he had come within two yards of the girl. And each day that passed found him more nearly up to his eyebrows in the tender emotion.

He thought of Mary when he was changing his wet shoes; he dreamed of her while putting flannel next his skin; he yearned for her over the evening arrowroot. Why, the man was such a slave to his devotion that he actually went to the length of purloining small articles belonging to her. Two days after Mary's arrival Rollo Podmarsh was driving off the first tee with one of her handkerchiefs, a powder-puff, and a dozen hairpins secreted in his left breast-pocket. When dressing for dinner he used to take them out and look at them, and at night he slept with them under his pillow. Heavens, how he loved that girl!

One evening when they had gone out into the garden together to look at the new moon – Rollo, by his mother's advice, wearing a woollen scarf to protect his throat – he endeavoured to bring the conversation round to the important subject. Mary's last remark had been about earwigs. Considered as a cue, it lacked a subtle something; but Rollo was not the man to be discouraged by that.

'Talking of earwigs, Miss Kent,' he said, in a low musical voice, 'have you ever been in love?'

Mary was silent for a moment before replying.

'Yes, once. When I was eleven. With a conjurer who came to perform at my birthday-party. He took a rabbit and two eggs out of my hair, and life seemed one grand sweet song.'

'Never since then?'

'Never.'

'Suppose – just for the sake of argument – suppose you ever did love anyone – er – what sort of a man would it be?'

'A hero,' said Mary, promptly.

'A hero?' said Rollo, somewhat taken aback. 'What sort of hero?'

'Any sort. I could only love a really brave man – a man who had done some wonderful heroic action.'

'Shall we go in?' said Rollo, hoarsely. 'The air is a little chilly.'

We have now, therefore, arrived at a period in Rollo Podmarsh's career which might have inspired those lines of Henley's about 'the night that covers me, black as the pit from pole to pole.' What with one thing and another, he was in an almost Job-like condition of despondency. I say 'one thing and another,' for it was not only hopeless love that weighed him down. In addition to being hopelessly in love, he was greatly depressed about his golf.

On Rollo in his capacity of golfer I have so far not dwelt. You have probably allowed yourself, in spite of the significant episode of the pipe, to dismiss him as one of those placid, contented – shall I say dilettante? – golfers who are so frequent in these degenerate days. Such was not the case. Outwardly placid, Rollo was consumed inwardly by an ever-burning fever of ambition. His aims were not extravagant. He did not want to become amateur champion, nor even to win a monthly medal; but he did, with his whole soul, desire one of these days to go round the course in under a hundred. This feat accomplished, it was his intention to set the seal on his golfing career by playing a real money-match; and already he had selected his opponent, a certain Colonel Bodger, a tottery performer of advanced years who for the last decade had been a martyr to lumbago.

But it began to look as if even the modest goal he had marked out for himself were beyond his powers. Day after day he would step on to the first tee, glowing with zeal and hope, only to crawl home in the quiet evenfall with another hundred and twenty on his card. Little wonder, then, that he began to lose his appetite and would moan feebly at the sight of a poached egg.

With Mrs Podmarsh sedulously watching over her son's health, you might have supposed that this inability on his part to teach the foodstuffs to take a joke would have caused consternation in the home. But it so happened that Rollo's mother had recently been reading a medical treatise in which an eminent physician stated that we all eat too much nowadays, and that the secret of a happy life is to lay off the carbohydrates to some extent. She was, therefore, delighted to observe the young man's moderation in the matter of food, and frequently held him up as an example to be noted and followed by little Lettice Willoughby, her grand-daughter, who was a good and consistent trencherwoman, particularly rough on the puddings. Little Lettice, I should mention, was the daughter of Rollo's sister Enid, who lived in the neighbourhood. Mrs Willoughby had been compelled to go away on a visit a few days before and had left her child with Mrs Podmarsh during her absence.

You can fool some of the people all the time, but Lettice Willoughby was not of the type that is easily deceived. A nice, old-fashioned child would no doubt have accepted without questioning her grand-mother's dictum that roly-poly pudding could not fail to hand a devastating wallop to the blood-pressure, and that to take two helpings of it was practically equivalent to walking right into the family vault. A child with less decided opinions of her own would have been impressed by the spectacle of her uncle refusing sustenance, and would have received without demur the statement that he did it because he felt that abstinence was good for his health. Lettice was a modern child and knew better. She had had experience of this loss of appetite and its significance. The first symptom which had preceded the demise of poor old Ponto, who had recently handed in his portfolio after holding office for ten years as the Willoughby family dog, had been this same disinclination to absorb nourishment. Besides, she was an observant child, and had not failed to note the haggard misery in her uncle's eyes. She tackled him squarely on the subject one morning after breakfast. Rollo had retired into the more distant parts of the garden, and was leaning forward, when she found him, with his head buried in his hands.

'Hallo, uncle,' said Lettice.

Rollo looked up wanly.

'Ah, child!' he said. He was fond of his niece.

'Aren't you feeling well, uncle?'

'Far, far from well.'

'It's old age, I expect,' said Lettice.

'I feel old,' admitted Rollo. 'Old and battered. Ah, Lettice, laugh and be gay while you can.'

'All right, uncle.'

'Make the most of your happy, careless, smiling, halcyon childhood.'

'Right-o, uncle.'

'When you get to my age, dear, you will realise that it is a sad, hopeless world. A world where, if you keep your head down, you forget to let the club-head lead: where even if you do happen by a miracle to keep 'em straight with your brassie, you blow up on the green and foozle a six-inch putt.'

Lettice could not quite understand what Uncle Rollo was talking about, but she gathered broadly that she had been correct in supposing him to be in a bad state, and her warm, childish heart was filled with pity for him. She walked thoughtfully away, and Rollo resumed his reverie.

Into each life, as the poet says, some rain must fall. So much had recently been falling into Rollo's that, when Fortune at last sent along a belated sunbeam, it exercised a cheering effect out of all proportion to its size. By this I mean that when, some four days after his conversation with Lettice, Mary Kent asked him to play golf with her, he read into the invitation a significance which only a lover could have seen in it. I will not go so far as to say that Rollo Podmarsh looked on Mary Kent's suggestion that they should have a round together as actually tantamount to a revelation of undying love; but he certainly regarded it as a most encouraging sign. It seemed to him that things were beginning to move, that Rollo Preferred were on a rising market. Gone was the gloom of the past days. He forgot those sad, solitary wanderings of his in the bushes at the bottom of the garden; he forgot that his mother had bought him a new set of winter woollies which felt like horsehair; he forgot that for the last few evenings his arrowroot had tasted rummy. His whole mind was occupied with the astounding fact that she had voluntarily offered to play golf with him, and he walked out on to the first tee filled with a yeasty exhilaration which nearly caused him to burst into song.

'How shall we play?' asked Mary. 'I am a twelve. What is your handicap?'

Rollo was under the disadvantage of not actually possessing a handicap. He had a sort of private system of book-keeping of his own by which he took strokes over if they did not seem to him to be up to sample, and allowed himself five-foot putts at discretion. So he had never actually handed in the three cards necessary for handicapping purposes.

'I don't exactly know,' he said. 'It's my ambition to get round in under a hundred, but I've never managed it yet.'

'Never?'

'Never! It's strange, but something always seems to go wrong.'

'Perhaps you'll manage it to-day,' said Mary, encouragingly, so encouragingly that it was all that Rollo could do to refrain from flinging himself at her feet and barking like a dog. 'Well, I'll start you two holes up, and we'll see how we get on. Shall I take the honour?'

She drove off one of those fair-to-medium balls which go with a twelve handicap. Not a great length, but nice and straight.

'Splendid!' cried Rollo, devoutly.

'Oh, I don't know,' said Mary. 'I wouldn't call it anything special.'

Titanic emotions were surging in Rollo's bosom as he addressed his ball. He had never felt like this before, especially on the first tee – where as a rule he found himself overcome with a nervous humility.

'Oh, Mary! Mary!' he breathed to himself as he swung.

You who squander your golden youth fooling about on a bowling-green will not understand the magic of those three words. But if you were a golfer, you would realise that in selecting just that invocation to breathe to himself Rollo Podmarsh had hit, by sheer accident, on the ideal method of achieving a fine drive. Let me explain. The first two words, tensely breathed, are just sufficient to take a man with the proper slowness to the top of his swing; the first syllable of the second 'Mary' exactly coincides with the striking of the ball; and the final 'ry!' takes care of the follow-through. The consequence was that Rollo's ball, instead of hopping down the hill like an embarrassed duck, as was its usual practice, sang off the tee with a scream like a shell, nodded in passing to Mary's ball, where it lay some hundred and fifty yards down the course, and, carrying on from there, came to rest within easy distance of the green. For the first time in his golfing life Rollo Podmarsh had hit a nifty.

Mary followed the ball's flight with astonished eyes.

'But this will never do!' she exclaimed. 'I can't possibly start you two up if you're going to do this sort of thing.'

Rollo blushed.

'I shouldn't think it would happen again,' he said. 'I've never done a drive like that before.'

'But it must happen again,' said Mary, firmly. 'This is evidently your day. If you don't get round in under a hundred to-day, I shall never forgive you.'

Rollo shut his eyes, and his lips moved feverishly. He was registering a vow that, come what might, he would not fail her. A minute later he was holing out in three, one under bogey.

The second hole is the short lake-hole. Bogey is three, and Rollo generally did it in four; for it was his custom not to count any balls he might sink in the water, but to start afresh with one which happened to get over, and then take three putts. But to-day something seemed to tell him that he would not require the aid of this ingenious system. As he took his mashie from the bag, he *knew* that his first shot would soar successfully on to the green.

'Ah, Mary!' he breathed as he swung.

These subtleties are wasted on a worm, if you will pardon the expression, like yourself, who, possibly owing to a defective education, is content to spend life's spring-time rolling wooden balls across a lawn; but I will explain that in altering and shortening his soliloquy at this juncture Rollo had done the very thing any good pro. would have recommended. If he had murmured, 'Oh, Mary! Mary!' as before he would have over-swung. 'Ah, Mary!' was exactly right for a half-swing with the mashie. His ball shot up in a beautiful arc, and trickled to within six inches of the hole.

Mary was delighted. There was something about this big, diffident man which had appealed from the first to everything in her that was motherly.

'Marvellous!' she said. 'You'll get a two. Five for the first two holes! Why, you simply must get round in under a hundred now.' She swung, but too lightly; and her ball fell in the water. 'I'll give you this,' she said, without the slightest chagrin, for this girl had a beautiful nature. 'Let's get on to the third. Four up! Why, you're wonderful!'

And not to weary you with too much detail, I will simply remark that, stimulated by her gentle encouragement, Rollo Podmarsh actually came off the ninth green with a medal-score of forty-six for the half-round. A ten on the seventh had spoiled his card to some extent, and a nine on the eighth had not helped, but nevertheless here he was in forty-six, with the easier half of the course before him. He tingled all over – partly because he was wearing the new winter woollies to which I have alluded previously, but principally owing to triumph, elation, and love. He gazed at Mary as Dante might have gazed at Beatrice on one of his particularly sentimental mornings.

Mary uttered an exclamation.

'Oh, I've just remembered,' she exclaimed. 'I promised to write last night to Jane Simpson and give her that new formula for knitting jumpers. I think I'll 'phone her now from the club-house and then it'll be off my mind. You go on to the tenth, and I'll join you there.'

Rollo proceeded over the brow of the hill to the tenth tee, and was filling in the time with practice-swings when he heard his name spoken.

'Good gracious, Rollo! I couldn't believe it was you at first.'

He turned to see his sister, Mrs Willoughby, the mother of the child Lettice.

'Hallo!' he said. 'When did you get back?'

'Late last night. Why, it's extraordinary!'

'Hope you had a good time. What's extraordinary? Listen, Enid. Do you know what I've done? Forty-six for the first nine! Forty-six! And holing out every putt.'

'Oh, then that accounts for it.'

'Accounts for what?'

'Why, your looking so pleased with life. I got an idea from Letty, when she wrote to me, that you were at death's door. Your gloom seems to have made a deep impression on the child. Her letter was full of it.'

Rollo was moved.

'Dear little Letty! She is wonderfully sympathetic.'

'Well, I must be off now,' said Enid Willoughby. 'I'm late. Oh, talking of Letty. Don't children say the funniest things! She wrote in her letter that you were very old and wretched and that she was going to put you out of your misery.'

'Ha ha ha!' laughed Rollo.

'We had to poison poor old Ponto the other day, you know, and poor little Letty was inconsolable till we explained to her that it was really the kindest thing to do, because he was so old and ill. But just imagine her thinking of wanting to end *your* sufferings!'

'Ha ha!' laughed Rollo. 'Ha ha h—!'

His voice trailed off into a broken gurgle. Quite suddenly a sinister thought had come to him.

The arrowroot had tasted rummy!

'Why, what on earth is the matter?' asked Mrs Willoughby, regarding his ashen face.

Rollo could find no words. He yammered speechlessly. Yes, for several nights the arrowroot had tasted very rummy. Rummy! There was no other adjective. Even as he plied the spoon he had said to himself: 'This arrowroot tastes rummy!' And – he uttered a sharp yelp as he remembered – it had been little Lettice who had brought it to him. He recollected being touched at the time by the kindly act.

'What *is* the matter, Rollo?' demanded Mrs Willoughby, sharply. 'Don't stand there looking like a dying duck.'

'I am a dying duck,' responded Rollo, hoarsely. 'A dying man, I mean. Enid, that infernal child has poisoned me!'

'Don't be ridiculous! And kindly don't speak of her like that!'

'I'm sorry. I shouldn't blame her, I suppose. No doubt her motives were good. But the fact remains.'

'Rollo, you're too absurd.'

'But the arrowroot tasted rummy.'

'I never knew you could be such an idiot,' said his exasperated sister with sisterly outspokenness. 'I thought you would think it quaint. I thought you would roar with laughter.'

'I did – till I remembered about the rumminess of the arrowroot.'

Mrs Willoughby uttered an impatient exclamation and walked away.

Rollo Podmarsh stood on the tenth tee, a volcano of mixed emotions. Mechanically he pulled out his pipe and lit it. But he found that he could not smoke. In this supreme crisis of his life tobacco seemed to have lost its magic. He put the pipe back in his pocket and gave himself up to his thoughts. Now terror gripped him; anon a sort of gentle melancholy. It was so hard that he should be compelled to leave the world just as he had begun to hit 'em right.

And then in the welter of his thoughts there came one of practical value. To wit, that by hurrying to the doctor's without delay he might yet be saved. There might be antidotes.

He turned to go and there was Mary Kent standing beside him with her bright, encouraging smile.

'I'm sorry I kept you so long,' she said. 'It's your honour. Fire away, and remember that you've got to do this nine in fifty-three at the outside.'

Rollo's thoughts flitted wistfully to the snug surgery where Dr. Brown was probably sitting at this moment surrounded by the finest antidotes.

'Do you know, I think I ought to—'

'Of course you ought to,' said Mary. 'If you did the first nine in forty-six, you can't possibly take fifty-three coming in.'

For one long moment Rollo continued to hesitate – a moment during which the instinct of self-preservation seemed as if it must win the day. All his life he had been brought up to be nervous about his health, and panic gripped him. But there is a deeper, nobler instinct than that of self-preservation – the instinctive desire of a golfer who is at the top of his form to go on and beat his medal-score record. And little by little this grand impulse began to dominate Rollo. If, he felt, he went off now to take antidotes, the doctor might possibly save his life; but reason told him that never again would he be likely to do the first nine in forty-six. He would have to start all over afresh.

Rollo Podmarsh hesitated no longer. With a pale, set face he teed up his ball and drove.

If I were telling this story to a golfer instead of to an excrescence – I use the word in the kindliest spirit – who spends his time messing about on a bowling-green, nothing would please me better than to describe shot by shot Rollo's progress over the remaining nine holes. Epics have been written with less material. But these details would, I am aware, be wasted on you.

Let it suffice that by the time his last approach trickled on to the eighteenth green he had taken exactly fifty shots.

'Three for it!' said Mary Kent. 'Steady now! Take it quite easy and be sure to lay your second dead.'

It was prudent counsel, but Rollo was now thoroughly above himself. He had got his feet wet in a puddle on the sixteenth, but he did not care. His winter woollies seemed to be lined with ants, but he ignored them. All he knew was that he was on the last green in ninety-six, and he meant to finish in style. No tame three putts for him! His ball was five yards away, but he aimed for the back of the hole and brought his putter down with a whack. Straight and true the ball sped, hit the tin, jumped high in the air, and fell into the hole with a rattle.

'Oo!' cried Mary.

Rollo Podmarsh wiped his forehead and leaned dizzily on his putter. For a moment so intense is the fervour induced by the game of games, all he could think of was that he had gone round in ninety-seven. Then, as one waking from a trance, he began to appreciate his position. The fever passed, and a clammy dismay took possession of him. He had achieved his life's ambition; but what now? Already he was conscious of a curious discomfort within him. He felt as he supposed Italians of the Middle Ages must have felt after dropping in to take pot-luck with the Borgias. It was hard. He had gone round in ninety-seven, but he could never take the next step in the career which he had mapped out in his dreams – the money-match with the lumbago-stricken Colonel Bodger.

Mary Kent was fluttering round him, bubbling congratulations, but Rollo sighed.

'Thanks,' he said. 'Thanks very much. But the trouble is, I'm afraid I'm going to die almost immediately. I've been poisoned!'

'Poisoned!'

'Yes. Nobody is to blame. Everything was done with the best intentions. But there it is.'

'But I don't understand.'

Rollo explained. Mary listened pallidly.

'Are you sure?' she gasped.

'Quite sure,' said Rollo, gravely. 'The arrowroot tasted rummy.'

'But arrowroot always does.'

Rollo shook his head.

'No,' he said. 'It tastes like warm blotting-paper, but not rummy.'

Mary was sniffing.

'Don't cry,' urged Rollo, tenderly. 'Don't cry.'

'But I must. And I've come out without a handkerchief.'

'Permit me,' said Rollo, producing one of her best from his left breast-pocket.

'I wish I had a powder-puff,' said Mary.

'Allow me,' said Rollo. 'And your hair has become a little disordered. If I may—' And from the same reservoir he drew a handful of hairpins.

Mary gazed at these exhibits with astonishment.

'But these are mine,' she said.

'Yes. I sneaked them from time to time.'

'But why?'

'Because I loved you,' said Rollo. And in a few moving sentences which I will not trouble you with he went on to elaborate this theme.

Mary listened with her heart full of surging emotions, which I cannot possibly go into if you persist in looking at that damned watch of yours. The scales had fallen from her eyes. She had thought slightingly of this man because he had been a little over-careful of his health, and all the time he had had within him the potentiality of heroism. Something seemed to snap inside her.

'Rollo!' she cried, and flung herself into his arms.

'Mary!' muttered Rollo, gathering her up.

'I told you it was all nonsense,' said Mrs Willoughby, coming up at this tense moment and going on with the conversation where she had left off. 'I've just seen Letty, and she said she meant to put you out of your misery but the chemist wouldn't sell her any poison, so she let it go.'

Rollo disentangled himself from Mary.

'What?' he cried.

Mrs Willoughby repeated her remarks.

'You're sure?' he said.

'Of course I'm sure.'

'Then why did the arrowroot taste rummy?'

'I made inquiries about that. It seems that mother was worried about your taking to smoking, and she found an advertisement in one of the magazines about the Tobacco Habit Cured in Three Days by a secret method without the victim's knowledge. It was a gentle, safe, agreeable method of eliminating the nicotine poison from the system, strengthening the weakened membranes, and overcoming the craving; so she put some in your arrowroot every night.'

There was a long silence. To Rollo Podmarsh it seemed as though the sun had suddenly begun to shine, the birds to sing, and the grasshoppers to toot. All Nature was one vast substantial smile. Down in the valley by the second hole he caught sight of Wallace Chesney's Plus Fours gleaming as their owner stooped to play his shot, and it seemed to him that he had never in his life seen anything so lovely.

'Mary,' he said, in a low, vibrant voice, 'will you wait here for me? I want to go into the club-house for a moment.'

'To change your wet shoes?'

'No!' thundered Rollo. 'I'm never going to change my wet shoes again in my life.' He felt in his pocket, and hurled a box of patent pills far into the undergrowth. 'But I *am* going to change my winter woollies. And when I've put those dashed barbed-wire entanglements into the club-house furnace, I'm going to 'phone to old Colonel Bodger. I hear his lumbago's worse than ever. I'm going to fix up a match with him for a shilling a hole. And if I don't lick the boots off him you can break the engagement!'

'My hero!' murmured Mary.

Rollo kissed her, and with long, resolute steps strode to the club-house.

There was a sound of revelry by night, for the first Saturday in June had arrived and the Golf Club was holding its monthly dance. Fairy lanterns festooned the branches of the chestnut trees on the terrace above the ninth green, and from the big dining-room, cleared now of its tables and chairs, came a muffled slithering of feet and the plaintive sound of saxophones moaning softly like a man who has just missed a short putt. In a basket-chair in the shadows, the Oldest Member puffed a cigar and listened, well content. His was the peace of the man who has reached the age when he is no longer expected to dance.

A door opened, and a young man came out of the club-house. He stood on the steps with folded arms, gazing to left and right. The Oldest Member, watching him from the darkness, noted that he wore an air of gloom. His brow was furrowed and he had the indefinable look of one who has been smitten in the spiritual solar plexus.

Yes, where all around him was joy, jollity, and song, this young man brooded.

The sound of a high tenor voice, talking rapidly and entertain-ingly on the subject of modern Russian thought, now intruded itself on the peace of the night. From the farther end of the terrace a girl came into the light of the lantern, her arm in that of a second young man. She was small and pretty, he tall and intellectual. The light shone on his high forehead and glittered on his tortoiseshell-rimmed spectacles. The girl was gazing up at him with reverence and adoration, and at the sight of these twain the youth on the steps appeared to undergo some sort of spasm. His face became contorted and he wobbled. Then, with a gesture of sublime despair, he tripped over the mat and stumbled back into the club-house. The couple passed on and disappeared, and the Oldest Member had the night to himself, until the door opened once more and the club's courteous and efficient secretary trotted down the steps. The scent of the cigar drew him to where the Oldest Member sat, and he dropped into the chair beside him.

'Seen young Ramage to-night?' asked the secretary.

'He was standing on those steps only a moment ago,' replied the Oldest Member. 'Why do you ask?'

'I thought perhaps you might have had a talk with him and found out what's the matter. Can't think what's come to him to-night. Nice, civil boy as a rule, but just now, when I was trying to tell him about my short approach on the fifth this afternoon, he was positively abrupt. Gave a sort of hollow gasp and dashed away in the middle of a sentence.'

The Oldest Member sighed.

'You must overlook his brusqueness,' he said. 'The poor lad is passing through a trying time. A short while back I was the spectator of a little drama that explains everything. Mabel Patmore is flirting disgracefully with that young fellow Purvis.'

'Purvis? Oh, you mean the man who won the club Bowls Championship last week?'

'I can quite believe that he may have disgraced himself in the manner you describe,' said the Sage, coldly. 'I know he plays that noxious game. And it is for that reason that I hate to see a nice girl like Mabel Patmore, who only needs a little more steadiness off the tee to become a very fair golfer, wasting her time on him. I suppose his attraction lies in the fact that he has a great flow of conversation, while poor Ramage is, one must admit, more or less of a dumb Isaac. Girls are too often snared by a glib tongue. Still, it is a pity, a great pity. The whole affair recalls irresistibly to my mind the story—'

The secretary rose with a whirr like a rocketing pheasant.

'—the story,' continued the Sage, 'of Jane Packard, William Bates, and Rodney Spelvin – which, as you have never heard it, I will now proceed to relate.'

'Can't stop now, much as I should like—'

'It is a theory of mine,' proceeded the Oldest Member, attaching himself to the other's coat-tails, and pulling him gently back into his seat, 'that nothing but misery can come of the union between a golfer and an outcast whose soul has not been purified by the noblest of games. This is well exemplified by the story of Jane Packard, William Bates, and Rodney Spelvin.'

'All sorts of things to look after—'

'That is why I am hoping so sincerely that there is nothing more serious than a temporary flirtation in this business of Mabel Patmore and bowls-playing Purvis. A girl in whose life golf has become a factor, would be mad to trust her happiness to a blister whose idea of enjoyment is trundling wooden balls across a lawn. Sooner or later he is certain to fail her in some crisis. Lucky for her if this failure occurs before the marriage knot has been inextricably tied and so opens her eyes to his inadequacy – as was the case in the matter of Jane Packard, William Bates, and Rodney Spelvin. I will now,' said the Oldest

Member, 'tell you all about Jane Packard, William Bates, and Rodney Spelvin.'

The secretary uttered a choking groan.

'I shall miss the next dance,' he pleaded.

'A bit of luck for some nice girl,' said the Sage, equably.

He tightened his grip on the other's arm.

Jane Packard and William Bates (said the Oldest Member) were not, you must understand, officially engaged. They had grown up together from childhood, and there existed between them a sort of understanding – the understanding being that, if ever William could speed himself up enough to propose, Jane would accept him, and they would settle down and live stodgily and happily ever after. For William was not one of your rapid wooers. In his affair of the heart he moved somewhat slowly and ponderously, like a motor-lorry, an object which both in physique and temperament he greatly resembled. He was an extraordinarily large, powerful, ox-like young man, who required plenty of time to make up his mind about any given problem. I have seen him in the club dining-room musing with a thoughtful frown for fifteen minutes on end while endeavouring to weigh the rival merits of a chump chop and a sirloin steak as a luncheon dish. A placid, leisurely man, I might almost call him lymphatic. I *will* call him lymphatic. He was lymphatic.

The first glimmering of an idea that Jane might possibly be a suitable wife for him had come to William some three years before this story opens. Having brooded on the matter tensely for six months, he then sent her a bunch of roses. In the October of the following year, nothing having occurred to alter his growing conviction that she was an attractive girl, he presented her with a two-pound box of assorted chocolates. And from then on his progress, though not rapid, was continuous, and there seemed little reason to doubt that, should nothing come about to weaken Jane's regard for him, another five years or so would see the matter settled.

And it did not appear likely that anything would weaken Jane's regard. They had much in common, for she was a calm, slow-moving person, too. They had a mutual devotion to golf, and played together every day; and the fact that their handicaps were practically level formed a strong bond. Most divorces, as you know, spring from the fact that the husband is too markedly superior to his wife at golf; this leading him, when she starts criticising his relations, to say bitter and unforgivable things about her mashie-shots. Nothing of this kind could happen with William and Jane. They would build their life on a solid foundation of sympathy and understanding. The years would find them consoling and encouraging each other, happy married lovers. If, that is to say, William ever got round to proposing.

It was not until the fourth year of this romance that I detected the first sign of any alteration in the schedule. I had happened to call on the Packards one afternoon and found them all out except Jane. She gave me tea and conversed for a while, but she seemed distrait. I had known her since she wore rompers, so felt entitled to ask if there was anything wrong.

'Not exactly wrong,' said Jane, and she heaved a sigh.

'Tell me,' I said.

She heaved another sigh.

'Have you ever read *The Love that Scorches*, by Luella Periton Phipps?' she asked.

I said I had not.

'I got it out of the library yesterday,' said Jane, dreamily, 'and finished it at three this morning in bed. It is a very, very beautiful book. It is all about the desert and people riding on camels and a wonderful Arab chief with stern, yet tender, eyes, and a girl called Angela, and oases and dates and mirages, and all like that. There is a chapter where the Arab chief seizes the girl and clasps her in his arms and she feels his hot breath searing her face and he flings her on his horse and they ride off and all around was sand and night, and the mysterious stars. And somehow – oh, I don't know—'

She gazed yearningly at the chandelier.

'I wish mother would take me to Algiers next winter,' she murmured, absently. 'It would do her rheumatism so much good.'

I went away frankly uneasy. These novelists, I felt, ought to be more careful. They put ideas into girls' heads and made them dissatisfied. I determined to look William up and give him a kindly word of advice. It was no business of mine, you may say, but they were so ideally suited to one another that it seemed a tragedy that anything should come between them. And Jane was in a strange mood. At any moment, I felt, she might take a good, square look at William and wonder what she could ever have seen in him. I hurried to the boy's cottage.

'William,' I said, 'as one who dandled you on his knee when you were a baby, I wish to ask you a personal question. Answer me this, and make it snappy. Do you love Jane Packard?'

A look of surprise came into his face, followed by one of intense thought. He was silent for a space.

'Who, me?' he said at length.

'Yes, you.'

'Jane Packard?'

'Yes, Jane Packard.'

'Do I love Jane Packard?' said William, assembling the material and arranging it neatly in his mind.

He pondered for perhaps five minutes.

'Why, of course I do,' he said.

'Splendid!'

'Devotedly, dash it!'

'Capital!'

'You might say madly.'

I tapped him on his barrel-like chest.

'Then my advice to you, William Bates, is to tell her so.'

'Now that's rather a brainy scheme,' said William, looking at me admiringly. 'I see exactly what you're driving at. You mean it would kind of settle things, and all that?'

'Precisely.'

'Well, I've got to go away for a couple of days to-morrow – it's the Invitation Tournament at Squashy Hollow – but I'll be back on Wednesday. Suppose I take her out on the links on Wednesday and propose?'

'A very good idea.'

'At the sixth hole, say?'

'At the sixth hole would do excellently.'

'Or the seventh?'

'The sixth would be better. The ground slopes from the tee, and you would be hidden from view by the dog-leg turn.'

'Something in that.'

'My own suggestion would be that you somehow contrive to lead her into that large bunker to the left of the sixth fairway.'

'Why?'

'I have reason to believe that Jane would respond more readily to your wooing were it conducted in some vast sandy waste. And there is another thing,' I proceeded, earnestly, 'which I must impress upon you. See that there is nothing tame or tepid about your behaviour when you propose. You must show zip and romance. In fact, I strongly recommend you, before you even say a word to her, to seize her and clasp her in your arms and let your hot breath sear her face.'

'Who, me?' said William.

'Believe me, it is what will appeal to her most.'

'But, I say! Hot breath, I mean! Dash it all, you know, what?'

'I assure you it is indispensable.'

'Seize her?' said William blankly.

'Precisely.'

'Clasp her in my arms?'

'Just so.'

William plunged into silent thought once more.

'Well, you *know*, I suppose,' he said at length. 'You've had experience, I take it. Still— Oh, all right, I'll have a stab at it.'

'There spoke the true William Bates!' I said. 'Go to it, lad, and Heaven speed your wooing!'

In all human schemes – and it is this that so often brings failure to the subtlest strategists – there is always the chance of the Unknown Factor popping up, that unforeseen X for which we have made no allowance and which throws our whole plan of campaign out of gear. I had not anticipated anything of the kind coming along to mar the arrangements on the present occasion; but when I reached the first tee on the Wednesday afternoon to give William Bates that last word of encouragement, which means so much, I saw that I had been too sanguine. William had not yet arrived, but Jane was there, and with her a tall, slim, dark-haired, sickeningly romantic-looking youth in faultlessly fitting serge. A stranger to me. He was talking to her in a musical undertone, and she seemed to be hanging on his words. Her beautiful eyes were fixed on his face, and her lips slightly parted. So absorbed was she that it was not until I spoke that she became aware of my presence.

'William not arrived yet?'

She turned with a start.

'William? Hasn't he? Oh! No, not yet. I don't suppose he will be long. I want to introduce you to Mr Spelvin. He has come to stay with the Wyndhams for a few weeks. He is going to walk round with us.'

Naturally this information came as a shock to me, but I masked my feelings and greeted the young man with a well-assumed cordiality.

'Mr George Spelvin, the actor?' I asked, shaking hands.

'My cousin,' he said. 'My name is Rodney Spelvin. I do not share George's histrionic ambitions. If I have any claim to – may I say renown? – it is as a maker of harmonies.'

'A composer, eh?'

'Verbal harmonies,' explained Mr Spelvin. 'I am, in my humble fashion, a poet.'

'He writes the most beautiful poetry,' said Jane, warmly. 'He has just been reciting some of it to me.'

'Oh, that little thing?' said Mr Spelvin, deprecatingly. 'A mere *morceau.* One of my juvenilia.'

'It was too beautiful for words,' persisted Jane.

'Ah, you,' said Mr Spelvin, 'have the soul to appreciate it. I could wish that there were more like you, Miss Packard. We singers have much to put up with in a crass and materialistic world. Only last week a man, a coarse editor, asked me what my sonnet, "Wine of Desire," *meant.*' He laughed indulgently. 'I gave him answer, 'twas a sonnet, not a mining prospectus.'

'It would have served him right,' said Jane, heatedly, 'if you had pasted him one on the nose!'

At this point a low whistle behind me attracted my attention, and I turned to perceive William Bates towering against the sky-line.

'Hoy!' said William.

I walked to where he stood, leaving Jane and Mr Spelvin in earnest conversation with their heads close together.

'I say,' said William, in a rumbling undertone, 'who's the bird with Jane?'

'A man named Spelvin. He is visiting the Wyndhams. I suppose Mrs Wyndham made them acquainted.'

'Looks a bit of a Gawd-help-us,' said William critically.

'He is going to walk round with you.'

It was impossible for a man of William Bates's temperament to start, but his face took on a look of faint concern.

'Walk round with us?'

'So Jane said.'

'But look here,' said William. 'I can't possibly seize her and clasp her in my arms and do all that hot-breath stuff with this pie-faced exhibit hanging round on the outskirts.'

'No, I fear not.'

'Postpone it, then, what?' said William, with unmistakable relief. 'Well, as a matter of fact, it's probably a good thing. There was a most extraordinarily fine steak-and-kidney pudding at lunch, and, between ourselves, I'm not feeling what you might call keyed up to anything in the nature of a romantic scene. Some other time, eh?'

I looked at Jane and the Spelvin youth, and a nameless apprehension swept over me. There was something in their attitude which I found alarming. I was just about to whisper a warning to William not to treat this new arrival too lightly, when Jane caught sight of him and called him over and a moment later they set out on their round.

I walked away pensively. This Spelvin's advent, coming immediately on top of that book of desert love, was undeniably sinister. My heart sank for William, and I waited at the club-house to have a word with him, after his match. He came in two hours later, flushed and jubilant.

'Played the game of my life!' he said. 'We didn't hole out all the putts, but, making allowance for everything, you can chalk me up an eighty-three. Not so bad, eh? You know the eighth hole? Well, I was a bit short with my drive, and found my ball lying badly for the brassy, so I took my driving-iron and with a nice easy swing let the pill have it so squarely on the seat of the pants that it flew—'

'Where is Jane?' I interrupted.

'Jane? Oh, the bloke Spelvin has taken her home.'

'Beware of him, William!' I whispered, tensely. 'Have a care, young Bates! If you don't look out, you'll have him stealing Jane from you. Don't laugh. Remember that I saw them together before you arrived. She was gazing into his eyes as a desert maiden might gaze into the eyes of a sheik. You don't seem to realise, wretched William Bates, that Jane is an extremely romantic girl. A fascinating stranger like this, coming suddenly into her life, may well snatch her away from you before you know where you are.'

'That's all right,' said William, lightly. 'I don't mind admitting that the same idea occurred to me. But I made judicious inquiries on the way round, and found out that the fellow's a poet. You don't seriously expect me to believe that there's any chance of Jane falling in love with a poet?'

He spoke incredulously, for there were three things in the world that he held in the smallest esteem – slugs, poets, and caddies with hiccups.

'I think it extremely possible, if not probable,' I replied.

'Nonsense!' said William. 'And, besides, the man doesn't play golf. Never had a club in his hand, and says he never wants to. That's the sort of fellow he is.'

At this, I confess, I did experience a distinct feeling of relief. I could imagine Jane Packard, stimulated by exotic literature, committing many follies, but I was compelled to own that I could not conceive of her giving her heart to one who not only did not play golf but had no desire to play it. Such a man, to a girl of her fine nature and correct upbringing, would be beyond the pale. I walked home with William in a calm and happy frame of mind.

I was to learn but one short week later that Woman is the unfathomable, incalculable mystery, the problem we men can never hope to solve.

The week that followed was one of much festivity in our village. There were dances, picnics, bathing-parties, and all the other adjuncts of high summer. In these William Bates played but a minor part. Dancing was not one of his gifts. He swung, if called upon, an amiable shoe, but the disposition in the neighbourhood was to refrain from calling upon him; for he had an incurable habit of coming down with his full weight upon his partner's toes, and many a fair girl had had to lie up for a couple of days after collaborating with him in a fox-trot.

Picnics, again, bored him, and he always preferred a round on the links to the merriest bathing-party. The consequence was that he kept practically aloof from the revels, and all through the week Jane Packard was squired by Rodney Spelvin. With Spelvin she swayed over the waxed floor; with Spelvin she dived and swam; and it was Spelvin who, with zealous hand, brushed ants off her mayonnaise and squashed wasps with a chivalrous teaspoon. The end was inevitable. Apart from anything else, the moon was at its full and many of these picnics were held at night. And you know what that means. It was about ten days later that William Bates came to me in my little garden with an expression on his face like a man who didn't know it was loaded.

'I say,' said William, 'you busy?'

I emptied the remainder of the water-can on the lobelias, and was at his disposal.

'I say,' said William, 'rather a rotten thing has happened. You know Jane?'

I said I knew Jane.

'You know Spelvin?'

I said I knew Spelvin.

'Well, Jane's gone and got engaged to him,' said William, aggrieved.

'What?'

'It's a fact.'

'Already?'

'Absolutely. She told me this morning. And what I want to know,' said the stricken boy, sitting down thoroughly unnerved on a basket of strawberries, 'is, where do I get off?'

My heart bled for him, but I could not help reminding him that I had anticipated this.

'You should not have left them so much alone together,' I said. 'You must have known that there is nothing more conducive to love than the moon in June. Why, songs have been written about it. In fact, I cannot at the moment recall a song that has not been written about it.'

'Yes, but how was I to guess that anything like this would happen?' cried William, rising and scraping strawberries off his person. 'Who would ever have supposed Jane Packard would leap off the dock with a fellow who doesn't play golf?'

'Certainly, as you say, it seems almost incredible. You are sure you heard her correctly? When she told you about the engagement, I mean. There was no chance that you could have misunderstood?'

'Not a bit of it. As a matter of fact, what led up to the thing, if you know what I mean, was me proposing to her myself. I'd been thinking a lot during the last ten days over what you said to me about that, and the more I thought of it the more of a sound egg the notion seemed. So I got her alone up at the club-house and said, "I say, old girl, what about it?" and she said, "What about what?" and I said, "What about marrying me? Don't if you don't want to, of course," I said, "but I'm bound to say it looks pretty good to me." And then she said she loved another – this bloke Spelvin, to wit. A nasty jar, I can tell you, it was. I was just starting off on a round, and it made me hook my putts on every green.'

'But did she say specifically that she was engaged to Spelvin?'

'She said she loved him.'

'There may be hope. If she is not irrevocably engaged the fancy may pass. I think I will go and see Jane and make tactful inquiries.'

'I wish you would,' said William. 'And, I say, you haven't any stuff that'll take strawberry-juice off a fellow's trousers, have you?'

My interview with Jane that evening served only to confirm the bad news. Yes, she was definitely engaged to the man Spelvin. In a burst of girlish confidence she told me some of the details of the affair.

'The moon was shining and a soft breeze played in the trees,' she said. 'And suddenly he took me in his arms, gazed deep into my eyes, and cried, "I love you! I worship you! I adore you! You are the tree on which the fruit of my life hangs; my mate; my woman; predestined to me since the first star shone up in yonder sky!"'

'Nothing,' I agreed, 'could be fairer than that. And then?' I said, thinking how different it all must have been from William Bates's miserable, limping proposal.

'Then we fixed it up that we would get married in September.'

'You are sure you are doing wisely?' I ventured.

Her eyes opened.

'Why do you say that?'

'Well, you know, whatever his other merits – and no doubt they are numerous – Rodney Spelvin does *not* play golf.'

'No, but he's very broad-minded about it.'

I shuddered. Women say these things so lightly.

'Broad-minded?'

'Yes. He has no objection to my going on playing. He says he likes my pretty enthusiasms.'

There seemed nothing more to say on that subject.

'Well,' I said, 'I am sure I wish you every happiness. I had hoped, of course – but never mind that.'

'What?'

'I had hoped, as you insist on my saying it, that you and William Bates—'

A shadow passed over her face. Her eyes grew sad.

'Poor William! I'm awfully sorry about that. He's a dear.'

'A splendid fellow,' I agreed.

'He has been so wonderful about the whole thing. So many men would have gone off and shot grizzly bears or something. But William just said "Right-o!" in a quiet voice, and he's going to caddy for me at Mossy Heath next week.'

'There is good stuff in the boy.'

'Yes.' She sighed. 'If it wasn't for Rodney— Oh, well!'

I thought it would be tactful to change the subject.

'So you have decided to go to Mossy Heath again?'

'Yes. And I'm really going to qualify this year.'

The annual Invitation Tournament at Mossy Heath was one of the most important fixtures of our local female golfing year. As is usual with these affairs, it began with a medal-play qualifying round, the thirty-two players with the lowest net scores then proceeding to fight it out during the remainder of the week by match-play. It gratified me to hear Jane speak so confidently of her chances, for this was the fourth year she had entered, and each time, though she had started out with the brightest prospects, she had failed to survive the qualifying round. Like so many golfers, she was fifty per cent. better at match-play than at medal-play. Mossy Heath, being a championship course, is full of nasty pitfalls, and on each of the three occasions on which she had tackled it one very bad hole had undone all her steady work on the other seventeen and ruined her card. I was delighted to find her so undismayed by failure.

'I am sure you will,' I said. 'Just play your usual careful game.'

'It doesn't matter what sort of a game I play this time,' said Jane, jubilantly. 'I've just heard that there are only thirty-two entries this year, so that everybody who finishes is bound to qualify. I have simply got to get round somehow, and there I am.'

'It would seem somewhat superfluous in these circumstances to play a qualifying round at all.'

'Oh, but they must. You see, there are prizes for the best three scores, so they have to play it. But isn't it a relief to know that, even if I come to grief on that beastly seventh, as I did last year, I shall still be all right?'

'It is, indeed. I have a feeling that once it becomes a matter of match-play you will be irresistible.'

'I do hope so. It would be lovely to win with Rodney looking on.'

'Will he be looking on?'

'Yes. He's going to walk round with me. Isn't it sweet of him?'

Her *fiancé*'s name having slid into the conversation again, she seemed inclined to become eloquent about him. I left her, however, before she could begin. To one so strongly pro-William as myself, eulogistic prattle about Rodney Spelvin was repugnant. I disapproved entirely of this infatuation of hers. I am not a narrow-minded man; I quite appreciate the fact that non-golfers are entitled to marry; but I could not countenance their marrying potential winners of the Ladies' Invitation Tournament at Mossy Heath.

The Greens Committee, as greens committees are so apt to do in order to justify their existence, have altered the Mossy Heath course considerably since the time of which I am speaking, but they have left the three most poisonous holes untouched. I refer to the fourth, the seventh, and the fifteenth. Even a soulless Greens Committee seems to have realised that golfers, long-suffering though they are, can be pushed too far, and that the addition of even a single extra bunker to any of these dreadful places would probably lead to armed riots in the club-house.

Jane Packard had done well on the first three holes, but as she stood on the fourth tee she was conscious, despite the fact that this seemed to be one of her good days, of a certain nervousness; and oddly enough, great as was her love for Rodney Spelvin, it was not his presence that gave her courage, but the sight of William Bates's large, friendly face and the sound of his pleasant voice urging her to keep her bean down and refrain from pressing.

As a matter of fact, to be perfectly truthful, there was beginning already to germinate within her by this time a faint but definite regret that Rodney Spelvin had decided to accompany her on this qualifying round. It was sweet of him to bother to come, no doubt, but still there was something about Rodney that did not seem to blend with the holy atmosphere of a championship course. He was the one romance of her life and their souls were bound together for all eternity, but the fact remained that he did not appear to be able to keep still while she was making her shots, and his light humming, musical though it was, militated against accuracy on the green. He was humming now as she addressed her ball, and for an instant a spasm of irritation shot through her. She fought it down bravely and concentrated on her drive, and when the ball soared over the cross-bunker she forgot her annoyance. There is nothing so mellowing, so conducive to sweet and genial thoughts, as a real juicy one straight down the middle, and this was a pipterino.

'Nice work,' said William Bates, approvingly.

Jane gave him a grateful smile and turned to Rodney. It was his appreciation that she wanted. He was not a golfer, but even he must be able to see that her drive had been something out of the common.

Rodney Spelvin was standing with his back turned, gazing out over the rolling prospect, one hand shading his eyes.

'That vista there,' said Rodney. 'That calm, wooded hollow, bathed in the golden sunshine. It reminds me of the island valley of Avilion—'

'Did you see my drive, Rodney?'

'—where falls not rain nor hail nor any snow, nor ever wind blows loudly. Eh? Your drive? No, I didn't.'

Again Jane Packard was aware of that faint, wistful regret. But this was swept away a few moments later in the ecstasy of a perfect iron-shot which plunked her ball nicely on to the green. The last time she had played this hole she had taken seven, for all round the plateau green are sinister sand-bunkers, each beckoning the ball into its hideous depths; and now she was on in two and life was very sweet. Putting was her strong point, so that there was no reason why she should not get a snappy four on one of the nastiest holes on the course. She glowed with a strange emotion as she took her putter, and as she bent over her ball the air seemed filled with soft music.

It was only when she started to concentrate on the line of her putt that this soft music began to bother her. Then, listening, she became aware that it proceeded from Rodney Spelvin. He was standing immediately behind her, humming an old French love-song. It was the sort of old French love-song to which she could have listened for hours in some scented garden under the young May moon, but on the green of the fourth at Mossy Heath it got right in amongst her nerve-centres.

'Rodney, *please!*'

'Eh?'

Jane found herself wishing that Rodney Spelvin would not say 'Eh?' whenever she spoke to him.

'Do you mind not humming?' said Jane. 'I want to putt.'

'Putt on, child, putt on,' said Rodney Spelvin, indulgently. 'I don't know what you mean, but, if it makes you happy to putt, putt to your heart's content.'

Jane bent over her ball again. She had got the line now. She brought back her putter with infinite care.

'My God!' exclaimed Rodney Spelvin, going off like a bomb.

Jane's ball, sharply jabbed, shot past the hole and rolled on about three yards. She spun round in anguish. Rodney Spelvin was pointing at the horizon.

'*What* a bit of colour!' he cried. 'Did you ever see such a bit of colour?'

'Oh, Rodney!' moaned Jane.

'Eh?'

Jane gulped and walked to her ball. Her fourth putt trickled into the hole.

'Did you win?' said Rodney Spelvin, amiably.

Jane walked to the fifth tee in silence.

The fifth and sixth holes at Mossy Heath are long, but they offer little trouble to those who are able to keep straight. It is as if the architect of the course had relaxed over these two in order to ensure that his malignant mind should be at its freshest and keenest when he came to design the pestilential seventh. This seventh, as you may remember, is the hole at which Sandy McHoots, then Open Champion, took an eleven on an important occasion. It is a short hole, and a full mashie will take you nicely on to the green, provided you can carry the river that frolics just beyond the tee and seems to plead with you to throw it a ball to play with. Once on the green, however, the problem is to stay there. The green itself is about the size of a drawing-room carpet, and in the summer, when the ground is hard, a ball that has not the maximum of back-spin is apt to touch lightly and bound off into the river beyond; for this is an island green, where the stream bends like a serpent. I refresh your memory with these facts in order that you may appreciate to the full what Jane Packard was up against.

The woman with whom Jane was partnered had the honour, and drove a nice high ball which fell into one of the bunkers to the left. She was a silent, patient-looking woman, and she seemed to regard this as perfectly satisfactory. She withdrew from the tee and made way for Jane.

'Nice work!' said William Bates, a moment later. For Jane's ball, soaring in a perfect arc, was dropping, it seemed, on the very pin.

'Oh, Rodney, look!' cried Jane.

'Eh?' said Rodney Spelvin.

His remark was drowned in a passionate squeal of agony from his betrothed. The most poignant of all tragedies had occurred. The ball, touching the green, leaped like a young lamb, scuttled past the pin, and took a running dive over the cliff.

There was a silence. Jane's partner, who was seated on the bench by the sand-box reading a pocket edition in limp leather of Vardon's *What Every Young Golfer Should Know*, with which she had been refreshing herself at odd moments all through the round, had not observed the incident. William Bates, with the tact of a true golfer, refrained from comment. Jane was herself swallowing painfully. It was left to Rodney Spelvin to break the silence.

'Good!' he said.

Jane Packard turned like a stepped-on worm.

'What do you mean, good?'

'You hit your ball farther than she did.'

'I sent it into the river,' said Jane, in a low, toneless voice.

'Capital!' said Rodney Spelvin, delicately masking a yawn with two fingers of his shapely right hand. 'Capital! Capital!'

Her face contorted with pain, Jane put down another ball.

'Playing three,' she said.

The student of Vardon marked the place in her book with her thumb, looked up, nodded, and resumed her reading.

'Nice w—' began William Bates, as the ball soared off the tee, and checked himself abruptly. Already he could see that the unfortunate girl had put too little beef into it. The ball was falling, falling. It fell. A crystal fountain flashed up towards the sun. The ball lay floating on the bosom of the stream, only some few feet short of the island. But, as has been well pointed out, that little less and how far away!

'Playing five!' said Jane, between her teeth.

'What,' inquired Rodney Spelvin, chattily, lighting a cigarette, 'is the record break?'

'Playing *five*,' said Jane, with a dreadful calm, and gripped her mashie.

'Half a second,' said William Bates, suddenly. 'I say, I believe you could play that last one from where it floats. A good crisp slosh with a niblick would put you on, and you'd be there in four, with a chance for a five. Worth trying, what? I mean, no sense in dropping strokes unless you have to.'

Jane's eyes were gleaming. She threw William a look of infinite gratitude.

'Why, I believe I could!'

'Worth having a dash.'

'There's a boat down there!'

'I could row,' said William.

'I could stand in the middle and slosh,' cried Jane.

'And what's-his-name – *that*,' said William, jerking his head in the direction of Rodney Spelvin, who was strolling up and down behind the tee, humming a gay Venetian barcarolle, 'could steer.'

'William,' said Jane, fervently, 'you're a darling.'

'Oh, I don't know,' said William, modestly.

'There's no one like you in the world. Rodney!'

'Eh?' said Rodney Spelvin.

'We're going out in that boat. I want you to steer.'

Rodney Spelvin's face showed appreciation of the change of programme. Golf bored him, but what could be nicer than a gentle row in a boat.

'Capital!' he said. 'Capital! Capital!'

There was a dreamy look in Rodney Spelvin's eyes as he leaned back with the tiller-ropes in his hands. This was just his idea of the proper way of passing a summer afternoon. Drifting lazily over the silver surface of the stream. His eyes closed. He began to murmur softly:

'All to-day the slow sleek ripples hardly bear up shoreward, Charged with sighs more light than laughter, faint and fair, Like a woodland lake's weak wavelets lightly lingering forward, Soft and listless as the— Here! Hi!'

For at this moment the silver surface of the stream was violently split by a vigorously-wielded niblick, the boat lurched drunkenly, and over his Panama-hatted head and down his grey-flannelled torso there descended a cascade of water.

'Here! Hi!' cried Rodney Spelvin.

He cleared his eyes and gazed reproachfully. Jane and William Bates were peering into the depths.

'I missed it,' said Jane.

'There she spouts!' said William, pointing. 'Ready?'

Jane raised her niblick.

'Here! Hi!' bleated Rodney Spelvin, as a second cascade poured damply over him.

He shook the drops off his face, and perceived that Jane was regarding him with hostility.

'I do wish you wouldn't talk just as I am swinging,' she said, pettishly. 'Now you've made me miss it again! If you can't keep quiet, I wish you wouldn't insist on coming round with one. Can you see it, William?'

'There she blows,' said William Bates.

'Here! You aren't going to do it *again* are you?' cried Rodney Spelvin.

Jane bared her teeth.

'I'm going to get that ball on to the green if I have to stay here all night,' she said.

Rodney Spelvin looked at her and shuddered. Was this the quiet, dreamy girl he had loved? This Mænad? Her hair was lying in damp wisps about her face, her eyes were shining with an unearthly light.

'No, but really—' he faltered.

Jane stamped her foot.

'What *are* you making all this fuss about, Rodney?' she snapped. 'Where is it, William?'

'There she dips,' said William. 'Playing six.'

'Playing six.'

'Let her go,' said William.

'Let her go it is!' said Jane.

A perfect understanding seemed to prevail between these two.

Splash!

The woman on the bank looked up from her Vardon as Rodney Spelvin's agonised scream rent the air. She saw a boat upon the water, a man rowing the boat, another man, hatless, gesticulating in the stern, a girl beating the water with a niblick. She nodded placidly and understandingly. A niblick was the club she would have used herself in such circumstances. Everything appeared to her entirely regular and orthodox. She resumed her book.

Splash!

'Playing fifteen,' said Jane.

'Fifteen is right,' said William Bates.

Splash! Splash! Splash!

'Playing forty-four.'

'Forty-four is correct.'

Splash! Splash! Splash! Splash!

'Eighty-three?' said Jane, brushing the hair out of her eyes.

'No. Only eighty-two,' said William Bates.

'Where is it?'

'There she drifts.'

A dripping figure rose violently in the stern of the boat, spouting water like a public fountain. For what seemed to him like an eternity Rodney Spelvin had ducked and spluttered and writhed, and now it came to him abruptly that he was through. He bounded from his seat, and at the same time Jane swung with all the force of her supple body. There was a splash beside which all the other splashes had been as nothing. The boat overturned and went drifting away. Three bodies plunged into the stream. Three heads emerged from the water.

The woman on the bank looked absently in their direction. Then she resumed her book.

'It's all right,' said William Bates, contentedly. 'We're in our depth.'

'My bag!' cried Jane. 'My bag of clubs!'

'Must have sunk,' said William.

'Rodney,' said Jane, 'my bag of clubs is at the bottom somewhere. Dive under and swim about and try to find it.'

'It's bound to be around somewhere,' said William Bates encouragingly.

Rodney Spelvin drew himself up to his full height. It was not an easy thing to do, for it was muddy where he stood, but he did it.

'Damn your bag of clubs!' he bellowed, lost to all shame. 'I'm going home!'

With painful steps, tripping from time to time and vanishing beneath the surface, he sloshed to the shore. For a moment he paused on the bank, silhouetted against the summer sky, then he was gone.

Jane Packard and William Bates watched him go with amazed eyes.

'I never would have dreamed,' said Jane, dazedly, 'that he was that sort of man.'

'A bad lot,' said William Bates.

'The sort of man to be upset by the merest trifle!'

'Must have a naturally bad disposition,' said William Bates.

'Why, if a little thing like this could make him so rude and brutal and horrid, it wouldn't be *safe* to marry him!'

'Taking a big chance,' agreed William Bates. 'Sort of fellow who would water the cat's milk and kick the baby in the face.' He took a deep breath and disappeared. 'Here are your clubs, old girl,' he said, coming to the surface again. 'Only wanted a bit of looking for.'

'Oh, William,' said Jane, 'you are the most wonderful man on earth!'

'Would you go as far as that?' said William.

'I was mad, mad, ever to get engaged to that brute!'

'Now there,' said William Bates, removing an eel from his left breast-pocket, 'I'm absolutely with you. Thought so all along, but didn't like to say so. What I mean is, a girl like you – keen on golf and all that sort of thing – ought to marry a chap like me – keen on golf and everything of that description.'

'William,' cried Jane, passionately, detaching a newt from her right ear, 'I will!'

'Silly nonsense, when you come right down to it, your marrying a fellow who doesn't play golf. Nothing in it.'

'I'll break off the engagement the moment I get home.'

'You couldn't make a sounder move, old girl.'

'William!'

'Jane!'

The woman on the bank, glancing up as she turned a page, saw a man and a girl embracing, up to their waists in water. It seemed to have nothing to do with her. She resumed her book.

Jane looked lovingly into William's eyes.

'William,' she said, 'I think I have loved you all my life.'

'Jane,' said William, 'I'm dashed sure I've loved *you* all *my* life. Meant to tell you so a dozen times, but something always seemed to come up.'

'William,' said Jane, 'you're an angel and a darling. Where's the ball?'

'There she pops.'

'Playing eighty-four?'

'Eighty-four it is,' said William. 'Slow back, keep your eye on the ball, and don't press.'

The woman on the bank began Chapter Twenty-five.

The side-door leading into the smoking-room opened, and the golf-club's popular and energetic secretary came trotting down the steps on to the terrace above the ninth green. As he reached the gravel, a wandering puff of wind blew the door to with a sharp report, and the Oldest Member, who had been dozing in a chair over his *Wodehouse on the Niblick*, unclosed his eyes, blinking in the strong light. He perceived the secretary skimming to and fro like a questing dog.

'You have lost something?' he inquired, courteously.

'Yes, a book. I wish,' said the secretary, annoyed, 'that people would leave things alone. You haven't seen a novel called *The Man with the Missing Eyeball* anywhere about, have you? I'll swear I left it on one of these seats when I went in to lunch.'

'You are better without it,' said the Sage, with a touch of austerity. 'I do not approve of these trashy works of fiction. How much more profitably would your time be spent in mastering the contents of such a volume as I hold in my hand. This is the real literature.'

The secretary drew nearer, peering discontentedly about him; and as he approached the Oldest Member sniffed inquiringly.

'What,' he said, 'is that odour of—? Ah, I see that you are

wearing them in your buttonhole. White violets,' he murmured. 'White violets. Dear me!'

The secretary smirked.

'A girl gave them to me,' he said, coyly. 'Nice, aren't they?' He squinted down complacently at the flowers, thus missing a sudden sinister gleam in the Oldest Member's eye – a gleam which, had he been on his guard, would have sent him scudding over the horizon; for it was the gleam which told that the Sage had been reminded of a story.

'White violets,' said the Oldest Member, in a meditative voice. 'A curious coincidence that you should be wearing white violets and looking for a work of fiction. The combination brings irresistibly to my mind—'

Realising his peril too late, the secretary started violently. A gentle hand urged him into the adjoining chair.

'—the story,' proceeded the Oldest Member, 'of William Bates, Jane Packard, and Rodney Spelvin.'

The secretary drew a deep breath of relief and the careworn look left his face.

'It's all right,' he said, briskly. 'You told me that one only the other day. I remember every word of it. Jane Packard got engaged to Rodney Spelvin, the poet, but her better feelings prevailed in time, and she broke it off and married Bates, who was a golfer. I recall the whole thing distinctly. This man Bates was an unromantic sort of chap, but he loved Jane Packard devotedly. Bless my soul, how it all comes back to me! No need to tell it me at all.'

'What I am about to relate now,' said the Sage, tightening his grip on the other's coat-sleeve, 'is another story about William Bates, Jane Packard, and Rodney Spelvin.'

* * *

Inasmuch (said the Oldest Member) as you have not forgotten the events leading up to the marriage of William Bates and Jane Packard, I will not repeat them. All I need say is that that curious spasm of romantic sentiment which had caused Jane to fall temporarily under the spell of a man who was not only a poet but actually a non-golfer appeared to have passed completely away, leaving no trace behind. From the day she broke off her engagement to Spelvin and plighted her troth to young Bates, nothing could have been more eminently sane and satisfactory than her behaviour. She seemed entirely her old self once more. Two hours after William had led her down the aisle, she and he were out on the links, playing off the final of the Mixed Foursomes, which – and we all thought it the best of omens for their married happiness – they won hands down. A deputation of all that was best and fairest in the village then escorted them to the station to see them off on their honeymoon, which was to be spent in a series of visits to well-known courses throughout the country.

Before the train left, I took young William aside for a moment. I had known both him and Jane since childhood, and the success of their union was very near my heart.

'William,' I said, 'a word with you.'

'Make it snappy,' said William.

'You have learned by this time,' I said, 'that there is a strong romantic streak in Jane. It may not appear on the surface, but it is there. And this romantic streak will cause her, like so many wives, to attach an exaggerated importance to what may seem to you trivial things. She will expect from her husband not only love and a constant tender solicitude—'

'Speed it up,' urged William.

'What I am trying to say is that, after the habit of wives,

she will expect you to remember each year the anniversary of your wedding day, and will be madder than a wet hen if you forget it.'

'That's all right. I thought of that myself.'

'It is not all right,' I insisted. 'Unless you take the most earnest precautions, you are absolutely certain to forget. A year from now you will come down to breakfast, and Jane will say to you, "Do you know what day it is to-day?" and you will answer "Tuesday" and reach for the ham and eggs, thus inflicting on her gentle heart a wound from which it will not readily recover.'

'Nothing like it,' said William, with extraordinary confidence. 'I've got a system calculated to beat the game every time. You know how fond Jane is of white violets?'

'Is she?'

'She loves 'em. The bloke Spelvin used to give her a bunch every day. That's how I got the idea. Nothing like learning the shots from your opponent. I've arranged with a florist that a bunch of white violets is to be shipped to Jane every year on this day. I paid five years in advance. I am, therefore, speaking in the most conservative spirit, on velvet. Even if I forget the day, the violets will be there to remind me. I've looked at it from every angle, and I don't see how it can fail. Tell me frankly, is the scheme a wam or is it not?'

'A most excellent plan,' I said, relieved. And the next moment the train came in. I left the station with my mind at rest. It seemed to me that the only possible obstacle to the complete felicity of the young couple had been removed.

Jane and William returned in due season from their honeymoon, and settled down to the normal life of a healthy young couple. Each day they did their round in the morning and their two rounds in the afternoon, and after dinner they would sit hand in hand in the peaceful dusk, reminding one another of the best shots they had brought off at the various holes. Jane would describe to William how she got out of the bunker on the fifth, and William would describe to Jane the low raking wind-cheater he did on the seventh, and then for a moment they would fall into that blissful silence which only true lovers know, until William, illustrating his remarks with a walking-stick, would show Jane how he did that pin-splitter with the mashie on the sixteenth. An ideally happy union, one would have said.

But all the while a little cloud was gathering. As the anniversary of their wedding day approached, a fear began to creep into Jane's heart that William was going to forget it. The perfect husband does not wait till the dawning of the actual day to introduce the anniversary *motif* into his conversation. As long as a week in advance he is apt to say, dreamily, 'About this time a year ago I was getting the old silk hat polished up for the wedding,' or 'Just about now, a year ago, they sent home the sponge-bag trousers, as worn, and I tried them on in front of the looking-glass.' But William said none of these things. Not even on the night before the all-important date did he make any allusion to it, and it was with a dull feeling of foreboding that Jane came down to breakfast next morning.

She was first at the table, and was pouring out the coffee when William entered. He opened the morning paper and started to peruse its contents in silence. Not a yip did he let out of him to the effect that this was the maddest, merriest day of all the glad new year.

'William,' said Jane.

'Hullo?'

'William,' said Jane, and her voice trembled a little, 'what day is it to-day?'

William looked at her over the paper, surprised.

'Wednesday, old girl,' he replied. 'Don't you remember that yesterday was Tuesday? Shocking memory you've got.'

He then reached out for the sausages and bacon and resumed his reading.

'Jane,' he said, suddenly. 'Jane, old girl, there's something I want to tell you.'

'Yes?' said Jane, her heart beginning to flutter.

'Something important.'

'Yes?'

'It's about these sausages. They are the very best,' said William, earnestly, 'that I have ever bitten. Where did you get them?'

'From Brownlow.'

'Stick to him,' said William.

Jane rose from the table and wandered out into the garden. The sun shone gaily, but for her the day was bleak and cold. That William loved her she did not doubt. But that streak of romance in her demanded something more than mere placid love. And when she realised that the poor mutt with whom she had linked her lot had forgotten the anniversary of their wedding-day first crack out of the box, her woman's heart was so wounded that for two pins she could have beaned him with a brick.

It was while she was still brooding in this hostile fashion that she perceived the postman coming up the garden. She went to meet him, and was handed a couple of circulars and a mysterious parcel. She broke the string, and behold! a cardboard box containing white violets.

Jane was surprised. Who could be sending her white violets? No message accompanied them. There was no clue whatever to their origin. Even the name of the florist had been omitted.

'Now, who—?' mused Jane, and suddenly started as if she had received a blow. Rodney Spelvin! Yes, it must be he. How many a bunch of white violets had he given her in the brief course of their engagement! This was his poetic way of showing her that he had not forgotten. All was over between them, she had handed him his hat and given him the air, but he still remembered.

Jane was a good and dutiful wife. She loved her William, and no others need apply. Nevertheless, she was a woman. She looked about her cautiously. There was nobody in sight. She streaked up to her room and put the violets in water. And that night, before she went to bed, she gazed at them for several minutes with eyes that were a little moist. Poor Rodney! He could be nothing to her now, of course, but a dear lost friend; but he had been a good old scout in his day.

It is not my purpose to weary you with repetitious detail in this narrative. I will, therefore, merely state that the next year and the next year and the year after that precisely the same thing took place in the Bateses' home. Punctually every September the seventh William placidly forgot, and punctually every September the seventh the sender of the violets remembered. It was about a month after the fifth anniversary, when William had got his handicap down to nine and little Braid Vardon Bates, their only child, had celebrated his fourth birthday, that Rodney Spelvin, who had hitherto confined himself to poetry, broke out in a new place and inflicted upon the citizenry a novel entitled *The Purple Fan*.

I saw the announcement of the publication in the papers; but beyond a passing resolve that nothing would induce me to read the thing I thought no more of the matter. It is always thus with life's really significant happenings. Fate sneaks its deadliest wallops in on us with such seeming nonchalance. How could I guess what that book was to do to the married happiness of Jane and William Bates?

In deciding not to read *The Purple Fan* I had, I was to discover, over-estimated my powers of resistance. Rodney Spelvin's novel turned out to be one of those things which it is impossible not to read. Within a week of its appearance it had begun to go through the country like Spanish influenza; and, much as I desired to avoid it, a perusal was forced on me by sheer weight of mass-thinking. Every paper that I picked up contained reviews of the book, references to it, letters from the clergy denouncing it; and when I read that three hundred and sixteen mothers had signed a petition to the authorities to have it suppressed, I was reluctantly compelled to spring the necessary cash and purchase a copy.

I had not expected to enjoy it, and I did not. Written in the neo-decadent style, which is so popular nowadays, its preciosity offended me; and I particularly objected to its heroine, a young woman of a type which, if met in real life, only ingrained chivalry could have prevented a normal man from kicking extremely hard. Having skimmed through it, I gave my copy to the man who came to inspect the drains. If I had any feeling about the thing, it was a reflection that, if Rodney Spelvin had had to get a novel out of his system, this was just the sort of novel he was bound to write. I remember experiencing a thankfulness that he had gone so entirely out of Jane's life. How little I knew!

* * *

Jane, like every other woman in the village, had bought her copy of *The Purple Fan*. She read it surreptitiously, keeping it concealed, when not in use, beneath a cushion on the Chesterfield. It was not its general tone that caused her to do this, but rather the subconscious feeling that she, a good wife, ought not to be deriving quite so much enjoyment from the work of a man who had occupied for a time such a romantic place in her life.

For Jane, unlike myself, adored the book. Eulalie French, its heroine, whose appeal I had so missed, seemed to her the most fascinating creature she had ever encountered.

She had read the thing through six times when, going up to town one day to do some shopping, she ran into Rodney Spelvin. They found themselves standing side by side on the pavement, waiting for the traffic to pass.

'Rodney!' gasped Jane.

It was a difficult moment for Rodney Spelvin. Five years had passed since he had last seen Jane, and in those five years so many delightful creatures had made a fuss of him that the memory of the girl to whom he had once been engaged for a few weeks had become a little blurred. In fact, not to put too fine a point on it, he had forgotten Jane altogether. The fact that she had addressed him by his first name seemed to argue that they must have met at some time somewhere; but, though he strained his brain, absolutely nothing stirred.

The situation was one that might have embarrassed another man, but Rodney Spelvin was a quick thinker. He saw at a glance that Jane was an extremely pretty girl, and it was his guiding rule in life never to let anything like that get past him. So he clasped her hand warmly, allowed an expression of amazed delight to sweep over his face, and gazed tensely into her eyes.

'You!' he murmured, playing it safe. 'You, little one!'

Jane stood five feet seven in her stockings and had a fore-arm like the village blacksmith's, but she liked being called 'little one.'

'How strange that we should meet like this!' she said, blushing brightly.

'After all these years,' said Rodney Spelvin, taking a chance. It would be a nuisance if it turned out that they had met at a studio-party the day before yesterday, but something seemed to tell him that she dated back a goodish way. Besides, even if they had met the day before yesterday, he could get out of it by saying that the hours had seemed like years. For you cannot stymie these modern poets. The boys are there.

'More than five,' murmured Jane.

'Now where the deuce was I five years ago?' Rodney Spelvin asked himself.

Jane looked down at the pavement and shuffled her left shoe nervously.

'I got the violets, Rodney,' she said.

Rodney Spelvin was considerably fogged, but he came back strongly.

'That's good!' he said. 'You got the violets? That's capital. I was wondering if you would get the violets.'

'It was like you to send them.'

Rodney blinked, but recovered himself immediately. He waved his hand with a careless gesture, indicative of restrained nobility.

'Oh, as to that—!'

'Especially as I'm afraid I treated you rather badly. But it really was for the happiness of both of us that I broke off the engagement. You do understand that, don't you?'

A light broke upon Rodney Spelvin. He had been confident

that it would if he only stalled along for awhile. Now he placed this girl. She was Jane something, the girl he had been engaged to. By Jove, yes. He knew where he was now.

'Do not let us speak of it,' he said, registering pain. It was quite easy for him to do this. All there was to it was tightening the lips and drawing up the left eyebrow. He had practised it in front of his mirror, for a fellow never knew when it might not come in useful.

'So you didn't forget me, Rodney?'

'Forget you!'

There was a short pause.

'I read your novel,' said Jane. 'I loved it.'

She blushed again, and the colour in her cheeks made her look so remarkably pretty that Rodney began to feel some of the emotions which had stirred him five years ago. He decided that this was a good thing and wanted pushing along.

'I hoped that you might,' he said in a low voice, massaging her hand. He broke off and directed into her eyes a look of such squashy sentimentality that Jane reeled where she stood. 'I wrote it for you,' he added, simply.

Jane gasped.

'For me?'

'I supposed you would have guessed,' said Rodney. 'Surely you saw the dedication?'

The Purple Fan had been dedicated, after Rodney Spelvin's eminently prudent fashion, to 'One Who Will Understand.' He had frequently been grateful for the happy inspiration.

'The dedication?'

'"To One Who Will Understand",' said Rodney, softly. 'Who would that be but you?'

'Oh, Rodney!'

'And didn't you recognise Eulalie, Jane? Surely you cannot have failed to recognise Eulalie?'

'Recognise her?'

'I drew her from you,' said Rodney Spelvin.

Jane's mind was in a whirl as she went home in the train. To have met Rodney Spelvin again was enough in itself to stimulate into activity that hidden pulse of romance in her. To discover that she had been in his thoughts so continuously all these years and that she still held such sway over his faithful heart that he had drawn the heroine of his novel from her was simply devastating. Mechanically she got out at the right station and mechanically made her way to the cottage. She was relieved to find that William was still out on the links. She loved William devotedly, of course, but just at the moment he would have been in the way; for she wanted a quiet hour with *The Purple Fan*. It was necessary for her to re-read in the light of this new knowledge the more important of the scenes in which Eulalie French figured. She knew them practically by heart already, but nevertheless she wished to read them again. When William returned, warm and jubilant, she was so absorbed that she only just had time to slide the book under the sofa-cushion before the door opened.

Some guardian angel ought to have warned William Bates that he was selecting a bad moment for his re-entry into the home, or at least to have hinted that a preliminary wash and brush-up would be no bad thing. There had been rain in the night, causing the links to become a trifle soggy in spots, and William was one of those energetic golfers who do not spare themselves. The result was that his pleasant features were a good deal obscured by mud. An explosion-shot out of the bunker on the fourteenth had filled his hair with damp sand, and his shoes were a disgrace to any refined home. No, take him for all in all, William did not look his best. He was fine if the sort of man you admired was the brawny athlete straight from the dust of the arena; but on a woman who was picturing herself the heroine of *The Purple Fan* he was bound to jar. Most of the scenes in which Eulalie French played anything like a fat part took place either on moonlight terraces or in beautifully furnished studios beneath the light of Oriental lamps with pink silk shades, and all the men who came in contact with her – except her husband, a clodhopping brute who spent most of his time in riding-kit – were perfectly dressed and had dark, clean-cut, sensitive faces.

William, accordingly, induced in Jane something closely approximating to the heeby-jeebies.

'Hullo, old girl!' said William, affectionately. 'You back? What have you been doing with yourself?'

'Oh, shopping,' said Jane, listlessly.

'See anyone you knew?'

For a moment Jane hesitated.

'Yes,' she said. 'I met Rodney Spelvin.'

Jealousy and suspicion had been left entirely out of William Bates's make-up. He did not start and frown; he did not clutch the arm of his chair; he merely threw back his head and laughed like a hyæna. And that laugh wounded Jane more than the most violent exhibition of mistrust could have done.

'Good Lord!' gurgled William, jovially. 'You don't mean to say that bird is still going around loose? I should have thought he would have been lynched years ago. Looks like negligence somewhere.'

There comes a moment in married life when every wife gazes

squarely at her husband and the scales seem to fall from her eyes and she sees him as he is – one of Nature's Class A fatheads. Fortunately for married men, these times of clear vision do not last long, or there would be few homes left unbroken. It was so that Jane gazed at William now, but unhappily her conviction that he was an out-size in rough-neck chumps did not pass. Indeed, all through that evening it deepened. That night she went to bed feeling for the first time that, when the clergyman had said, 'Wilt thou, Jane?' and she had replied, in the affirmative, a mean trick had been played on an inexperienced girl.

And so began that black period in the married life of Jane and William Bates, the mere recollection of which in after years was sufficient to put them right off their short game and even to affect their driving from the tee. To William, having no clue to the cause of the mysterious change in his wife, her behaviour was inexplicable. Had not her perfect robustness made such a theory absurd, he would have supposed that she was sickening for something. She golfed now intermittently, and often with positive reluctance. She was frequently listless and distrait. And there were other things about her of which he disapproved.

'I say, old girl,' he said one evening, 'I know you won't mind my mentioning it, and I don't suppose you're aware of it yourself, but recently you've developed a sort of silvery laugh. A nasty thing to have about the home. Try to switch it off, old bird, would you mind?'

Jane said nothing. The man was not worth answering. All through the pages of *The Purple Fan*, Eulalie French's silvery laugh had been highly spoken of and greatly appreciated by one and all. It was the thing about her that the dark, clean-cut, sensitive-faced men most admired. And the view Jane took of the matter was that if William did not like it the poor fish could do the other thing.

But this brutal attack decided her to come out into the open with the grievance which had been vexing her soul for weeks past.

'William,' she said, 'I want to say something. William, I am feeling stifled.'

'I'll open the window.'

'Stifled in this beastly little village, I mean,' said Jane, impatiently. 'Nobody ever does anything here except play golf and bridge, and you never meet an artist-soul from one year's end to the other. How can I express myself? How can I be myself? How can I fulfil myself?'

'Do you want to?' asked William, somewhat out of his depth.

'Of course I want to. And I shan't be happy unless we leave this ghastly place and go to live in a studio in town.'

William sucked thoughtfully at his pipe. It was a tense moment for a man who hated metropolitan life as much as he did. Nevertheless, if the solution of Jane's recent weirdness was simply that she had got tired of the country and wanted to live in town, to the town they must go. After a first involuntary recoil, he nerved himself to the martyrdom like the fine fellow he was.

'We'll pop off as soon as I can sell the house,' he said.

'I can't wait as long as that. I want to go now.'

'All right,' said William, amiably. 'We'll go next week.'

William's forebodings were quickly fulfilled. Before he had been in the Metropolis ten days he realised that he was up against it as he had never been up against it before. He and Jane and little Braid Vardon had established themselves in what the house-agent described as an attractive bijou studio-apartment in the heart of the artistic quarter. There was a nice bedroom for Jane, a delightful cupboard for Braid Vardon, and a cosy corner behind a Japanese screen for William. Most compact. The rest of the place consisted of a room with a large skylight, handsomely furnished with cushions and samovars, where Jane gave parties to the intelligentsia.

It was these parties that afflicted William as much as anything else. He had not realised that Jane intended to run a *salon*. His idea of a pleasant social evening was to have a couple of old friends in for a rubber of bridge, and the almost nightly incursion of a horde of extraordinary birds in floppy ties stunned him. He was unequal to the situation from the first. While Jane sat enthroned on her cushion, exchanging gay badinage with rising young poets and laughing that silvery laugh of hers, William would have to stand squashed in a corner, trying to hold off some bobbed-haired female who wanted his opinion of Augustus John.

The strain was frightful, and, apart from the sheer discomfort of it, he found to his consternation that it was beginning to affect his golf. Whenever he struggled out from the artistic zone now to one of the suburban courses, his jangled nerves unfitted him for decent play. Bit by bit his game left him. First he found that he could not express himself with the putter. Then he began to fail to be himself with the mashie-niblick. And when at length he discovered that he was only fulfilling himself about every fifth shot off the tee he felt that this thing must stop.

The conscientious historian will always distinguish carefully between the events leading up to a war and the actual occurrence

THE HEART OF A GOOF

resulting in the outbreak of hostilities. The latter may be, and generally is, some almost trivial matter, whose only importance is that it fulfils the function of the last straw. In the case of Jane and William what caused the definite rift was Jane's refusal to tie a can to Rodney Spelvin.

The author of *The Purple Fan* had been from the first a leading figure in Jane's salon. Most of those who attended these functions were friends of his, introduced by him, and he had assumed almost from the beginning the demeanour of a master of the revels. William, squashed into his corner, had long gazed at the man with sullen dislike, yearning to gather him up by the slack of his trousers and heave him into outer darkness; but it is improbable that he would have overcome his native amiability sufficiently to make any active move, had it not been for the black mood caused by his rotten golf. But one evening, when, coming home after doing the Mossy Heath course in five strokes over the hundred, he found the studio congested with Rodney Spelvin and his friends, many of them playing ukeleles, he decided that flesh and blood could bear the strain no longer.

As soon as the last guest had gone he delivered his ultimatum.

'Listen, Jane,' he said. 'Touching on this Spelvin bloke.'

'Well?' said Jane, coldly. She scented battle from afar.

'He gives me a pain in the neck.'

'Really?' said Jane, and laughed a silvery laugh.

'Don't do it, old girl,' pleaded William, wincing.

'I wish you wouldn't call me "old girl".'

'Why not?'

'Because I don't like it.'

'You used to like it.'

'Well, I don't now.'

'Oh!' said William, and ruminated awhile. 'Well, be that as it may,' he went on, 'I want to tell you just one thing. Either you throw the bloke Spelvin out on his left ear and send for the police if he tries to get in again, or I push off. I mean it! I absolutely push off.'

There was a tense silence.

'Indeed?' said Jane at last.

'Positively push off,' repeated William, firmly. 'I can stand a lot, but pie-faced Spelvin tries human endurance too high.'

'He is not pie-faced,' said Jane, warmly.

'He is pie-faced,' insisted William. 'Come round to the Vienna Bon-Ton Bakery to-morrow and I will show you an individual custard-pie that might be his brother.'

'Well, I am certainly not going to be bullied into giving up an old friend just because—'

William stared.

'You mean you won't hand him the mitten?'

'I will not.'

'Think what you are saying, Jane. You positively decline to give this false-alarm the quick exit?'

'I do.'

'Then,' said William, 'all is over. I pop off.'

Jane stalked without a word into her bedroom. With a mist before his eyes William began to pack. After a few moments he tapped at her door.

'Jane.'

'Well?'

'I'm packing.'

'Indeed?'

'But I can't find my spare mashie.'

'I don't care.'

William returned to his packing. When it was finished, he stole to her door again. Already a faint stab of remorse was becoming blended with his just indignation.

'Jane.'

'Well?'

'I've packed.'

'Really?'

'And now I'm popping.'

There was silence behind the door.

'I'm popping, Jane,' said William. And in his voice, though he tried to make it cold and crisp, there was a note of wistfulness.

Through the door there came a sound. It was the sound of a silvery laugh. And as he heard it William's face hardened. Without another word he picked up his suit-case and golf-bag, and with set jaw strode out into the night.

One of the things that tend to keep the home together in these days of modern unrest is the fact that exalted moods of indignation do not last. William, released from the uncongenial atmosphere of the studio, proceeded at once to plunge into an orgy of golf that for awhile precluded regret. Each day he indulged his starved soul with fifty-four holes, and each night he sat smoking in bed, pleasantly fatigued, reviewing the events of the past twelve hours with complete satisfaction. It seemed to him that he had done the good and sensible thing.

And then, slowly at first, but day by day more rapidly, his mood began to change. That delightful feeling of jolly freedom ebbed away.

It was on the morning of the tenth day that he first became definitely aware that all was not well. He had strolled out on the links after breakfast with a brassy and a dozen balls for a bit of practice, and, putting every ounce of weight and muscle into the stroke, brought off a snifter with his very first shot. Straight and true the ball sped for the distant green, and William, forgetting everything in the ecstasy of the moment, uttered a gladsome cry.

'How about that one, old girl?' he exclaimed.

And then, with a sudden sinking of the heart, he realised that he was alone.

An acute spasm of regret shot through William's massive bosom. In that instant of clear thinking he understood that golf is not all. What shall it profit a man that he do the long hole in four, if there is no loving wife at his elbow to squeak congratulations? A dull sensation of forlorn emptiness afflicted William Bates. It passed, but it had been. And he knew it would come again.

It did. It came that same afternoon. It came next morning. Gradually it settled like a cloud on his happiness. He did his best to fight it down. He increased his day's output to sixty-three holes, but found no relief. When he reflected that he had had the stupendous luck to be married to a girl like Jane and had chucked the thing up, he could have kicked himself round the house. He was in exactly the position of the hero of the movie when the sub-title is flashed on the screen: 'Came a Day When Remorse Bit Like An Adder Into Roland Spenlow's Soul.' Of all the chumps who had ever tripped over themselves and lost a good thing, from Adam downwards, he, he told himself, was the woollen-headedest.

On the fifteenth morning it began to rain.

Now, William Bates was not one of your fair-weather golfers. It took more than a shower to discourage him. But this was real rain, with which not even the stoutest enthusiast could cope. It poured down all day in a solid sheet and set the seal on his melancholy. He pottered about the house, sinking deeper and deeper into the slough of despond, and was trying to derive a little faint distraction from practising putts into a tooth-glass when the afternoon post arrived.

There was only one letter. He opened it listlessly. It was from Jukes, Enderby, and Miller, florists, and what the firm wished to ascertain was whether, his deposit on white violets to be despatched annually to Mrs William Bates being now exhausted, he desired to renew his esteemed order. If so, on receipt of the money they would spring to the task of sending same.

William stared at the letter dully. His first impression was that Jukes, Enderby, and Miller were talking through their collective hats. White violets? What was all this drivel about white violets? Jukes was an ass. He knew nothing about white violets. Enderby was a fool. What had he got to do with white violets? Miller was a pin-head. He had never deposited any money to have white violets despatched.

William gasped. Yes, by George, he had, though, he remembered with a sudden start. So he had, by golly! Good gosh! it all came back to him. He recalled the whole thing, by Jove! Crikey, yes!

The letter swam before William's eyes. A wave of tenderness engulfed him. All that had passed recently between Jane and himself was forgotten – her weirdness, her wish to live in the Metropolis, her silvery laugh – everything. With one long, loving gulp, William Bates dashed a not unmanly tear from his eye and, grabbing a hat and raincoat, rushed out of the house and sprinted for the station.

* * *

At about the hour when William flung himself into the train, Jane was sitting in her studio-apartment, pensively watching little Braid Vardon as he sported on the floor. An odd melancholy had gripped her. At first she had supposed that this was due to the rain, but now she was beginning to realise that the thing went much deeper than that. Reluctant though she was to confess it, she had to admit that what she was suffering from was a genuine soul-sadness, due entirely to the fact that she wanted William.

It was strange what a difference his going had made. William was the sort of fellow you shoved into a corner and forgot about, but when he was not there the whole scheme of things seemed to go blooey. Little by little, since his departure, she had found the fascination of her surroundings tending to wane, and the glamour of her new friends had dwindled noticeably. Unless you were in the right vein for them, Jane felt, they could be an irritating crowd. They smoked too many cigarettes and talked too much. And not far from being the worst of them, she decided, was Rodney Spelvin. It was with a sudden feeling of despair that she remembered that she had invited him to tea this afternoon and had got in a special seed-cake for the occasion. The last thing in the world that she wanted to do was to watch Rodney Spelvin eating cake.

It is a curious thing about men of the Spelvin type, how seldom they really last. They get off to a flashy start and for a while convince impressionable girls that the search for a soul-mate may be considered formally over; but in a very short while reaction always sets in. There had been a time when Jane could have sat and listened to Rodney Spelvin for hours on end. Then she began to feel that from fifteen to twenty minutes was about sufficient. And now the mere thought of having to listen to him at all was crushing her like a heavy burden.

She had got thus far in her meditations when her attention was attracted to little Braid Vardon, who was playing energetically in a corner with some object which Jane could not distinguish in the dim light.

'What have you got there, dear?' she asked.

'Wah,' said little Braid, a child of few words, proceeding with his activities.

Jane rose and walked across the room. A sudden feeling had come to her, the remorseful feeling that for some time now she had been neglecting the child. How seldom nowadays did she trouble to join in his pastimes!

'Let mother play too,' she said, gently. 'What are you playing? Trains?'

'Golf.'

Jane uttered a sharp exclamation. With a keen pang she saw that what the child had got hold of was William's spare mashie. So he had left it behind after all! Since the night of his departure it must have been lying unnoticed behind some chair or sofa.

For a moment the only sensation Jane felt was an accentuation of that desolate feeling which had been with her all day. How many a time had she stood by William and watched him foozle with this club! Inextricably associated with him it was, and her eyes filled with sudden tears. And then she was abruptly conscious of a new, a more violent emotion, something akin to panic fear. She blinked, hoping against hope that she had been mistaken. But no. When she opened her eyes and looked again she saw what she had seen before.

The child was holding the mashie all wrong.

'Braid!' gasped Jane in an agony.

All the mother-love in her was shrieking at her, reproaching her. She realised now how paltry, how greedily self-centred she had been. Thinking only of her own pleasures, how sorely she had neglected her duty as a mother! Long ere this, had she been worthy of that sacred relation, she would have been brooding over her child, teaching him at her knee the correct Vardon grip, shielding him from bad habits, seeing to it that he did not get his hands in front of the ball, putting him on the right path as regarded the slow back-swing. But, absorbed in herself, she had sacrificed him to her shallow ambitions. And now there he was, grasping the club as if it had been a spade and scooping with it like one of those twenty-four handicap men whom the hot weather brings out on seaside links.

She shuddered to the very depths of her soul. Before her eyes there rose a vision of her son, grown to manhood, reproaching her. 'If you had but taught me the facts of life when I was a child, mother,' she seemed to hear him say, 'I would not now be going round in a hundred and twenty, rising to a hundred and forty in anything like a high wind.'

She snatched the club from his hands with a passionate cry. And at this precise moment in came Rodney Spelvin, all ready for tea.

'Ah, little one!' said Rodney Spelvin, gaily.

Something in her appearance must have startled him, for he stopped and looked at her with concern.

'Are you ill?' he asked.

Jane pulled herself together with an effort.

'No, quite well. Ha, ha!' she replied, hysterically.

She stared at him wildly, as she might have stared at a cater-pillar in her salad. If it had not been for this man, she felt, she would have been with William in their snug little cottage, a happy wife. If it had not been for this man, her only child would have been laying the foundations of a correct swing under the eyes of a conscientious pro. If it had not been for this man— She waved him distractedly to the door.

'Good-bye,' she said. 'Thank you so much for calling.'

Rodney Spelvin gaped. This had been the quickest and most tealess tea-party he had ever assisted at.

'You want me to go?' he said, incredulously.

'Yes, go! go!'

Rodney Spelvin cast a wistful glance at the gate-leg table. He had had a light lunch, and the sight of the seed-cake affected him deeply. But there seemed nothing to be done. He moved reluctantly to the door.

'Well, good-bye,' he said. 'Thanks for a very pleasant afternoon.'

'So glad to have seen you,' said Jane, mechanically.

The door closed. Jane returned to her thoughts. But she was not alone for long. A few minutes later there entered the female cubist painter from downstairs, a manly young woman with whom she had become fairly intimate.

'Oh, Bates, old chap!' said the cubist painter.

Jane looked up.

'Yes, Osbaldistone?'

'Just came in to borrow a cigarette. Used up all mine.'

'So have I, I'm afraid.'

'Too bad. Oh, well,' said Miss Osbaldistone, resignedly, 'I suppose I'll have to go out and get wet. I wish I had had the sense to stop Rodney Spelvin and send him. I met him on the stairs.'

'Yes, he was in here just now,' said Jane.

Miss Osbaldistone laughed in her hearty manly way.

'Good boy, Rodney,' she said, 'but too smooth for my taste. A little too ready with the salve.'

'Yes?' said Jane, absently.

'Has he pulled that one on you yet about your being the original of the heroine of *The Purple Fan*?'

'Why, yes,' said Jane, surprised. 'He did tell me that he had drawn Eulalie from me.'

Her visitor emitted another laugh that shook the samovars.

'He tells every girl he meets the same thing.'

'What!'

'Oh yes. It's his first move. He actually had the nerve to try to spring it on me. Mind you, I'm not saying it's a bad stunt. Most girls like it. You're sure you've no cigarettes? No? Well, how about a shot of cocaine? Out of that too? Oh, well, I'll be going, then. Pip-pip, Bates.'

'Toodle-oo, Osbaldistone,' said Jane, dizzily. Her brain was reeling. She groped her way to the table, and in a sort of trance cut herself a slice of cake.

'Wah!' said little Braid Vardon. He toddled forward, anxious to count himself in on the share-out.

Jane gave him some cake. Having ruined his life, it was, she felt, the least she could do. In a spasm of belated maternal love she also slipped him a jam-sandwich. But how trivial and useless these things seemed now.

'Braid!' she cried, suddenly.

'What?'

'Come here.'

'Why?'

'Let mother show you how to hold that mashie.'

'What's a mashie?'

A new gash opened in Jane's heart. Four years old, and he

didn't know what a mashie was. And at only a slightly advanced age Bobby Jones had been playing in the American Open Championship.

'This is a mashie,' she said, controlling her voice with difficulty.

'Why?'

'It is called a mashie.'

'What is?'

'This club.'

'Why?'

The conversation was becoming too metaphysical for Jane. She took the club from him and closed her hands over it.

'Now, look, dear,' she said, tenderly. 'Watch how mother does it. She puts the fingers—'

A voice spoke, a voice that had been absent all too long from Jane's life.

'You'll pardon me, old girl, but you've got the right hand much too far over. You'll hook for a certainty.'

In the doorway, large and dripping, stood William. Jane stared at him dumbly.

'William!' she gasped at length.

'Hullo, Jane!' said William. 'Hullo, Braid! Thought I'd look in.'

There was a long silence.

'Beastly weather,' said William.

'Yes,' said Jane.

'Wet and all that,' said William.

'Yes,' said Jane.

There was another silence.

'Oh, by the way, Jane,' said William. 'Knew there was something I wanted to say. You know those violets?'

'Violets?'

'White violets. You remember those white violets I've been sending you every year on our wedding anniversary? Well, what I mean to say, our lives are parted and all that sort of thing, but you won't mind if I go on sending them – what? Won't hurt you, what I'm driving at, and'll please me, see what I mean? So, well, to put the thing in a nutshell, if you haven't any objection, that's that.'

Jane reeled against the gate-leg table.

'William! Was it you who sent those violets?'

'Absolutely. Who did you think it was?'

'William!' cried Jane, and flung herself into his arms.

William scooped her up gratefully. This was the sort of thing he had been wanting for weeks past. He could do with a lot of this. He wouldn't have suggested it himself, but, seeing that she felt that way, he was all for it.

'William,' said Jane, 'can you ever forgive me?'

'Oh, rather,' said William. 'Like a shot. Though, I mean to say, nothing to forgive, and all that sort of thing.'

'We'll go back right away to our dear little cottage.'

'Fine!'

'We'll never leave it again.'

'Topping!'

'I love you,' said Jane, 'more than life itself.'

'Good egg!' said William.

Jane turned with shining eyes to little Braid Vardon.

'Braid, we're going home with daddy!'

'Where?'

'Home. To our little cottage.'

'What's a cottage?'

'The house where we used to be before we came here.'

'What's here?'

'This is.'

'Which?'

'Where we are now.'

'Why?'

'I'll tell you what, old girl,' said William. 'Just shove a green-baize cloth over that kid, and then start in and brew me about five pints of tea as strong and hot as you can jolly well make it. Otherwise I'm going to get the cold of a lifetime.'

It was an afternoon on which one would have said that all Nature smiled. The air was soft and balmy; the links, fresh from the rains of spring, glistened in the pleasant sunshine; and down on the second tee young Clifford Wimple, in a new suit of plus-fours, had just sunk two balls in the lake, and was about to sink a third. No element, in short, was lacking that might be supposed to make for quiet happiness.

And yet on the forehead of the Oldest Member, as he sat beneath the chestnut tree on the terrace overlooking the ninth green, there was a peevish frown; and his eye, gazing down at the rolling expanse of turf, lacked its customary genial bene-volence. His favourite chair, consecrated to his private and personal use by unwritten law, had been occupied by another. That is the worst of a free country – liberty so often degenerates into licence.

The Oldest Member coughed.

'I trust,' he said, 'you find that chair comfortable?'

The intruder, who was the club's hitherto spotless secretary, glanced up in a goofy manner.

'Eh?'

'That chair – you find it fits snugly to the figure?'

'Chair? Figure? Oh, you mean this chair? Oh yes.'

'I am gratified and relieved,' said the Oldest Member.

There was a silence.

'Look here,' said the secretary, 'what would you do in a case like this? You know I'm engaged?'

'I do. And no doubt your *fiancée* is missing you. Why not go in search of her?'

'She's the sweetest girl on earth.'

'I should lose no time.'

'But jealous. And just now I was in my office, and that Mrs Pettigrew came in to ask if there was any news of the purse which she lost a couple of days ago. It had just been brought to my office, so I produced it; whereupon the infernal woman, in a most unsuitably girlish manner, flung her arms round my neck and kissed me on my bald spot. And at that moment Adela came in. Death,' said the secretary, 'where is thy sting?'

The Oldest Member's pique melted. He had a feeling heart.

'Most unfortunate. What did you say?'

'I hadn't time to say anything. She shot out too quick.'

The Oldest Member clicked his tongue sympathetically.

'These misunderstandings between young and ardent hearts are very frequent,' he said. 'I could tell you at least fifty cases of the same kind. The one which I will select is the story of Jane Packard, William Bates, and Rodney Spelvin.'

'You told me that the other day. Jane Packard got engaged to Rodney Spelvin, the poet, but the madness passed and she married William Bates, who was a golfer.'

'This is another story of the trio.'

'You told me that one, too. After Jane Packard married William Bates she fell once more under the spell of Spelvin, but repented in time.'

'This is still another story. Making three in all.'

The secretary buried his face in his hands.

'Oh, well,' he said, 'go ahead. What does anything matter now?'

'First,' said the Oldest Member, 'let us make ourselves comfortable. Take this chair. It is easier than the one in which you are sitting.'

'No, thanks.'

'I insist.'

'Oh, all right.'

'Woof!' said the Oldest Member, settling himself luxuriously.

With an eye now full of kindly good-will, he watched young Clifford Wimple play his fourth. Then, as the silver drops flashed up into the sun, he nodded approvingly and began.

The story which I am about to relate (said the Oldest Member) begins at a time when Jane and William had been married some seven years. Jane's handicap was eleven, William's twelve, and their little son, Braid Vardon, had just celebrated his sixth birthday.

Ever since that dreadful time, two years before, when, lured by the glamour of Rodney Spelvin, she had taken a studio in the artistic quarter, dropped her golf, and practically learned to play the ukelele, Jane had been unremitting in her efforts to be a good mother and to bring up her son on the strictest principles. And, in order that his growing mind might have every chance, she had invited William's younger sister, Anastatia, to spend a week or two with them and put the child right on the true functions of the mashie. For Anastatia had reached the semi-finals of the last year's Ladies' Open Championship and, unlike many excellent players, had the knack of teaching.

On the evening on which this story opens the two women

were sitting in the drawing-room, chatting. They had finished tea; and Anastatia, with the aid of a lump of sugar, a spoon, and some crumbled cake, was illustrating the method by which she had got out of the rough on the fifth at Squashy Hollow.

'You're wonderful!' said Jane, admiringly. 'And such a good influence for Braid! You'll give him his lesson to-morrow afternoon as usual?'

'I shall have to make it the morning,' said Anastatia. 'I've promised to meet a man in town in the afternoon.'

As she spoke there came into her face a look so soft and dreamy that it roused Jane as if a bradawl had been driven into her leg. As her history has already shown, there was a strong streak of romance in Jane Bates.

'Who is he?' she asked, excitedly.

'A man I met last summer,' said Anastatia.

And she sighed with such abandon that Jane could no longer hold in check her womanly nosiness.

'Do you love him?' she cried.

'Like bricks,' whispered Anastatia.

'Does he love you?'

'Sometimes I think so.'

'What's his name?'

'Rodney Spelvin.'

'What!'

'Oh, I know he writes the most awful bilge,' said Anastatia, defensively, misinterpreting the yowl of horror which had proceeded from Jane. 'All the same, he's a darling.'

Jane could not speak. She stared at her sister-in-law aghast. Although she knew that if you put a driver in her hands she could paste the ball into the next county, there always seemed to her something fragile and helpless about Anastatia. William's sister was one of those small, rose-leaf girls with big blue eyes to whom good men instinctively want to give a stroke a hole and on whom bad men automatically prey. And when Jane reflected that Rodney Spelvin had to all intents and purposes preyed upon herself, who stood five foot seven in her shoes and, but for an innate love of animals, could have felled an ox with a blow, she shuddered at the thought of how he would prey on this innocent half-portion.

'You really love him?' she quavered.

'If he beckoned to me in the middle of a medal round, I would come to him,' said Anastatia.

Jane realised that further words were useless. A sickening sense of helplessness obsessed her. Something ought to be done about this terrible thing, but what could she do? She was so ashamed of her past madness that not even to warn this girl could she reveal that she had once been engaged to Rodney Spelvin herself; that he had recited poetry on the green while she was putting; and that, later, he had hypnotised her into taking William and little Braid to live in a studio full of samovars. These revelations would no doubt open Anastatia's eyes, but she could not make them.

And then, suddenly, Fate pointed out a way.

It was Jane's practice to go twice a week to the cinema palace in the village; and two nights later she set forth as usual and took her place just as the entertainment was about to begin.

At first she was only mildly interested. The title of the picture, 'Tried in the Furnace,' had suggested nothing to her. Being a regular patron of the silver screen, she knew that it might quite easily turn out to be an educational film on the subject of clinker-coal. But as the action began to develop she found herself leaning forward in her seat, blindly crushing a caramel between her fingers. For scarcely had the operator started to turn the crank when inspiration came to her.

Of the main plot of 'Tried in the Furnace' she retained, when finally she reeled out into the open air, only a confused recollection. It had something to do with money not bringing happiness or happiness not bringing money, she could not remember which. But the part which remained graven upon her mind was the bit where Gloria Gooch goes by night to the apartments of the libertine, to beg him to spare her sister, whom he has entangled in his toils.

Jane saw her duty clearly. She must go to Rodney Spelvin and conjure him by the memory of their ancient love to spare Anastatia.

It was not the easiest of tasks to put this scheme into operation. Gloria Gooch, being married to a scholarly man who spent nearly all his time in a library a hundred yards long, had been fortunately situated in the matter of paying visits to libertines; but for Jane the job was more difficult. William expected her to play a couple of rounds with him in the morning and another in the afternoon, which rather cut into her time. However, Fate was still on her side, for one morning at breakfast William announced that business called him to town.

'Why don't you come too?' he said.

Jane started.

'No. No, I don't think I will, thanks.'

'Give you lunch somewhere.'

'No. I want to stay here and do some practice-putting.'

'All right. I'll try to get back in time for a round in the evening.'

Remorse gnawed at Jane's vitals. She had never deceived

William before. She kissed him with even more than her usual fondness when he left to catch the ten-forty-five. She waved to him till he was out of sight; then, bounding back into the house, leaped at the telephone and, after a series of conversations with the Marks-Morris Glue Factory, the Poor Pussy Home for Indigent Cats, and Messrs. Oakes, Oakes, and Parbury, dealers in fancy goods, at last found herself in communication with Rodney Spelvin.

'Rodney?' she said, and held her breath, fearful at this breaking of a two years' silence and yet loath to hear another strange voice say 'Wadnumjerwant?' 'Is that you, Rodney?'

'Yes. Who is that?'

'Mrs Bates. Rodney, can you give me lunch at the Alcazar to-day at one?'

'Can I!' Not even the fact that some unknown basso had got on the wire and was asking if that was Mr Bootle could blur the enthusiasm in his voice. 'I should say so!'

'One o'clock, then,' said Jane. His enthusiastic response had relieved her. If by merely speaking she could stir him so, to bend him to her will when they met face to face would be pie.

'One o'clock,' said Rodney.

Jane hung up the receiver and went to her room to try on hats.

The impression came to Jane, when she entered the lobby of the restaurant and saw him waiting, that Rodney Spelvin looked somehow different from the Rodney she remembered. His handsome face had a deeper and more thoughtful expression, as if he had been through some ennobling experience.

'Well, here I am,' she said, going to him and affecting a jauntiness which she did not feel.

He looked at her, and there was in his eyes that unmistakable goggle which comes to men suddenly addressed in a public spot by women whom, to the best of their recollection, they do not know from Eve.

'How are you?' he said. He seemed to pull himself together. 'You're looking splendid.'

'You're looking fine,' said Jane.

'You're looking awfully well,' said Rodney.

'You're looking awfully well,' said Jane.

'You're looking fine,' said Rodney.

There was a pause.

'You'll excuse me glancing at my watch,' said Rodney. 'I have an appointment to lunch with – er – somebody here, and it's past the time.'

'But you're lunching with me,' said Jane, puzzled.

'With you?'

'Yes. I rang you up this morning.'

Rodney gaped.

'Was it you who 'phoned? I thought you said "Miss Bates."'

'No, Mrs Bates.'

'Mrs Bates?'

'Mrs Bates.'

'Of course. You're Mrs Bates.'

'Had you forgotten me?' said Jane, in spite of herself a little piqued.

'Forgotten you, dear lady! As if I could!' said Rodney, with a return of his old manner. 'Well, shall we go in and have lunch?'

'All right,' said Jane.

She felt embarrassed and ill at ease. The fact that Rodney had obviously succeeded in remembering her only after the effort of a lifetime seemed to her to fling a spanner into the machinery of her plans at the very outset. It was going to be difficult, she

THE PURIFICATION OF RODNEY SPELVIN

realised, to conjure him by the memory of their ancient love to spare Anastatia; for the whole essence of the idea of conjuring anyone by the memory of their ancient love is that the party of the second part should be aware that there ever was such a thing.

At the luncheon-table conversation proceeded fitfully. Rodney said that this morning he could have sworn it was going to rain, and Jane said she had thought so, too, and Rodney said that now it looked as if the weather might hold up, and Jane said Yes, didn't it? and Rodney said he hoped the weather would hold up because rain was such a nuisance, and Jane said Yes, wasn't it? Rodney said yesterday had been a nice day, and Jane said Yes, and Rodney said that it seemed to be getting a little warmer, and Jane said Yes, and Rodney said that summer would be here any moment now, and Jane said Yes, wouldn't it? and Rodney said he hoped it would not be too hot this summer, but that, as a matter of fact, when you came right down to it, what one minded was not so much the heat as the humidity, and Jane said Yes, didn't one?

In short, by the time they rose and left the restaurant, not a word had been spoken that could have provoked the censure of the sternest critic. Yet William Bates, catching sight of them as they passed down the aisle, started as if he had been struck by lightning. He had happened to find himself near the Alcazar at lunch-time and had dropped in for a chop; and, peering round the pillar which had hidden his table from theirs, he stared after them with saucer-like eyes.

'Oh, dash it!' said William.

This William Bates, as I have indicated in my previous references to him, was not an abnormally emotional or temperamental man. Built physically on the lines of a motor-lorry, he had much of that vehicle's placid and even phlegmatic outlook on life. Few things had the power to ruffle William, but, unfortunately, it so happened that one of these things was Rodney Spelvin. He had never been able entirely to overcome his jealousy of this man. It had been Rodney who had come within an ace of scooping Jane from him in the days when she had been Miss Packard. It had been Rodney who had temporarily broken up his home some years later by persuading Jane to become a member of the artistic set. And now, unless his eyes jolly well deceived him, this human gumboil was once more busy on his dastardly work. Too dashed thick, was William's view of the matter; and he gnashed his teeth in such a spasm of resentful fury that a man lunching at the next table told the waiter to switch off the electric fan, as it had begun to creak unendurably.

Jane was reading in the drawing-room when William reached home that night.

'Had a nice day?' asked William.

'Quite nice,' said Jane.

'Play golf?' asked William.

'Just practised,' said Jane.

'Lunch at the club?'

'Yes.'

'I thought I saw that bloke Spelvin in town,' said William.

Jane wrinkled her forehead.

'Spelvin? Oh, you mean Rodney Spelvin? Did you? I see he's got a new book coming out.'

'You never run into him these days, do you?'

'Oh no. It must be two years since I saw him.'

'Oh?' said William. 'Well, I'll be going upstairs and dressing.'

It seemed to Jane, as the door closed, that she heard a curious clicking noise, and she wondered for a moment if little Braid had got out of bed and was playing with the Mah-Jongg counters. But it was only William gnashing his teeth.

There is nothing sadder in this life than the spectacle of a husband and wife with practically identical handicaps drifting apart; and to dwell unnecessarily on such a spectacle is, to my mind, ghoulish. It is not my purpose, therefore, to weary you with a detailed description of the hourly widening of the breach between this once ideally united pair. Suffice it to say that within a few days of the conversation just related the entire atmosphere of this happy home had completely altered. On the Tuesday, William excused himself from the morning round on the plea that he had promised Peter Willard a match, and Jane said What a pity! On Tuesday afternoon William said that his head ached, and Jane said Isn't that too bad? On Wednesday morning William said he had lumbago, and Jane, her sensitive feelings now deeply wounded, said Oh, had he? After that, it came to be agreed between them by silent compact that they should play together no more.

Also, they began to avoid one another in the house. Jane would sit in the drawing-room, while William retired down the passage to his den. In short, if you had added a couple of ikons and a photograph of Trotsky, you would have had a *mise en scène* which would have fitted a Russian novel like the paper on the wall.

One evening, about a week after the beginning of this tragic state of affairs, Jane was sitting in the drawing-room, trying to read *Braid on Taking Turf*. But the print seemed blurred and the philosophy too metaphysical to be grasped. She laid the book down and stared sadly before her.

Every moment of these black days had affected Jane like a

stymie on the last green. She could not understand how it was that William should have come to suspect, but that he did suspect was plain; and she writhed on the horns of a dilemma. All she had to do to win him back again was to go to him and tell him of Anastatia's fatal entanglement. But what would happen then? Undoubtedly he would feel it his duty as a brother to warn the girl against Rodney Spelvin; and Jane instinctively knew that William warning anyone against Rodney Spelvin would sound like a private of the line giving his candid opinion of the sergeant-major.

Inevitably, in this case, Anastatia, a spirited girl and deeply in love, would take offence at his words and leave the house. And if she left the house, what would be the effect on little Braid's mashie-play? Already, in less than a fortnight, the gifted girl had taught him more about the chip-shot from ten to fifteen yards off the green than the local pro. had been able to do in two years. Her departure would be absolutely disastrous.

What it amounted to was that she must sacrifice her husband's happiness or her child's future; and the problem of which was to get the loser's end was becoming daily more insoluble.

She was still brooding on it when the postman arrived with the evening mail, and the maid brought the letters into the drawing-room.

Jane sorted them out. There were three for William, which she gave to the maid to take to him in his den. There were two for herself, both bills. And there was one for Anastatia, in the well-remembered handwriting of Rodney Spelvin.

Jane placed this letter on the mantelpiece, and stood looking at it like a cat at a canary. Anastatia was away for the day, visiting friends who lived a few stations down the line; and every womanly instinct in Jane urged her to get hold of a kettle and steam the gum off the envelope. She had almost made up her mind to disembowel the thing and write 'Opened in error' on it, when the telephone suddenly went off like a bomb and nearly startled her into a decline. Coming at that moment it sounded like the Voice of Conscience.

'Hullo?' said Jane.

'Hullo!' replied a voice.

Jane clucked like a hen with uncontrollable emotion. It was Rodney.

'Is that you?' asked Rodney.

'Yes,' said Jane.

And so it was, she told herself.

'Your voice is like music,' said Rodney.

This may or may not have been the case, but at any rate it was exactly like every other female voice when heard on the telephone. Rodney prattled on without a suspicion.

'Have you got my letter yet?'

'No,' said Jane. She hesitated. 'What was in it?' she asked, tremulously.

'It was to ask you to come to my house to-morrow at four.'

'To your house!' faltered Jane.

'Yes. Everything is ready. I will send the servants out, so that we shall be quite alone. You will come, won't you?'

The room was shimmering before Jane's eyes, but she regained command of herself with a strong effort.

'Yes,' she said. 'I will be there.'

She spoke softly, but there was a note of menace in her voice. Yes, she would indeed be there. From the very moment when this man had made his monstrous proposal, she had been asking herself what Gloria Gooch would have done in a crisis like this. And the answer was plain. Gloria Gooch, if her sister-in-law was intending to visit the apartments of a libertine, would have gone there herself to save the poor child from the consequences of her infatuated folly.

'Yes,' said Jane, 'I will be there.'

'You have made me the happiest man in the world,' said Rodney. 'I will meet you at the corner of the street at four, then.' He paused. 'What is that curious clicking noise?' he asked.

'I don't know,' said Jane. 'I noticed it myself. Something wrong with the wire, I suppose.'

'I thought it was somebody playing the castanets. Until to-morrow, then, good-bye.'

'Good-bye.'

Jane replaced the receiver. And William, who had been listening to every word of the conversation on the extension in his den, replaced his receiver, too.

Anastatia came back from her visit late that night. She took her letter, and read it without comment. At breakfast next morning she said that she would be compelled to go into town that day.

'I want to see my dressmaker,' she said.

'I'll come, too,' said Jane. 'I want to see my dentist.'

'So will I,' said William. 'I want to see my lawyer.'

'That will be nice,' said Anastatia, after a pause.

'Very nice,' said Jane, after another pause.

'We might all lunch together,' said Anastatia. 'My appointment is not till four.'

'I should love it,' said Jane. 'My appointment is at four, too.'

'So is mine,' said William.

'What a coincidence!' said Jane, trying to speak brightly.

'Yes,' said William. He may have been trying to speak brightly, too; but, if so, he failed. Jane was too young to have seen Salvini in 'Othello,' but, had she witnessed that great tragedian's performance, she could not have failed to be struck by the resemblance between his manner in the pillow scene and William's now.

'Then shall we all lunch together?' said Anastatia.

'I shall lunch at my club,' said William, curtly.

'William seems to have a grouch,' said Anastatia.

'Ha!' said William.

He raised his fork and drove it with sickening violence at his sausage.

So Jane had a quiet little woman's lunch at a confectioner's alone with Anastatia. Jane ordered a tongue-and-lettuce sandwich, two macaroons, marsh-mallows, ginger-ale and cocoa; and Anastatia ordered pineapple chunks with whipped cream, tomatoes stuffed with beetroot, three dill pickles, a raspberry nut sundae, and hot chocolate. And, while getting outside this garbage, they talked merrily, as women will, of every subject but the one that really occupied their minds. When Anastatia got up and said good-bye with a final reference to her dressmaker, Jane shuddered at the depths of deceit to which the modern girl can sink.

It was now about a quarter to three, so Jane had an hour to kill before going to the rendezvous. She wandered about the streets, and never had time appeared to her to pass so slowly, never had a city been so congested with hard-eyed and suspicious citizens. Every second person she met seemed to glare at her as if he or she had guessed her secret.

The very elements joined in the general disapproval. The sky had turned a sullen grey, and far-away thunder muttered faintly, like an impatient golfer held up on the tee by a slow foursome.

It was a relief when at length she found herself at the back of Rodney Spelvin's house, standing before the scullery window, which it was her intention to force with the pocket-knife won in happier days as second prize in a competition at a summer hotel for those with handicaps above eighteen.

But the relief did not last long. Despite the fact that she was about to enter this evil house with the best motives, a sense of almost intolerable guilt oppressed her. If William should ever get to know of this! Wow! felt Jane.

How long she would have hesitated before the window, one cannot say. But at this moment, glancing guiltily round, she happened to catch the eye of a cat which was sitting on a near-by wall, and she read in this cat's eye such cynical derision that the urge came upon her to get out of its range as quickly as possible. It was a cat that had manifestly seen a lot of life, and it was plainly putting an entirely wrong construction on her behaviour. Jane shivered, and, with a quick jerk, prised the window open and climbed in.

It was two years since she had entered this house, but once she had reached the hall she remembered its topography perfectly. She mounted the stairs to the large studio sitting-room on the first floor, the scene of so many Bohemian parties in that dark period of her artistic life. It was here, she knew, that Rodney would bring his victim.

The studio was one of those dim, over-ornamented rooms which appeal to men like Rodney Spelvin. Heavy curtains hung in front of the windows. One corner was cut off by a high-backed Chesterfield. At the far end was an alcove, curtained like the windows. Once Jane had admired this studio, but now it made her shiver. It seemed to her one of those nests in which, as the sub-title of *Tried in the Furnace* had said, only eggs of evil are hatched. She paced the thick carpet restlessly, and suddenly there came to her the sound of footsteps on the stairs.

Jane stopped, every muscle tense. The moment had arrived. She faced the door, tight-lipped. It comforted her a little in this crisis to reflect that Rodney was not one of those massive Ethel M. Dell libertines who might make things unpleasant for an intruder. He was only a welter-weight egg of evil; and, if he tried to start anything, a girl of her physique would have little or no difficulty in knocking the stuffing out of him.

The footsteps reached the door. The handle turned. The door opened. And in strode William Bates, followed by two men in bowler hats.

'Ha!' said William.

Jane's lips parted, but no sound came from them. She staggered back a pace or two. William, advancing into the centre of the room, folded his arms and gazed at her with burning eyes.

'So,' said William, and the words seemed forced like drops of vitriol from between his clenched teeth, 'I find you here, dash it!'

Jane choked convulsively. Years ago, when an innocent child, she had seen a conjurer produce a rabbit out of a top-hat which an instant before had been conclusively proved to be empty. The sudden apparition of William affected her with much the same sensations as she had experienced then.

'How-ow-ow—?' she said.

'I beg your pardon?' said William, coldly.

'How-ow-ow—?'

'Explain yourself,' said William.

'How-ow-ow did you get here? And who-oo-oo are these men?'

William seemed to become aware for the first time of the

presence of his two companions. He moved a hand in a hasty gesture of introduction.

'Mr Reginald Brown and Mr Cyril Delancey – my wife,' he said, curtly.

The two men bowed slightly and raised their bowler hats.

'Pleased to meet you,' said one.

'Most awfully charmed,' said the other.

'They are detectives,' said William.

'Detectives!'

'From the Quick Results Agency,' said William. 'When I became aware of your clandestine intrigue, I went to the agency and they gave me their two best men.'

'Oh, well,' said Mr Brown, blushing a little.

'Most frightfully decent of you to put it that way,' said Mr Delancey.

William regarded Jane sternly.

'I knew you were going to be here at four o'clock,' he said. 'I overheard you making the assignation on the telephone.'

'Oh, William!'

'Woman,' said William, 'where is your paramour?'

'Really, really,' said Mr Delancey, deprecatingly.

'Keep it clean,' urged Mr Brown.

'Your partner in sin, where is he? I am going to take him and tear him into little bits and stuff him down his throat and make him swallow himself.'

'Fair enough,' said Mr Brown.

'Perfectly in order,' said Mr Delancey.

Jane uttered a stricken cry.

'William,' she screamed, 'I can explain all.'

'All?' said Mr Delancey.

'All?' said Mr Brown.

'All,' said Jane.

'All?' said William.

'All,' said Jane.

William sneered bitterly.

'I'll bet you can't,' he said.

'I'll bet I can,' said Jane.

'Well?'

'I came here to save Anastatia.'

'Anastatia?'

'Anastatia.'

'My sister?'

'Your sister.'

'His sister Anastatia,' explained Mr Brown to Mr Delancey in an undertone.

'What from?' asked William.

'From Rodney Spelvin. Oh, William, can't you understand?'

'No, I'm dashed if I can.'

'I, too,' said Mr Delancey, 'must confess myself a little fogged. And you, Reggie?'

'Completely, Cyril,' said Mr Brown, removing his bowler hat with a puzzled frown, examining the maker's name, and putting it on again.

'The poor child is infatuated with this man.'

'With the bloke Spelvin?'

'Yes. She is coming here with him at four o'clock.'

'Important,' said Mr Brown, producing a note-book and making an entry.

'Important, if true,' agreed Mr Delancey.

'But I heard you making the appointment with the bloke Spelvin over the 'phone,' said William.

'He thought I was Anastatia. And I came here to save her.'

* * *

William was silent and thoughtful for a few moments.

'It all sounds very nice and plausible,' he said, 'but there's just one thing wrong. I'm not a very clever sort of bird, but I can see where your story slips up. If what you say is true, where is Anastatia?'

'Just coming in now,' whispered Jane. 'Hist!'

'Hist, Reggie!' whispered Mr Delancey.

They listened. Yes, the front door had banged, and feet were ascending the staircase.

'Hide!' said Jane, urgently.

'Why?' said William.

'So that you can overhear what they say and jump out and confront them.'

'Sound,' said Mr Delancey.

'Very sound,' said Mr Brown.

The two detectives concealed themselves in the alcove. William retired behind the curtains in front of the window. Jane dived behind the Chesterfield. A moment later the door opened.

Crouching in her corner, Jane could see nothing, but every word that was spoken came to her ears; and with every syllable her horror deepened.

'Give me your things,' she heard Rodney say, 'and then we will go upstairs.'

Jane shivered. The curtains by the window shook. From the direction of the alcove there came a soft scratching sound, as the two detectives made an entry in their note-books.

For a moment after this there was silence. Then Anastatia uttered a sharp, protesting cry.

'Ah, no, no! Please, please!'

'But why not?' came Rodney's voice.

'It is wrong – wrong.'

'I can't see why.'

'It is, it is! You must not do that. Oh, please, please don't hold so tight.'

There was a swishing sound, and through the curtains before the window a large form burst. Jane raised her head above the Chesterfield.

William was standing there, a menacing figure. The two detectives had left the alcove and were moistening their pencils. And in the middle of the room stood Rodney Spelvin, stooping slightly and grasping Anastatia's parasol in his hands.

'I don't get it,' he said. 'Why is it wrong to hold the dam' thing tight?' He looked up and perceived his visitors. 'Ah, Bates,' he said, absently. He turned to Anastatia again. 'I should have thought that the tighter you held it, the more force you would get into the shot.'

'But don't you see, you poor zimp,' replied Anastatia, 'that you've got to keep the ball straight. If you grip the shaft as if you were a drowning man clutching at a straw and keep your fingers under like that, you'll pull like the dickens and probably land out of bounds or in the rough. What's the good of getting force into the shot if the ball goes in the wrong direction, you cloth-headed goof?'

'I see now,' said Rodney, humbly. 'How right you always are!'

'Look here,' interrupted William, folding his arms. 'What is the meaning of this?'

'You want to grip firmly but lightly,' said Anastatia.

'Firmly but lightly,' echoed Rodney.

'What is the meaning of this?'

'And with the fingers. Not with the palms.'

'What is the meaning of this?' thundered William. 'Anastatia, what are you doing in this man's rooms?'

'Giving him a golf lesson, of course. And I wish you wouldn't interrupt.'

'Yes, yes,' said Rodney, a little testily. 'Don't interrupt, Bates, there's a good fellow. Surely you have things to occupy you elsewhere?'

'We'll go upstairs,' said Anastatia, 'where we can be alone.'

'You will not go upstairs,' barked William.

'We shall get on much better there,' explained Anastatia. 'Rodney has fitted up the top-floor back as an indoor practising room.'

Jane darted forward with a maternal cry.

'My poor child, has the scoundrel dared to delude you by pretending to be a golfer? Darling, he is nothing of the kind.'

Mr Reginald Brown coughed. For some moments he had been twitching restlessly.

'Talking of golf,' he said, 'it might interest you to hear of a little experience I had the other day at Marshy Moor. I had got a nice drive off the tee, nothing record-breaking, you understand, but straight and sweet. And what was my astonishment on walking up to play my second to find—'

'A rather similar thing happened to me at Windy Waste last Tuesday,' interrupted Mr Delancey. 'I had hooked my drive the merest trifle, and my caddie said to me, "You're out of bounds." "I am not out of bounds," I replied, perhaps a little tersely, for the lad had annoyed me by a persistent habit of sniffing. "Yes, you are out of bounds," he said. "No, I am not out of bounds," I retorted. Well, believe me or believe me not, when I got up to my ball—'

'Shut up!' said William.

'Just as you say, sir,' replied Mr Delancey, courteously.

Rodney Spelvin drew himself up, and in spite of her loathing for his villainy Jane could not help feeling what a noble and romantic figure he made. His face was pale, but his voice did not falter.

'You are right,' he said. 'I am not a golfer. But with the help of this splendid girl here, I hope humbly to be one some day, Ah, I know what you are going to say,' he went on, raising a hand. 'You are about to ask how a man who has wasted his life as I have done can dare to entertain the mad dream of ever acquiring a decent handicap. But never forget,' proceeded Rodney, in a low, quivering voice, 'that Walter J. Travis was nearly forty before he touched a club, and a few years later he won the British Amateur.'

'True,' murmured William.

'True, true,' said Mr Delancey and Mr Brown. They lifted their bowler hats reverently.

'I am thirty-three years old,' continued Rodney, 'and for fourteen of those thirty-three years I have been writing poetry – aye, and novels with a poignant sex-appeal, and if ever I gave a thought to this divine game it was but to sneer at it. But last summer I saw the light.'

'Glory! Glory!' cried Mr Brown.

'One afternoon I was persuaded to try a drive. I took the club with a mocking, contemptuous laugh.' He paused, and a wild light came into his eyes. 'I brought off a perfect pip,' he said, emotionally. 'Two hundred yards and as straight as a whistle. And, as I stood there gazing after the ball, something seemed to run up my spine and bite me in the neck. It was the golf-germ.'

'Always the way,' said Mr Brown. 'I remember the first drive I ever made. I took a nice easy stance—'

'The first drive I made,' said Mr Delancey, 'you won't believe this, but it's a fact, was a full—'

'From that moment,' continued Rodney Spelvin, 'I have had but one ambition – to somehow or other, cost what it might, get down into single figures.' He laughed bitterly. 'You see,' he said, 'I cannot even speak of this thing without splitting my infinitives. And even as I split my infinitives, so did I split my drivers. After that first heavenly slosh I didn't seem able to do anything right.'

He broke off, his face working. William cleared his throat awkwardly.

'Yes, but dash it,' he said, 'all this doesn't explain why I find you alone with my sister in what I might call your lair.'

'The explanation is simple,' said Rodney Spelvin. 'This sweet girl is the only person in the world who seems able to simply and intelligently and in a few easily understood words make clear the knack of the thing. There is none like her, none. I have been to pro. after pro., but not one has been any good to me. I am a temperamental man, and there is a lack of sympathy and human understanding about these professionals which jars on my artist soul. They look at you as if you were a half-witted child. They click their tongues. They make odd Scotch noises. I could not endure the strain. And then this wonderful girl, to whom in a burst of emotion I had confided my unhappy case, offered to give me private lessons. So I went with her to some of those indoor practising places. But here, too, my sensibilities were racked by the fact that unsympathetic eyes observed me. So I fixed up a room here where we could be alone.'

'And instead of going there,' said Anastatia, 'we are wasting half the afternoon talking.'

William brooded for a while. He was not a quick thinker.

'Well, look here,' he said at length, 'this is the point. This is the nub of the thing. This is where I want you to follow me very closely. Have you asked Anastatia to marry you?'

'Marry me?' Rodney gazed at him, shocked. 'Have I asked her to marry me? I, who am not worthy to polish the blade of her niblick! I, who have not even a thirty handicap, ask a girl to marry me who was in the semi-final of last year's Ladies' Open! No, no, Bates, I may be a *vers-libre* poet, but I have some sense of what is fitting. I love her, yes. I love her with a fervour which causes me to frequently and for hours at a time lie tossing sleeplessly upon my pillow. But I would not dare to ask her to marry me.'

Anastatia burst into a peal of girlish laughter.

'You poor chump!' she cried. 'Is that what has been the matter all this time! I couldn't make out what the trouble was. Why, I'm crazy about you. I'll marry you any time you give the word.'

Rodney reeled.

'What!'

'Of course I will.'

'Anastatia!'

'Rodney!'

He folded her in his arms.

'Well, I'm dashed,' said William. 'It looks to me as if I had been making rather a lot of silly fuss about nothing. Jane, I wronged you.'

'It was my fault.'

'No, no!'

'Yes, yes!'

'Jane!'

'William!'

He folded her in his arms. The two detectives, having entered the circumstances in their note-books, looked at one another with moist eyes.

'Cyril!' said Mr Brown.

'Reggie!' said Mr Delancey.

Their hands met in a brotherly clasp.

'And so,' concluded the Oldest Member, 'all ended happily. The storm-tossed lives of William Bates, Jane Packard, and Rodney Spelvin came safely at long last into harbour. At the subsequent wedding William and Jane's present of a complete golfing outfit, including eight dozen new balls, a cloth cap, and a pair of spiked shoes, was generally admired by all who inspected the gifts during the reception.

'From that time forward the four of them have been inseparable. Rodney and Anastatia took a little cottage close to that of William and Jane, and rarely does a day pass without a close foursome between the two couples. William and Jane being steady tens and Anastatia scratch and Rodney a persevering eighteen, it makes an ideal match.'

'What does?' asked the secretary, waking from his reverie.

'This one.'

'Which?'

'I see,' said the Oldest Member, sympathetically, 'that your troubles, weighing on your mind, have caused you to follow my little narrative less closely than you might have done. Never mind, I will tell it again.'

'The story' (said the Oldest Member) 'which I am about to relate begins at a time when—'

TITLES IN THE COLLECTOR'S WODEHOUSE

Pearls, Girls and Monty Bodkin
A Pelican at Blandings
Performing Flea
Piccadilly Jim
Pigs Have Wings
Plum Pie
The Pothunters
A Prefect's Uncle
The Prince and Betty
Psmith in the City
Psmith, Journalist
Quick Service
Right Ho, Jeeves
Ring for Jeeves
Sam the Sudden
Service with a Smile
The Small Bachelor
Something Fishy

Something Fresh
Spring Fever
Stiff Upper Lip, Jeeves
Summer Lightning
Summer Moonshine
Sunset at Blandings
The Swoop!
Tales of St Austin's
Tales of Wrykyn and Elsewhere
Thank You, Jeeves
Ukridge
Uncle Dynamite
Uncle Fred in the Springtime
Uneasy Money
Very Good, Jeeves!
The White Feather
Young Men in Spats

This edition of P. G. Wodehouse has been prepared from the first British printing of each title.

The Collector's Wodehouse is printed on acid-free paper and set in Caslon, a typeface designed and engraved by William Caslon of William Caslon & Son, Letter-Founders in London around 1740.